'He did not ... my housekeep... become my mis...

'And are you happy that your brother has organised your future?' Sarah scoffed.

'Of course I'm not happy about it,' Gavin replied bluntly. 'But I am willing to accept it.'

'Because you want to claim your inheritance.' The statement was tinged with acrimony.

'Yes, I want my inheritance.'

Eyes that had become sleepy roved her figure.

'And I want you.'

Dear Reader

The path of true love never runs smooth, so the old saying goes, and I have written a duet of novels with those wise words in mind. In this first book, THE VIRTUOUS COURTESAN, it is certainly a fitting adage! The heroine, Sarah Marchant, has suffered a traumatic childhood. When her future is cruelly bound to that of Gavin Stone—something neither of them wants—it seems matters must only get worse...or will they?

The second story features Ruth Hayden as the heroine. Widowed when very young, she has also endured a great deal of heartache in her early years. Then Sir Clayton Powell arrives, with an offer that should benefit them both. But can a marriage without love survive?

2008 marks the tenth anniversary of the publication of MR TRELAWNEY'S PROPOSAL, my first Regency novel for Mills & Boon. It is, therefore, a double delight for me to be part of this year's centenary celebrations. Although I enjoy reading and writing historical fiction, it has been exciting to see the innovative and widening choice of books on offer by the world's most famous romance publisher. The Mills & Boon success story is heartening proof that, despite uncertain times, very many people continue to have an enduring love of reading all types of romance.

In this special year I would like to take the opportunity of thanking all my editors and all my readers, past and present.

Mary

THE VIRTUOUS COURTESAN

Mary Brendan

MILLS & BOON®

Pure reading pleasure™

First published in Great Britain 2008
Harlequin Mills & Boon Limited,
Eton House, 18-24 Paradise Road, Richmond, Surrey TW9 1SR

© Mary Brendan 2008

ISBN: 978 0 263 86266 9

Set in Times Roman 10½ on 13 pt.
04-0708-71734

Printed and bound in Spain
by Litografia Rosés S.A., Barcelona

THE VIRTUOUS
COURTESAN

Mary Brendan was born in North London, but now lives in rural Suffolk. She has always had a fascination with bygone days, and enjoys the research involved in writing historical fiction. When not at her word processor, she can be found trying to bring order to a large overgrown garden, or browsing local fairs and junk shops for that elusive bargain.

Recent novels by the same author:

WEDDING NIGHT REVENGE*
THE UNKNOWN WIFE*
A SCANDALOUS MARRIAGE*
THE RAKE AND THE REBEL*
A PRACTICAL MISTRESS†
THE WANTON BRIDE†

The Meredith Sisters
†*The Hunter Brothers*

Chapter One

It had been a calamitous few days for Joseph Pratt. Misfortune had first visited him on Monday when he had discovered his wife in bed with her young lover. On Wednesday he had lost thirty guineas on a wager, despite having it on excellent authority that the nag would secure a cup at the County races. Yesterday was no improvement; a rival firm of solicitors had poached one of his best clients. Now Friday had arrived and with it a raging toothache. Gingerly he probed the swelling with his tongue and flinched, whilst keeping his eyes fixed on the fellow seated opposite. Despite a throbbing gum his mouth stretched into a smirk, for he anticipated being soon so thoroughly entertained, it might compensate for his week of woe.

Beneath stubby fallen lashes, the lawyer took a summarising look at the preposterously handsome profile presented to him. The fellow was frowning out into a sunny afternoon and Joseph noted his honed, almost fleshless visage was unfashionably brown for a Mayfair dandy.

Mr Gavin Stone might possess an air of sleepy sophistication, but he obviously rose early enough on occasion to catch the sun and acquire a vulgar gypsy colouring. Joseph's covert appraisal of his visitor continued; in fact, he found it hard to look away for the man was quite different to the louche individual he had been expecting. Not that his late client, Edward Stone, had spoken much about his younger brother. But he had gleaned from odd comments that the fellow was a damnable rogue.

Presently the rogue's lips were compressed to a thin line and, if that alone did not signify his deep irritation, there were the long fingers drumming on a shiny boot perched atop an elegantly breeched knee. He might have a reputation as a libertine, and have his pockets to let, but he was not a man with whom one might take liberties, of that Joseph was sure.

Another look was slanted from beneath Joseph's sandy brows at the fellow lounging in a chair. He had a hand plunged negligently into a pocket, ruining the effect of a suit of clothes that, even to Joseph's jaundiced eye, looked to have cost a pretty city penny.

Joseph quickly averted his gaze as Gavin Stone lost interest in the pastoral scene beyond the window and cast a glower at the empty chair on his left. From the corner of his vision Joseph saw first one, then the other finely dressed long leg extend as they were stretched out. Joseph's lips twitched a little maliciously. It was a small chair for such a well-built man and no doubt, after almost three-quarters of an hour stuck within its cracked leather arms, Gavin Stone was feeling cramped. Suddenly his visitor's enviable physique was rudely impressed on him as the man surged to his feet.

The solicitor bent his head to peruse a document. Even when balled fists were planted gently on the edge of the desktop directly in his line of vision Joseph did not immediately look up. A moment later he met a penetrating blue gaze for he sensed that he continued to ignore Mr Stone at his peril.

'How much longer must we tarry over this?'

Joseph cleared his throat; the smirk had long since withered from his lips. 'I can only apologise, sir. My correspondence was most concise. The appointment was for one of the clock.' Rapidly blinking eyes sought the wall clock. 'I imagine Miss Marchant has been unavoidably delayed.'

'I imagine you are right.' Gavin's response was silky irony. 'But I am not prepared to wait for her any longer. We have given her the courtesy of forty wasted minutes. Let us proceed with the matter. You can advise the lady of her bequest at a later date.'

'I'm afraid I cannot, sir,' Joseph stressed in a horrified tone. 'My late client was most specific in his instructions. His last will and testament must not be read until both parties are present.'

'What?' Gavin cursed inaudibly and pivoted on a heel. When he spoke his back was to the lawyer and his voice was speciously calm. 'Why did you not inform me of this sooner?'

'You did not ask, sir, and earlier there seemed no need to bring it to your attention,' the lawyer argued.

Gavin's back teeth met as he sought to control his vexation at that reasonable defence. 'I intend travelling back to London this afternoon,' he informed Pratt curtly. 'I want to be on the road by three o'clock, four at the latest.'

Joseph grabbed at a little bell positioned on the edge of his desk. 'There is yet time, then. Perhaps some more refreshment…'

The brass implement was snatched away by Gavin before he could again be tormented by its feeble clatter. He abruptly replaced it on polished wood. He had been fobbed off already with weak tea and stilted chit-chat and had no further stomach for either. 'I think not… thank you,' he curtly declined further hospitality. 'I shall be at the Red Lion until four o'clock this afternoon. Should Miss…'

'Marchant,' the solicitor swiftly supplied the absentee's name.

'Quite…' Gavin muttered impatiently. 'Should she turn up before that time, send your clerk to the inn to inform me and I will endeavour to delay my departure. It is best to close this business today.'

It seemed that within one stride Gavin Stone's tall

figure was at the exit and he was stooping in anticipation of quitting the office through a low sloping portal. Slowly he straightened and frowned at the scrawny clerk who had silently appeared and was now in his way.

The young man stretched his neck in his stiff collar to take a peer around the broad chest blocking his vision.

'Excuse me, Mr Stone…Mr Pratt,' he piped. 'Miss Marchant is below and sends her apologies for her late arrival—shall I…?'

'Show her up…show her up,' Mr Pratt hissed impatiently, finishing the nervous youth's sentence for him. A flapping hand stressed the urgency to fetch her. 'There…she is at last arrived,' Joseph soothed. 'We might speedily set to and you will still be refreshed and away in good time.' He sidled closer. 'Please, sit down?' he hesitantly suggested, for the saturnine fellow remained close to the exit.

Gavin muttered something inaudible beneath his breath and, ignoring the invitation to be seated, strolled to an open window, braced a hand against the frame and moodily stared out. His dark humour started to evaporate as warm scented air teased his senses and he squinted against late summer sunlight.

At this time of the year this small country town was undeniably a pleasant spot. Picturesque cottages and the green sward of the town square could be seen from his vantage point. Pratt and Donaghue, the legal firm

whose letter concerning his brother's demise had
summoned him from London, held offices on the first
floor of a redbrick townhouse. The building was
flanked either side by similar properties with sturdy
entrance doors bearing brass nameplates of the
educated fellows trading within. Along both sides of a
narrow High Street were shops of varying sizes, some
with wares displayed outside. It appeared enough was
on offer in Willowdene to meet a person's needs.
Nevertheless, Gavin remained surprised that his brother
had some years ago relinquished his Mayfair lifestyle
to reside permanently in what, to Gavin, was simply a
quaint backwater.

'I'm so sorry to be late. I hope you have not been
greatly inconvenienced.'

Her voice was attractively youthful despite its note
of husky anxiety. Gavin slowly turned his head,
thinking it highly unlikely that Miss Marchant might
look as good as she sounded. If he was surprised by
what he saw, he restricted the emotion to a thoughtful
pursing of his lips.

When informed earlier this afternoon by Joseph Pratt
that a Miss Marchant had been named in his brother's
will, and would be joining them to hear of her bequest,
he had imagined a loyal spinster servant was to be hand-
somely rewarded for looking after Edward, and asked no
more.

Eddie had lived apart from his wife, Janet, for more
than fifteen years. In the absence of a wife to marshal

his household, it would be expected that a competent female would be hired to do so. Edward was ever a methodical man, if one disinclined to part with a penny more than he had to. It would not surprise Gavin one bit to find his brother's menials were all owed back pay.

But this was no middle-aged servant. He levelled a steady blue gaze on the slender young woman who was in the process of removing a bonnet from her pale blonde hair. She then stripped off her gloves, very quickly, as though to make up for lost time. This was a lady of refinement. Had she not already spoken and revealed her class, he would have known from her deportment and poise that she was gently bred. But what kept Gavin momentarily spellbound was her undeniable beauty. And then misanthropic thoughts started to fill his head.

His eyes narrowed and his mouth took on a cynical slant. Perhaps he was beginning to understand his brother's passion for the place. Considering the girl's obvious youth and breeding, his suspicions should have been dismissed as ridiculous. Nevertheless he continued to ponder whether Edward might not have been quite the pious prig he'd liked to make out.

'Umm…please sit here, Miss Marchant.' Joseph indicated a similar armchair to the one Gavin had vacated. 'And we can immediately begin. Mr Stone is impatient to get back to London tonight.'

Sarah Marchant took a step forward, her eyes again drawn to the imposing figure positioned by the window.

So this was Gavin Stone! He appeared stern, soberly dressed and nothing like the carefree wastrel Eddie's description had led her to imagine. But it was not just his appearance that surprised her; she had expected a younger version of Eddie, for he had said they were physically alike. Sarah suppressed a wry smile. Eddie had obviously wished it so. This man was far taller and broader than his older brother had been and, she had to admit, far more handsome. He had darker colouring than Eddie and a luxuriant mane of hair framing the rugged planes of his face. Eddie had fretted over losing what remained of his thinning locks by the time he reached forty. Poor Eddie had been two years short of that milestone birthday when he caught smallpox. Sarah swallowed the little ache in her throat at the memory of his horrible illness. Thankfully it had been of short duration and he had succumbed quickly to its ravages.

Sarah quickly averted her eyes. She had been staring in quite a vulgar fashion whilst she compared the brothers. Remembering her manners she dipped into a neat bob. She also delivered an apologetic smile despite his surly countenance. But then Sarah accepted Gavin Stone had every reason to be annoyed. In fairness she would not have been pleased either to have kicked her heels in Mr Pratt's office for so long. Before sitting down she made an effort to appear confident and briskly repeated her apology and strengthened her smile.

'I hope you were not delayed by anything unpleasant?'

Sarah's topaz eyes flicked to Gavin. He had uttered that in an odd tone…as though he expected her to furnish a reason for her tardiness. And now, far from appearing aloof, he had an amused, almost scornful look deep in his eyes that she found distinctly disquieting. 'A domestic matter, sir.' The concise information was quietly conveyed. She deliberately looked at the lawyer. A small nod of her blonde head indicated she was ready to proceed.

Joseph swung a sly glance from Mr Stone to Miss Marchant. He sensed a certain amount of friction between them already. Ten minutes hence, when the full extent of Edward Stone's last will and testament was made known to them, he expected sparks to fly. He coughed and collected his papers together in a businesslike manner. Although he knew each protagonist was perfectly aware of the other's identity, he made brief formal introductions. He could sense that Gavin Stone was intrigued and not a little impatient to know what part this lovely young woman had played in his brother's life.

Earlier, when he had attempted to while away time by making small talk with Gavin Stone, he had purposely steered conversation away from the lady on whom they waited. Too much information about her might alert him to what may lie ahead and thus spoil the sensational surprise.

Gavin settled himself back in the chair he had recently vacated, but in such a way that he now faced Miss Marchant rather than the desk behind which the lawyer was hunched.

Aware that she was under scrutiny, Sarah flicked up her dusky lashes to boldly gaze back. When that did not deter him, but rather intensified the amusement at the back of his eyes, she flushed. She sensed that Gavin Stone had already taken against her. Perhaps he thought she was about to snatch away his inheritance. Well, she knew she was not. Eddie had told her that the bulk of his estate would pass to his only sibling despite the fact he didn't like Gavin and rarely saw him. But he had promised to make adequate provision for her future. Today she was to find out what that was. She was hoping for a permanent tenancy of Elm Lodge, and an annuity. She flushed, ashamed of her mercenary thoughts. But then everybody must live…somehow… She just wished that there had been no need for her to participate in this pantomime in the lawyer's office today. In life, Eddie had chosen to avoid his brother; she was coming to wish he had afforded her that privilege after his death.

'I will come straight to the point,' Joseph said in a ponderous tone and swept a glance between the pair seated opposite. 'Mr Edward Stone, deceased, has left his entire estate and possessions to his brother, Mr Gavin Stone.' He paused for a moment to allow that information to be digested. 'However, there is a condition attached to the house in Brighton. The deceased's wife presently resides there and is to benefit from free and uninterrupted use of the house until she dies. Edward has also left his estranged wife a small sum of money to be paid as an annuity.' Another pause, then he added, 'It was not necessary that Janet Stone attend today. In fact, it was Edward's wish that she should not be invited to do so.'

Gavin slanted a look at the lady sitting adjacent. 'I see,' was all he said, but his eyes lingered on her.

Sarah felt the colour in her cheeks rising. The odious beast might have guessed the nature of the relationship between her and his brother, but did he have to make it quite so obvious that he disapproved?

She had been a mistress, but no marriage breaker. Edward and Janet Stone had lived apart for many years before Sarah had even met Eddie. She clasped her hands in her lap to steady them, determined to ignore his barbs. After all, people in glasshouses should not throw stones. And she'd heard enough about Gavin Stone's character to know he inhabited a very fragile domain. Having thus boosted her courage, she nevertheless wished that Eddie had shown more consideration for her feelings than to insist she attend, like a grasping harlot, and tolerate the company of two gentlemen she sensed held her in contempt.

'Now we come to the role Miss Marchant must play…' The lawyer coughed and stuck a finger between his collar and his rubicund neck. 'That is to say, Miss

Marchant is also mentioned in Mr Edward Stone's will. Her bequest is linked to yours, sir.' Despite the slick, quiet way in which he had introduced that last bit of information, a dangerous gleam immediately flared in Gavin's eyes, making Joseph hasten on. 'In order that your inheritance might be taken up, you must comply with Edward's stipulation that you continue to keep Miss Marchant in the manner to which she has become accustomed.'

Joseph sat back in his chair, his lids lowered to shield the fact that his eyes were excitedly batting between the couple in front of him. He had expected a stunned silence, but after many seconds, when all that could be heard was the clock ticking on the wall, he peeked up and ventured, 'Are there any questions?'

Finally Sarah broke free from her debilitating daze. It could not possibly be what she thought! Eddie would not do such a vile thing. He had said he was fond of her. There was a mistake…an infelicity in phrasing… 'Would you please repeat that last?' she murmured with a trembling smile.

'Yes…please repeat that,' Gavin uttered in a voice so consumed with icy rage that the lawyer again loosened his collar from his fiery neck.

'The gist of it is that you, Miss Marchant, will henceforth be protected by Mr Gavin Stone.' He turned a wary blinking eye on the dark face of the gentleman. 'For you, sir, the gist of it is that you must continue to pay for Miss Marchant's keep or you forfeit your inheritance.' He swivelled the papers about. 'Here…you may read it yourself,' he offered. 'If you refuse these terms and conditions, I'm afraid you will not receive a penny piece from your brother's estate and in six months' time the Crown may have it all.'

Further words of explanation from the lawyer were lost as Gavin sprang to his feet. 'Is this some kind of joke?' His eyes were fixed mercilessly on Sarah's whitening face. 'Did you know of this? Did you put this mischief in to my brother's head?'

The accusation and disgust in his voice fired Sarah's temper. Her head was flung back, sending blonde hair rippling about her shoulders. 'I assure you, sir, had I known of this I would not have bothered turning up at all today, late or early.' She jumped up, bristling with indignation. Barely a foot of space separated them. 'I am as shocked and appalled as you are.' She sent a look over his raw-boned face. Oh, he might have the veneer of quality, but close to she could tell a man who lived a debauched lifestyle. She had watched her papa drink and whore until he met his end in an ugly death. 'In fact, I might ask whether you had some hand in this devilish strategy,' she snapped out. 'Is your indignation real or subterfuge?' Sarah barely paused for breath before adding in a hiss, 'I cannot believe that Eddie would have done this without much persuading.'

Gavin took a pace towards her. Just one. But something in that slow determined movement made Sarah shrink back. 'You think I need to plot or use coercion to get a paramour?' he enquired softly.

A frisson of fear raced through Sarah. Far from his previous expression of faint amusement, he now looked perilously enraged. She regretted having spoken so impetuously, but found it impossible to either retract the accusation or apologise for it. 'I know you are a reprobate. Eddie told me,' she said in a wobbly voice. 'Will you deny it?'

'Would that he had mentioned you, madam,' Gavin drawled, ignoring the reference to his riotous reputation. 'Had he done so, I might have come and given my opinion of you whilst he was still alive. Then he would have known better than to attempt to foist you on to me.'

Joseph sank back in his chair and compressed his lips to stop a smile. Oh, entertainment, indeed! This was exceeding every expectation he'd had of a diverting scene taking place here today. Things were so fraught between them that he quite expected Miss Marchant might slap the insolent rogue's face. Her small hands were squeezed into fists at her side, and so tensely did she hold herself it seemed she might topple forwards.

Of course, Joseph had known for some while that Miss Marchant was Eddie Stone's mistress, as did most people hereabouts. But it was a discreet liaison and, after the first months of scandalous chatter, interest about them had died away. Little was known of Miss

Marchant for she kept herself to herself and lived on the very outskirts of town. She did not seek approval from the town's *grandes dames*, thus they could not withhold it. She did not attempt to socialise with them, thus they could not shun her.

As for Eddie, he had been thought an upstanding and popular fellow who was known to live apart from his crippled wife. He cared for Janet Stone, which was all people expected he might do in the circumstances, and if he sought comfort elsewhere…who could blame him? The mystery was, of course, why a genteel beauty such as Sarah Marchant would abase herself to become a gentleman's paramour when, clearly, she could have attracted offers of marriage before her reputation was irreparably sullied.

'You may have no fear of having me foisted upon you, sir. I refuse the terms.' That crisp statement was directed at the lawyer, jerking him from his musing. Sarah did not deign to give Gavin even a cursory glance. 'I have no desire to benefit from Edward's will and agree to sign whatever I must to make that final.'

'Umm…I'm afraid that makes no difference to—'

'Well, what does?' thundered Gavin before the lawyer could finish.

'Nothing, sir.'

'So we're stuck together in some unholy alliance?'

'If you will, sir,' Joseph said carefully and lowered his eyes.

Sarah flushed scarlet. The unfortunate choice of

words elicited imagery that was clear to her and obviously was to the gentlemen, too. She heard a sound that could have been a coarse laugh, but was probably a snort of anger issuing from Gavin Stone. Gathering up her bonnet and gloves in shaking hands, she took her leave without a single word. Her steps towards the door were rapid although a rational part of her mind hoped it did not look as though she fled from him. Within thirty seconds she was down the stairs and out in the mellow September sun.

Chapter Two

'Are you not going after her?'

Gavin levelled a narrowed gaze on the lawyer. The man had had the impertinence to sound quite disapproving. 'To what purpose?' he coolly enquired. 'So we might argue in the street and provide not just you, but the whole town with diversion?'

Joseph had the grace to glow whilst gesturing his innocence. 'Of course a scene would not be at all wise. But I imagined you hoped to come to some sort of arrangement with the young lady.'

'I think Miss Marchant has made it clear she would not want to consider an arrangement with me.'

'But you are not averse to an arrangement with her?' the lawyer prompted with sharp inquisitiveness.

Gavin strolled away from the window, from which vantage point he had watched the chit rush off as though the hounds of hell were on her heels. Either she'd been genuinely innocent of any hand in the scheme, and had meant what she said about forgoing her meal ticket, or she was a damn fine actress. For a man who had never experienced any difficulty in the art of seduction, that notion brought with it a crushing conclusion. There was a courtesan who might seriously choose to starve rather than sleep with him. Whereas he, if he were to be honest and circumstances had been different, would have sought to proposition her. She was one of the most divine-looking women he had ever met. And Heaven only knew he had enjoyed the company of quite a few alluring females. Why such a jewel was not dazzling the *ton* in Mayfair was as mystifying as why she had been attracted to Edward in the first place. An irritable sigh escaped Gavin. But nothing was as damnably vexing as his brother's decision to attach such bizarre terms to his inheritance.

If Edward had wanted his mistress to continue living in comfort on his death, why on earth had he not simply left her a tidy sum? She might be young, but she'd looked and sounded intelligent enough to manage her money. Or had Edward known his mistress to be an incorrigible spendthrift who might quickly run through her pension?

A rueful twitch lifted a corner of Gavin's mouth as he considered the possibility. Expensive mistresses were an enduring worry of which he had first-hand knowledge. Half his present financial problems had resulted from his current paramour's profligacy. The amount Elizabeth frittered on shoes alone would keep a family in modest comfort for several months of the year. Charitably he allowed that the blame for the other half of the pecuniary crisis in which he found himself fell squarely on his own shoulders. Gaming, horse-flesh, two new vehicles delivered to his mansion in Lansdowne Crescent in as many months....

But even the memory of his luxury purchases, and his wanton lover, could not keep his mind long in Mayfair.

The knowledge that his brother had kept an exquisitely beautiful woman was stirring a very unwelcome feeling in Gavin. He had not imagined Edward lived like a monk simply because he resided in the sticks and liked to moralise, but neither would he have imagined Edward capable of attracting such a gem. He swiftly banished the ridiculous idea that he might be jealous. Sibling rivalry between them had died with childhood and scraps over toys. As adults they had always been too different in character to covet what the other had. Or so he'd thought.

'Have you decided to return to London and give up your brother's bequest?' The lawyer interrupted Gavin's concentration with a doleful tone and a cautionary shake of the head. 'There is much at stake, you know: several fine properties and almost three thousand pounds annual income from the Willowdene estate. Then there is a not inconsiderable sum of cash in the bank and bonds—'

'I know I stand to lose a lot,' Gavin tetchily curtailed him.

'Indeed so, sir! A terrible waste it would be if it is taken by the Crown.' He tapped the document, inviting Gavin to check the threat. 'And you could put the funds to good use, I'm sure.'

Gavin shot a look at the smug fellow. So Joseph Pratt knew he spent beyond his means. But then, as Edward's man of business, he would naturally know that Edward had loaned him money, at an extortionate rate, once or twice.

'Does Miss Marchant have adequate private means or was she wholly dependent on my brother?'

'I'm not sure, sir,' Joseph answered with a frown. 'But I've always imagined her relationship with Mr Edward Stone was borne of necessity,' he added a mite too truthfully.

Gavin's cynical expression became more pronounced. 'Has she family hereabouts who might help her?' He didn't want it on his conscience that the chit might end up in the workhouse.

'I've not heard of any kith or kin. She has a couple of loyal old retainers who came from London with her. Due to the…*arrangement* between her and your brother, she naturally did not socialise with other ladies in town. For a while their relationship stirred much gossip, but that died away some time ago.'

'How long ago?' Gavin asked. He had judged her to be of tender age and had deduced that Edward must have quite recently taken up with her. Or perhaps she was blessed with more youthful looks than her years warranted.

Joseph sucked his teeth as he made a mental calculation. 'Oh, I should say it all started about three or four years ago now.' He gave Gavin a shrewd glance. The fellow's anger seemed to have been overtaken by a growing interest in Miss Marchant. 'Her young age gave rise to the worst of the chatter. But a lot of females are wed before they turn sixteen. And Sarah Marchant had already reached that very age by all accounts.'

Gavin's expression barely changed. But a sweeping look arced up and over the ceiling, displaying his disgust at what he'd just heard. Gavin had not bedded a woman that young since he was a teenager himself. But what really rankled was Edward's hypocrisy. His brother had readily given him the mantle of black sheep of the family despite having seduced a girl barely out of the schoolroom. The fact that Miss Marchant looked delectable enough to tempt a saint was hardly an excuse for such behaviour.

'Where does she presently reside?' Gavin asked abruptly.

'At Elm Lodge. It is one of the properties you now own, or will own if…' Joseph's voice faded and he gestured pointedly at the document in front of him. 'The Lodge is situated on the edge of the Willowdene estate by the woods.' After a few silent moments, when it seemed Gavin had plunged deep into thought, Joseph probed, 'It is almost a half-past three. Will you journey back to London today?'

Gavin cast a frown at the clock. He had quite forgotten that it had been his intention to rush back to Mayfair. It was now unthinkable to head home without seeing Sarah Marchant again. The need to stay was not just to do with securing his inheritance, though he needed the money. A quite vulgar curiosity about her was bedevilling him. He wanted to find out more about her; especially why she had slept with his dull brother to earn her keep.

'As you say,' he replied coolly, 'it is sensible that a solution of sorts be found. I shall remain at the Red Lion tonight and will contact you again regarding this vexing matter.'

'Why do you not stay at Willowdene Manor?' Joseph asked quickly as Gavin made to exit the room. 'I do not think any risk of infection lingers,' he reassured him. 'Edward was interred immediately and none of the staff succumbed.'

'It is not that. I'd sooner stay at the Red Lion as my time here is to be brief.' The excuse was valid, but only part of the reason for staying away from his brother's home. Gavin anticipated many questions from the staff at The Manor. Quite rightly they would be concerned for their jobs and pay until a new master took over and things were back to normal. At the moment he had no answers to give them. With a brusque nod for the lawyer, he ducked beneath the low beam and quit the room.

From the window Joseph Pratt watched the tall figure of Gavin Stone striding away. He noticed that minx Molly from the Red Lion giving him quite a bold smile and calling out to him before huddling, giggling, against her friend. Both girls turned to ogle as he strode past.

Joseph felt a prickle of envy. Gavin Stone was too damned handsome for his own good. That irritation apart, he oddly felt a sense of unease at what had occurred in his office this afternoon. He had relished the drama, but he certainly did not relish the possible outcome. Apart from other considerations, it would do his professional reputation no good. It might be construed that the Stone inheritance had been snatched away by the Crown because his good advice had been lacking rather than his late client's benevolence.

He had no real desire to see Gavin's fortune in jeopardy or Sarah made homeless. But then Joseph was sure, once her pride had been salved, that the young woman would come to her senses. It was a shame her lover had died, but unfortunate things occurred in life. Kept women were usually of a practical nature and accepted they must transfer their affections from time to time.

Miss Marchant had always seemed to him pleasant and polite and, of course, like any man, he could not fail to be smitten by her loveliness. In fact, he thought with a flash of inspiration, should Gavin Stone have spoiled his chances by being rude to her, perhaps a humble solicitor might wangle his way into favour. More modest terms would need to be negotiated, of course. But he could run to a small cottage and a stocked larder. Joseph turned from the window, grinning. And if he did take a beautiful young mistress it was no more than that cheating harlot, Mrs Rosamund Pratt, deserved!

Sarah sank onto the bale of hay and let the tears flow. Hateful man! Hateful man! The phrase flew back and forth in her agitated mind before bursting through small pearly teeth. But to which gentleman that insult was directed she could not have said: the smarmy lawyer, the mean lover, the insolent stranger—all deserved the epithet, and more besides.

A handkerchief was snatched from her reticule and held to her wet eyes. Had she not known Edward Stone's true character at all? How could he have acted so horridly? Eddie had not kept her in luxury, but neither had he been cruelly parsimonious. She had not gone without basic necessities. Now it seemed that to keep a roof over her head and bread on her plate she must apologise to his wastrel brother and then attempt to seduce him. The very idea made a sob of hysterical laughter choke her. She would rather… Her angry thoughts ebbed and stilled. What would she rather? Face destitution? Would she see Aunt Bea and Timothy starve?

Sarah felt a chill creep over her. It was unthinkable.

She wrung the little handkerchief in her fingers, until a ripping sound made her stop and push it back whence it came. Slender fingers smeared away the last of the tears on her cheeks and she gulped a calming breath. What was she to do? Even if she eventually managed to subdue her misgivings and pride enough to solicit Gavin Stone's protection, he had made it clear he didn't want her. In fact, he had made it clear that she disgusted him. He had even had the nerve to suggest that she might have plotted with Eddie to trap him. She had done no such thing but, in truth, she did regret having let the swine rile her. She had said things that were most unwise given her circumstances. Yet the greatest pity of it all was that her memory of Edward was now spoiled by a wrangle over his money.

She had been bitterly disappointed at not receiving the things she had wanted—Elm Lodge, an annuity of her own—but perhaps she had been hopelessly optimistic in thinking they might come to her. She had not been Edward's wife, neither had she been his only lover.

Edward had been quickly buried to allay fears of infection. Sarah had stayed away from the formal service and paid her respects privately, when the townspeople had gone from the graveside, but the other woman who had shared Edward's life had been there.

Christine Beauvoir had been accepted at the interment despite everybody knowing that she had been Edward's mistress for a long time. Her widow status conferred on her a certain respectability.

Yet she had been absent from the solicitor's office today. Her name had not been mentioned in Edward's will. Sarah knew the widow had her own property and income. She could only guess that Eddie had thought Christine had no need of any financial help from him on his demise.

A dejected grimace twisted her soft mouth. She was not so lucky. She must gratefully take the provision Eddie intended her to have. That conclusion brought her to a bitter truth: a suitable agreement with Gavin Stone must be reached. But she would not sleep with him. She had seen disgust in his eyes when he looked upon her face. How much more repulsive would she be to him when he first saw her naked in his bed?

Abruptly she gained her feet and began to pace to and fro, her full, soft lips compressed and her white brow puckered in concentration.

It was as Sarah was marching back and forth behind the tumbledown barn on the edge of town that Gavin caught sight of her. It was a mere glimpse of pale curls that first arrested his attention. A few moments later he spotted a swirl of grey skirt as she changed direction.

He settled back against the wall of the Red Lion's stables and plunged his hands into his pockets. She obviously had not fled far. He was glad she was still in the vicinity. He had not relished the idea of pursuing her to Elm Lodge like a draconian landlord about to claim *droit de seigneur*.

After a short surreptitious observation, he had seen

enough to be sure the woman was indeed Sarah Marchant. He guessed from her restless pacing that her frame of mind was similar to his own. With a wry smile he realised that now was probably as good a time as any to see if they could find a sensible solution to the damnable predicament Edward had landed them in.

'It seems we got off on the wrong foot. Shall we try again?'

Sarah swivelled about to see Gavin Stone brace a dark hand against the wall of the barn. Immediately her heart was jolted into pumping faster. Her mouth parted in readiness to spontaneously demand an apology for his boorish behaviour earlier. Her soft lips came together again without her having uttered a blameful word. He didn't look quite so arrogant or scornful now and, in any case, her opinion of his manners was irrelevant. He held the key to securing her family's continuing comfortable existence.

'That seems a sensible suggestion,' she coolly agreed and, simply to occupy her jittery nerves, collected her bonnet from the hay bale she'd sat upon. She had also moved away from the edge of the barn to conceal herself from inquisitive eyes. Her reputation might be thoroughly besmirched, but she had no wish to add to her infamy. If she were caught in broad daylight loitering behind a barn with a gentleman, it was likely to give the town's gossips a fine time.

Gavin moved closer, watching as she fiddled with

her hat, first winding the strings about her palm before immediately jerking them loose.

Obviously he had startled her by coming upon her so unexpectedly. He strolled into the barn and made a cursory inspection of the dilapidated state of it before wandering out again. She still seemed unsettled, so he walked the length of the building to give her a little longer to regain her composure.

'Please don't stand where you might be seen.' Sarah pursued him to the edge of the barn. She made as though to catch his sleeve and tug him backwards. Momentarily a small hand hovered in space before recoiling. 'It is best if we keep out of sight. I would not want any curious passerby to come and investigate what is going on.'

Gavin duly complied whilst emitting a rasping chuckle. 'In Mr Pratt's office you called me a reprobate. Are you now worried for my reputation?'

'Perhaps I am more concerned for mine,' Sarah remarked acidly. 'But then you believe I have no good name to keep, don't you?' she added quietly. She could tell he was about to humour her with polite lies and she'd rather not hear them. 'You are right, of course,' she interrupted him. 'I am not liked or welcomed here in town. But it does not do to flaunt my notoriety or unnecessarily rub people's noses in it.'

Gavin noticed the proud tilt to her chin, but she couldn't conceal the tremor in her voice. She might know she was despised, but she suffered for it. After three or more years as a courtesan one might have expected her to acquire an amount of robust defiance. Her vulnerability was rather sweet and stirred something akin to tenderness in him.

Within a moment he had quashed the noble emotion and reinstated a more cynical outlook. He had no idea whether Miss Marchant had gladly set on the path to ruination with a man old enough to be her father. Until he did, he would reserve judgement on how genuine was her trembling modesty and whether plucking at his heartstrings was simply part of a calculated act.

'Is it correct that you were just sixteen when Edward…?' Gavin hesitated, sought an inoffensive term. 'When he took you under his protection?'

'Yes, I was sixteen,' Sarah said. 'And I would rather not discuss it. It was a long time ago,' she said carefully. She had no intention of furnishing details of her affair with Edward to his brother. But neither did she want to rekindle friction between them. She was very conscious of the need to prolong this truce.

'Three years is not so long.' Gavin was not so easily deterred.

'It was four years ago. It seems a long time to me,' Sarah countered with grit in her voice and immediately turned the subject to the one presently most troubling to her. 'We must try to find a way to solve the problem of Edward's will. I'm sure you must want that too. It would be a great pity if you lost your inheritance.'

'Indeed, it would,' Gavin drily concurred.

Sarah ignored the ironic inflection in his voice. He thought she was showing him faux-concern in order to wheedle what she wanted out of him and secure her own future. It was true. A quick encompassing look roved over him. Oh, he might be far more handsome and sophisticated than Edward, but she would sooner have Edward any day.

She sensed Gavin Stone could be courteous and charming when it suited him—as it did now—but a latent and dangerous power seemed to lurk behind his measured words and smiles. He naturally wanted his bequest and she was the obstacle preventing him having it. Was Gavin Stone capable of resorting to devilry to get his money?

An anxious breath filled her lungs. She had earlier settled on an idea that seemed a very fair compromise. It was a simple plan, but she'd persevered with it because she recalled Mr Pratt had mentioned Gavin Stone wanted to hasten back to London. To expedite matters he might readily agree to her suggestion and return tomorrow. And that would suit her admirably.

'I live At Elm Lodge,' she blurted out. 'It is part of the estate that you have inherited.'

'I know.'

Sarah looked at him, hoping he might contribute more conversation. He did not. 'I hope you will not deem it an impertinence,' she quickly continued, 'but I have thought of a compromise that might benefit us both.'

A slight rise of his dark brows was not the encouragement she had hoped for, but did indicate that he was willing to listen to her idea.

'As you know, your brother resided at Willowdene Manor where there are plentiful staff. I have lived alone at the Lodge for three years and have just two servants who live out. Mr and Mrs Jackson help with cooking and gardening and so on. They have taken on other work too and have their own cottage in the village.'

'No.'

'You don't know what I'm going to say,' Sarah gasped out at that rude interruption.

'Yes, I do. You're going to say that you will dispense with their services and act as a housekeeper and gardener at the Lodge to earn the right to stay there.'

So he *had* known what she was going to say. But then it had hardly been an ingenious plan. 'Why will you not agree to it?' Sarah's demand was harsh with frustration. 'It will solve everything. You can honestly say to the executors that you are providing for me financially and thus will be able to legally claim your inheritance.'

'I have every intention of claiming my inheritance,' Gavin stressed softly. 'But not like that.'

Chapter Three

'Why ever not? Is it too simple a plan?'

'Simple plans are usually the best sort.'

'Well?' Sarah prompted, a glimmer of hope brightening her eyes and voice. 'Are you now persuaded towards it?'

'No.'

'To what do you object, sir?' Sarah demanded, barely suppressing her exasperation.

'Several things,' Gavin said. 'But let us start with the most obvious. If I wanted a housekeeper at Elm Lodge it would be more economic to employ Mrs Jackson.'

'But Maude cannot help you lay hands on your brother's fortune,' Sarah pointed out with a note of triumph. 'I alone can do that. My employment might be more costly, but also greatly beneficial.' Whilst willing him to agree to her logic, she came closer to look up expectantly into his darkly rugged features.

Within a moment she could feel heat prickling beneath her cheeks for eyes of cerulean blue were interestedly roving her face, lingering on her mouth. An odd feeling quickened her blood. It disturbed her so profoundly that she took an involuntary step back. If he thought to flatter her into accepting less than was her due, he was to be sorely disappointed. She would never be duped by a philanderer's artfulness.

He thought he had her measure. Perhaps he did, but she had his, too. Just a short time ago at the will reading he had been incensed and scornful of her. How different he seemed now he'd had time to reason that a gallant might do better than a tyrant. However much he was tempted to curse her to hell he needed her cooperation just as she needed his.

'I only want a small living allowance of fifty pounds per annum,' Sarah briskly informed him and peeked from beneath twin fans of dusky lashes to see what reaction that demand provoked. She could discern no change in his demeanour. He remained resting against the barn, indolently watching her.

She suspected he must eventually agree to her suggestion. There was too much at stake to reject a reasonable plan just because she'd been the one to voice it. If he wanted to puff up his ego by quibbling and driving a hard bargain, she was not about to indulge him.

'Why will you not agree?' she taunted him. 'Do you not want to return to Mr Pratt's office and tell him you can comply with the terms of your inheritance?'

'I would be delighted to do just that,' Gavin drawled. 'I imagine my bank would also rejoice at the news that they can give up hounding me for loan repayments.'

Sarah was suddenly assailed by a memory of her papa skulking behind drawn curtains when heavily in debt to the bank and in regular receipt of threatening missives. 'Very well,' she said calmly. 'I can tell you are not swayed by that offer. I am prepared to accept a lesser sum of forty pounds per annum just so we might both go home.'

A chuckle grazed Gavin's throat. 'I take it you don't play cards?'

'I do, but not very well. What made you say that?' she asked sharply, sensitive to being mocked.

'You have not mastered the art of bluffing, my dear,' he explained softly. 'You've disclosed your hand far too soon.'

He was laughing at her. Bright spots of colour burned in her cheeks. 'This is a matter of some gravity, not a silly game,' she snapped. 'I would sooner be direct and honest. I can only hope you might be too.'

Gavin bowed his head in humble acknowledgement of being chastised, but humour was still slanting his mouth. 'In my world, Miss Marchant, gambling is a matter of some gravity and not a silly game. And being direct and honest when the stakes are high is foolish.'

'And that, sir, is a helpful insight into your character, for which I thank you,' Sarah retorted primly. 'It is also another reason for me to want to speedily conclude

our business. You may then return to your world and
your sophisticated friends in London and leave me in
peace.'

That acerbic comment drew to an end Gavin's com-
fortably lounging stance. A lithe movement freed his
person from planked wood. He strolled closer, his
thorough appraisal bringing more blood to sting her
cheeks. 'For a woman who has spent all her adult life
as a harlot, you can appear a mite too sanctimonious,
my dear.' Gavin watched as the scarlet stain spread,
marring her flawless complexion. 'It seems Edward
took too many liberties with you,' he continued in a
sensual tone. 'As I see it, the worst by far was forcing
false piety down your throat.'

A small hand flew to Sarah's neck as though that
part of her anatomy was under assault. 'How dare
you!' she finally gasped. 'How dare you speak to me
like that.' She gritted through small pearly teeth, 'Your
brother always treated me with respect. He was a
decent man. He was kind.'

'Kind?' Gavin echoed sardonically. 'Was it kind of
him to leave you to the tender mercy of a brother he'd
slander as a reprobate?'

Sarah visibly winced at that. She had asked herself
the same question many times since she'd bolted from
the solicitor's office. If Edward had cared even a little
for her, it was indeed hard to understand why he would
put her future security in the hands of a man he'd described as a rake and a wastrel.

'Why do you think he did that?' Gavin asked abruptly.

'I'm sure he…I don't know…Edward was gravely ill,' she stuttered out, aware she was under intense scrutiny from narrowed blue eyes. 'The smallpox left him often delirious.'

'His doctor and his lawyer deemed him of sound mind to the very end. He was *compos mentis* when he dictated his instructions to Joseph Pratt. He knew what he was about.'

Sarah twirled agitatedly on the spot. 'What does it matter now?' Her small hands gestured hopelessness. 'Edward has gone and taken with him the reason we must endure this madness.' She pressed her brow with slender fingers as though she might smooth out the furrows there. 'Oh, how I wish that he were still here,' she whispered almost to herself.

'I'm sure you do.' Gavin's laugh was as mordant as had been his tone. 'A few months ago he was a healthy man in his prime. It must be galling having your meal ticket whipped away so unexpectedly.'

'I wish he were here because I miss him,' she enunciated icily, yet the grain of truth in his sarcasm made her voice quiver. Her main concern was how she would go on now Edward had left her with nothing of her own. She tilted her chin to glare at the stranger who held sway over her life. 'And my feelings for your brother are private and none of your concern.'

'Unfortunately my brother has seen fit to make your

very existence my concern.' It was a reminder issued in a voice of silky steel.

It had the effect of immediately goading Sarah into retaliation. 'Well, you may fret no longer that I will be a burden of unwanted responsibility.' A tiny part of her mind acknowledged that she was about to act rashly. Still she could not prevent the words erupting. 'I would sooner face penury than accept your charity.'

'I'm relieved to hear it,' Gavin said ironically. 'Charity is not at all what I have in mind for you, Miss Marchant. I intend you earn your keep.'

Swiftly Sarah settled her bonnet back on her head and tied the strings with unsteady fingers. Blood thundered at her temples, making her feel she might faint as she readied herself to leave. She could tell it was late afternoon as the sun was low and soon Mr Bloom would be closed for business. She must purchase laudanum from the apothecary before heading back home. But it was the unspoken question hovering between them that was really prompting her to speed away.

Several times since their encounter in Mr Pratt's office Sarah's mind had glanced away from an unpalatable truth. A virile man—and especially, as in this case an infamous womaniser—was unlikely to turn down the opportunity to bed a young woman passed on to him for that purpose. When one took into account that the fellow was required to pay for her board and lodging, the idea that he might do so simply from the goodness of his heart seemed ludicrous.

But Gavin's furious reaction on hearing of Edward's wishes had encouraged Sarah to hope they might find a less sordid solution to this conundrum. From the start Gavin Stone had seemed to her to be his own man and not a character to take easily to his brother manipulating him from the grave. But she could no longer deny that the fire in his eyes was generated as much by lust as anger. He might not like her, he might mock and scorn her and call her a harlot, but none of it would stop him wanting to sleep with her. And she was his for the taking…or so he thought…

'Good day to you, sir,' she said with admirable aplomb and attempted to stride past him.

'Are you about to run away again like a spoiled child because you cannot get your own way?' Gavin had stepped to block her path, but it was his comment, not his person, that brought her to a halt.

Her blonde head swayed back on her slender neck and she attacked him with fierce tawny eyes. 'I am not running away,' she informed him clearly. 'I am going because I refuse to participate in more pointless wrangling over Edward's will.' She sucked in a calming breath. 'You have rejected my very reasonable compromise, and so be it. For now it seems wise to part company and see if a solution can be found tomorrow. Perhaps by then a little of the hostility between us might have evaporated.' There was a brief pause before she added, 'Good day to you, sir.'

'I'm encouraged that you think there is yet hope for us, Miss Marchant.'

Sarah dodged past him and, when sure she was in no danger of being restrained, swished about to look back at him. 'And I'm encouraged, sir, that you did not immediately act petulantly and say you would be miles away in London tomorrow.' She hesitated at his silence and took a step closer to him again. She was now in a more logical frame of mind. The thought that he might return home had rendered her more anxious than annoyed. 'Are you going straight back to London?' she demanded to know.

'No. I have my petulance under control,' he wryly answered. He gazed indicatively at the golden orb settled on the horizon. 'It would be foolish to travel overnight and risk being set upon by felons. Should I expire also, I imagine you, Miss Marchant, would be in very dire straits.'

Sarah gave him a faux-sweet smile. 'Then I must wish you good health, sir, and safe journeys, till we have this sorted out to my liking.' She watched his amusement deepen, his mouth and eyes soften as he casually put his hands in to his pockets. At times he could look quite youthful and appealing when hard mockery was gone from his eyes and they shared a little joke…

Sarah put such silly sentiment from her mind. Just a short while ago he had insulted her, shown his disdain for a woman he classed as little more than a harlot. With a very brief nod she turned her back on him and grace-fully walked away.

* * *

Sarah caught Mr Bloom just as he was in the process of bolting the door to his apocothery. He slid back the bolts, welcomed her in, and served her the usual dose of laudanum.

If privately Daniel Bloom held an opinion on the quantity of the drug he sold to Miss Marchant, he kept his own counsel. She was a joy to behold and a good customer and it would not do to upset her. He watched her curvaceous figure with an appreciative eye as she turned from the counter, clutching her purchase. Time and again over the years he had deemed Edward Stone a lucky dog to have such a filly in his bed. But of course now Edward Stone was lucky no more...and it was whispered that neither was Miss Marchant...

Already there was a rumour in town that Miss Marchant had been so put out by what transpired at the will reading earlier that she'd run off in a fine old state. But then people were always looking for something to tattle over.

Daniel looked out of the shop window. Towards the eastern end of the High Street he could see the dogcart with old Matthew Jackson perched on the seat. He'd seen the fellow sitting like that, puffing on his pipe, for quite a long time. Daniel watched Sarah increase her pace as though she regretted being late for her lift home. Daniel shook his head in disbelief. For a woman who got through that amount of sedative she had a surprising amount of vim.

'I'm sorry to be late, Matthew,' Sarah burst out as she came within earshot of Maude's husband. He often brought her into town and always waited in the same spot for her to finish her business.

'Don't matter none,' the old fellow answered having removed the clay pipe. Once she had settled on the seat beside him, he gave her a grizzled look. 'All come right, has it?' It was Matthew's oblique way of asking whether she'd got a pleasing bequest from her protector's will.

Sarah summoned up a small smile and tried to look optimistic. 'Not quite,' she answered. 'But I've not yet lost hope that it will…eventually.'

Matthew grunted an unintelligible response, thrust the pipe back between his teeth, and set the horse in motion. After a few yards the pipe was removed again. 'Straight home?' he asked.

'No…' Sarah looked at the brown bottle clutched on her lap. 'No, to Aunt Bea's, please, Matthew.'

He grunted again and bashed out the pipe's contents on the side of the cart. Shaking his head dolefully, he gave his full attention to the road.

Gavin watched the cart pulling into the distance as he strolled back to the Red Lion. A look of frustration tautened his features. It was not solely due to the fact that the day was closing with his inheritance still hanging in the balance. Constantly pricking his mind was the wish that Edward's mistress might be as unappealing to him as had been his spouse.

Even when Janet had been a vivacious brunette of twenty with many admirers, he had not found her desirable. His feelings for Miss Sarah Marchant were, unfortunately, quite different. In the lawyer's office he had scorned Sarah for imagining that he might stoop to coerce a woman to sleep with him. At the time he had meant what he said: never in his life had he bedded an unwilling woman. But his attitude to her had undergone a subtle change, although he couldn't pinpoint when or why it had come about.

She was attractive, as befitted her line of work, but she also possessed a beguiling innocence.

He'd believed he knew the artful ways of courtesans. It was no idle boast that for over a decade and a half he'd kept company with women of every class and character. Never had he come across a woman as enigmatic as Sarah Marchant. He reluctantly accepted that it would be easy to become obsessed with his brother's mistress and the knowledge disturbed him. That way lay insanity.

They both knew where this situation must ultimately lead. If she had given him just a small sign that she might welcome his protection, he would have offered it. But she had sought to deflect his advances by offering to be his housekeeper.

He had considered—and rejected—employing her before she voiced the suggestion. Once he had curbed his initial anger on discovering that his brother was dictating to him from the grave, he'd accepted his responsibility to protect her. It was no hardship. He'd known from the moment he set eyes on her that he found her desirable.

The reason for her ruination he'd yet to discover, but it was likely to be the usual mundane tale: her well-to-do family had cast her out after a faithless lover in her youth had abandoned her to her fate. Gavin could not recall any such gossip over a Miss Marchant, but then, if she had always lived in the countryside, the scandal would not have reached London.

Whatever had occurred, it had not cowed her. He was not dealing with a timid mouse. From their conversations he knew she was intelligent and forthright. She could be wilful and passionate, too. Perhaps he was dealing with an artful schemer. Her subtle rejection might be a teasing ploy to aggravate his desire and increase her settlement. Gavin smiled ruefully. It wouldn't be the first time a particularly comely courtesan had managed to do that. But with his inheritance secure he could afford to be generous to his paramours without plunging himself into debt. The chit simply needed to say yes and he would undertake to look after her in style.

His intention was to take her to London with him and settle her close to his Mayfair mansion. What was there for her to object to in that? She might have been fond of Edward, but he was gone and his parting gift was that she be passed on like a family concubine to pleasure his heir. It was an act likely to crush tender memories in even the most loyal mistress.

Gavin had been aware he was under observation as he stood in contemplation of the cart disappearing into the distance. Now he turned his attention to his admirer. The saucy wench had been trying to catch his eye since he arrived at the Red Lion. He decided she was attractive enough to dampen the fire Miss Marchant had put in his loins. As he passed he gave Molly a wink that sent her, rosy-cheeked, scuttling into the kitchen to boast of her success to the other girls.

'Oh, I can't go on like this,' was Aunt Bea's flustered welcome as she opened the door to her niece and flapped her gloved hands at her.

'How has Tim been today?' Sarah asked quietly, for she was well aware of the cause of her aunt's agitation. She removed her bonnet and smoothed her blonde hair.

'In a temper,' her aunt responded pithily. 'And I'm in a mind to go out and let him stew in his own juice. Your brother should mind his manners, no matter his pitiful condition.'

'He cannot help his moods,' Sarah said softly. She indicated the laudanum in her hand. 'A draught of this is sure to calm him and ease his mood.'

'And thank Heavens for it.' With that announcement Aunt Beatrice took the drug and led the way into the front room of her neat cottage. She turned about and gave Sarah a penetrating look. 'Come, tell me everything. What happened this morning? Did you get the Lodge to live in and a pension as you hoped?'

Sarah shook her head.

'You must quit the Lodge? Edward left you a pension at least?' Beatrice said, a mixture of shock and outrage in her tone.

'No,' Sarah said and pulled a little face.

'Well…I never did! And him such a gentlemen. Or so he seemed.' Beatrice took an indignant march here and there in her small sitting room. 'Well, how are we all to live? The cupboards are nearly empty. Why did the tightfist want you to attend his will reading if he'd no intention of leaving you a bequest of some sort?'

'He did make me a bequest…of some sort,' Sarah admitted and close behind that declaration followed a small hysterical giggle.

Aunt Beatrice gave her an old-fashioned look. She crossed her thin arms over her narrow chest. 'Well, I'm pleased you can joke about it all, miss. When we're all in the workhouse you may not find it so amusing.' She huffed a sorry sigh and said more gently, 'Come, tell me what it was he left you.'

'His brother,' Sarah said.

Chapter Four

'Mr Pratt! It is a surprise to see you, sir.'

Joseph Pratt had advanced ahead of her housekeeper into the neatly furnished room Sarah used as a small parlour. Having given the fellow a glower for arriving at Elm Lodge uninvited, Maude Jackson withdrew and shut the door. For a moment she lingered with her good ear near the panels before removing herself to the kitchen.

Moments ago Sarah had been sorting through her jewellery box. Apart from a few family heirlooms left to her by her mama, she had no wish to keep the rest. All were pieces Edward had bought for her and she would sooner be rid of painful memories of him. She would also sooner have the cash they might raise. Now the casket was put aside and, with a perplexed expression, she got to her feet. It could only be a matter concerning Edward's will that brought Joseph Pratt to her door. She looked enquiringly at him, but no immediate explanation was forthcoming.

Joseph fiddled with his hat brim, his cheeks taking on a bashful glow. A smile slanted sideways at her before he burst out, 'I beg you will not deem my call an unpleasant surprise, Miss Marchant.'

Sarah's bemusement increased. 'I can only answer that when I know what prompted it, sir,' she returned politely. 'I imagine it concerns the business in your office yesterday.'

'Precisely…' The confirmation was issued with a sibilant throb.

'I hope there is no more bad news…' Sarah ventured, unable to properly decipher his queer attitude.

'No…no,' he reassured with a flap of a hand. 'Please do not alarm yourself.' A look of studied sympathy shaped his flaccid jowls. Inwardly he was gratified to learn that she considered the prospect of becoming Gavin Stone's mistress as *bad news*. 'I know the terms of the will must have come as a terrible shock and disappointment to you.'

His eyes were drawn to the open jewellery box. The sight of it boosted his confidence. Ladies sorted through their gems for only two reasons: to bestow them or to sell them. He came to the swift conclusion that Miss Marchant was taking stock of her assets so she might cash in. And that heightened his suspicion that she had not yet come to an arrangement with the deceased's brother.

Joseph had seen Gavin Stone earlier that day. Although they did no more than exchange a nod in greeting, the scowl the fellow had on his face was enough for Joseph to surmise that Gavin was no closer to securing his inheritance. But Edward's heir had six months in which to win over Miss Marchant before he lost his fortune. In the meantime the lady could either choose to swallow her pride and go to him or foster a little dalliance elsewhere to pay her bills. Joseph had deduced that she might prefer the latter simply to avoid the churlish rogue for as long as possible. In fact, he was increasingly hopeful Miss Marchant might be persuaded to accept discreet assistance from a personable lawyer…and naturally display ample gratitude for it.

Emboldened by what seemed to him perfect logic, Mr Pratt continued, 'It's my ardent wish that I might ease the…um…regrettable situation in which you find yourself, Miss Marchant. To that end I am begging you will favourably consider what I am about to put to you.'

Sarah looked up at him, a spark of hope livening her weary eyes. Had he come to tell her that he had discovered a legal solution to their woes? He was looking at her intently as though something of significance was on his mind. His language was rather flamboyant but then he might be anxious that before business was concluded she would fly off in a huff as she had yesterday.

'I…please do sit down, sir. Naturally I am interested in any suggestions that might improve my lot. I shall get Maude to fetch some tea.' Sarah's tone held muted excitement and she speedily set about summoning Maude to bring refreshments.

Joseph sat down, satisfaction settling on his features. Miss Marchant seemed to have grasped his meaning and was not too coy to show pleasure at it. He lounged back into the sofa and drove specks from his cuff with finger flicks. Her enthusiasm was to be expected. He was, after all, a pillar of Willowdene society. Miss Marchant was no doubt thanking her lucky stars that a charming and prosperous saviour had prevented her enduring the attentions of less worthy individuals.

Sarah returned to sit opposite her guest who had taken the space on the sofa she had vacated. She was eager to learn in what way he might ease her situation. But he remained stubbornly silent and was impertinently eyeing her jewellery.

'I expect you have been looking through your keepsakes.' Joseph continued peering judiciously into the casket. He had decided to kindly condescend to have tea and a little chat for her modesty's sake. He sighed, touched a finger to a silver bangle. 'Memories of the departed are a comfort at such times.'

'I have had my memories tarnished,' Sarah answered, truthfully.

'Quite.' Joseph sagely nodded. 'The prospect of being left in the care of a…shall we say…licentious fellow is not something a young lady of refinement ought ever to face.'

Clasping her hands in her lap Sarah leaned forward

in her chair. 'I think you are about to suggest an alternative,' she prompted. 'Please let me know what it is, sir. I am impatient to hear anything of benefit.'

Joseph goggled at her. He had been hoping for a positive response to his proposition but a little reticence—even if faked—would also have been welcome. He did not want his prize devalued by the knowledge that Miss Marchant bestowed her favours too easily. He looked at her lovely face, aglow with expectation, rosy lips parted in readiness to smile. He swallowed and eased his position, deciding her eagerness was quite charming for it was having the required effect. 'You have been treated badly, my dear,' he said hoarsely, 'but I can offer you not inconsiderable consolation. I only await your permission to describe the advantages to you.' He made to pluck one of Sarah's slender hands from her lap.

Sarah quickly withdrew her fingers, but sent him a tight smile. She needed no physical demonstration of his benevolence. His words would do very well. When he made another clumsy lunge for her midriff, she sprang to her feet and put distance between them. 'What advantages, sir?' she prompted rather impatiently.

Joseph was also on his feet, but he gave up his pursuit of Sarah. His attention had been drawn to a woman of more advanced years. Maude had reappeared, not bearing the tea tray, but news of another caller.

'Mr Gavin Stone is here, miss.'

That gentleman was strolling into the room before either of its occupants had fully digested news of his arrival.

'Mr Stone…' Sarah's flustered greeting drew a penetrating look from Gavin's deep blue eyes. His attention then flicked to her companion.

Joseph executed a very stiff bow and, with his sallow complexion mottling, stalked to the sofa to collect his hat whilst muttering about the need to take his leave.

'Don't go on my account,' Gavin said placidly. His tone seemed at odds with the long hard stare concentrated on the lawyer. It had the effect of hurrying Joseph towards the door.

The sight of Gavin Stone, attired in riding clothes with his black boots gleaming through a layer of dust, had unsettled Sarah for a moment. He had the look of a prosperous Romany come a-calling with his rugged tanned features and careless dark locks. Now, as the lawyer reached the door, Sarah quickly jerked herself to her senses. A suspicion niggled at her that this might be no chance meeting between the three of them, but something the gentlemen had deliberately concocted to browbeat her. Her conspiracy theory was soon quashed: Joseph Pratt looked distinctly put out by Gavin's arrival. She was, too, for had the lawyer not been about to expound on a way of improving her lot?

'You have not yet fully explained the reason for your visit, sir,' Sarah reminded him, skipping to the door to intercept his departure. 'We were talking of—'

'It is of no consequence now, Miss Marchant,' Joseph interrupted brusquely. His floridity increased until he was red to the roots of his receding hair. With a jerky bow he was soon gone from the room.

'How odd,' Sarah murmured to herself, unaware that her genuine puzzlement had caused Maude's gimlet eyes to slide to meet those of her remaining guest.

Maude had not liked the lawyer, but she'd welcomed this fellow turning up unexpectedly. She knew as soon as he gave his name that he had every right to be here. Gavin Stone was, of course, the wild brother who'd inherited the big estate and that included Elm Lodge. That aside, she'd also given him a once over and decided he was handsome enough to be as bad as he liked. Sometimes scoundrels changed when they found what they were looking for. And Maude reckoned, from the way that Gavin Stone was staring at Sarah, he'd met his match. Satisfaction writhed across her pursed lips. 'Shall I bring in the tea, miss?' Maude asked.

Sarah glanced at Gavin. They had parted yesterday on frosty terms. She did not want to offer him her hospitality, yet to deny him a cup of tea seemed mean. A glint of humour in his eyes betrayed that he was aware of her quandary.

'Yes…thank you, Maude.' The firm order for refreshment sent Maude immediately from the room.

To break the tense quiet Sarah blurted, 'Mr Pratt is quite an odd character, I think.'

'Do you? Why?' Gavin asked mildly.

'I'm still not sure what was his purpose in coming here today. I thought at one time he was about to tell me he had found a legal loophole through which we might both wriggle to freedom. But if that were so, he would have stayed to tell us. He went off in a peculiar mood, I thought.'

Gavin strolled closer to inspect the look of bewilderment on her face. He could detect no coyness, no sham modesty. She seemed genuinely unaware that the lawyer had designs on her virtue. Once again he was struck by her apparent innocence…her undeniable beauty. He could understand why Joseph Pratt had felt compelled to try his luck. Gavin imagined the lawyer would not be the only gentleman sniffing around Miss Marchant, spouting sympathy and suggestions.

'I think Mr Pratt was about to tell you he expected your personal attention in exchange for any assistance he offered.'

Sarah frowned and then her brow smoothed, her eyes widened in shock. Quickly she brought her soft lips together and turned away from him to shield her confusion. He would think that! The lecherous beast!

'I do not think you should judge every gentleman by your own lax morals, sir,' she retorted crisply. She twirled around to face him with her chin at a haughty angle. 'I found nothing…offensive…in Mr Pratt's behaviour.' The moment it was out, Sarah knew that declaration was not quite true. The lawyer had indeed tried to grab inappropriately at her person. The more she pondered on the encounter, the more she realised there had been ambiguity in his conversation too. Had she been a gullible fool not to realise he had an ulterior motive? Fast on the heels of that crushing thought came a yet worse one. Would others follow? Now Edward had gone, would she be seen as fair game?

Sarah knew she was pretty. From quite a young age her mother had told her she had been blessed with exceptional looks. Her dear mama had had great hopes that her beauty would lure a wealthy suitor and solve all their financial woes. But it wasn't to be.

More recently Edward Stone had praised her looks. In the sly eyes of some of the men hereabouts she'd seen reflected Edward's admiration. Oh, in front of their womenfolk they might purport to dislike her, but she'd sensed that privately they'd coveted Edward's young paramour.

And so did his brother.

Whatever Gavin thought of her as a person—and he had made his opinion of her clear yesterday when roundly attacking her character—it would not dampen his lust. The fact that she had a heart and a soul and a yearning for affection and respect would bother him not one jot. He was here today for the same reason as had been Joseph Pratt…to have her naked beneath him.

She sensed colour creep to stain her milky neck and

a hand moved involuntarily to shield it. Would he still lust after her if he knew that her body was not so pretty as her face?

'Please sit down, if you would like to.' The words were ejected in little above a whisper.

Gavin wordlessly declined the polite invitation by moving instead to take up a position by the chimney-piece. Sarah sat down, then wished she had not, for she could sense his pitiless gaze warming the top of her head.

'Joseph Pratt is unlikely to be the only gentleman interested in propositioning you.'

Sarah's small teeth sunk into her bottom lip. So he could read her thoughts too. She simply nodded and blinked.

'Is that what you want? A parade of gentlemen callers from which you might choose a wealthy candidate to keep you?'

Sarah flew to her feet, her fists gripped tight by her side. 'You know I do not! If that were all I wanted, I would have accepted my fate and settled on you. You will be richer than all of them put together once you have the Stone inheritance.'

'But I have not yet offered my services,' Gavin reminded quietly.

'You do not need to, sir,' Sarah replied damningly. 'You have said you will not forgo your inheritance and neither will you spare me.'

'Your complaints would be better directed at Edward. He engineered this bizarre scheme.'

Sarah could not argue with that. She expelled a sigh, gesturing hopelessly. 'At least you seem to have absolved me of any guilt in trying to trap you into it. For that I am grateful.'

'My conceit might suffer to admit it, but I know you would rather choose your future, as would I.' Gavin moved closer to watch her reaction to what he said next. 'And you? Do you still believe that I am wicked enough to have asked my brother to bequeath me his beautiful mistress?'

'As you say,' she said carefully, keen to foster the fragile harmony, 'neither of us wants to be shackled to a stranger.' Had she not been made of sterner stuff, she might have melted beneath the sultry sapphire gaze that had accompanied his compliment on her looks. But her memory was not so short. She had but recently been the butt of his scorn and insults.

'Perhaps it was Edward's intention that we no longer be strangers.'

'I would sooner he had introduced you in the normal way whilst he was alive,' Sarah commented pithily.

'Edward was always careful to keep out of sight anything of his I might have wanted.'

More subtle praise. She could not deny he was a skilful flirt. Again heat bled in to her cheeks. His rough-velvet voice allied with those steady predatory gazes combined to create quite a heady attack on the senses. Their conversation seemed no longer focused on material considerations, but had become quite intimate.

She felt suffocated, unable to rise to the challenge of playing his sophisticated game. She stepped away. 'Your reminiscence about your brother is not helping solve our predicament, sir,' she said briskly.

'But I think it is,' Gavin quietly begged to differ. 'We need to ascertain what reasons he might have had for wanting to entwine our lives upon his demise.' Gavin strolled to the window and looked out into woodland. 'He must have realised that this would come as a shock to us both. He had little fondness for me, I know, and if it is some sort of bad joke, I allow him his laugh. But you?' He turned and slanted Sarah a look. 'Were you at odds over something that might have prompted him to secretly seek revenge?'

'No,' Sarah hotly denied. 'Nothing like that passed between us. I believed we were friends till the end.'

'Friends?' Gavin echoed drily.

'Yes, friends,' Sarah repeated with some emphasis. 'It is possible for a man and a woman to share a friendship as well as a bed.'

Gavin bowed his head in mock humility. 'Thank you for that insight, Miss Marchant,' he drawled. 'Hard-hearted rakes do not know such things.'

'Neither do they know when to accept a very good deal.' She came closer to him to make her point. 'You will be better off having Elm Lodge occupied than empty. You are foolish not to immediately accept my suggestion to housekeep for you. A fortune is almost yours for a tenancy and a paltry annual sum.'

Gavin's smile deepened to a lazy chuckle. 'I'm almost persuaded,' he murmured infuriatingly.

Sarah flung herself around in a temper and stalked off two paces. 'I am done with trying to be reasonable.' She retraced those angry steps to glare up at him with sparking topaz eyes. 'I do not give a fig what becomes of you or your brother's inheritance. You may return to London empty-handed and end in the Fleet.' She sucked in a breath to add, 'Oh, I know you are a spend-thrift, too. I know all about you.'

'And are you going to return the compliment and tell me all about you?'

Sarah blanched, shrinking back a pace. She had not expected that unwanted question. She parted her soft lips to demand he take his leave, but was silenced by the sight of Maude entering with the tea tray. If the servant noticed her mistress's flushed cheeks and fiery eyes, or the tension vibrating her neat figure, she gave no sign. 'Shall I pour, miss?' she asked placidly.

'No…thank you,' Sarah added with a hint of apology for her brusqueness.

The brief interlude whilst Maude settled the tray on the table allowed her wits to curb her temper. She must secure essentials for her and her family. Once Maude had departed she enquired coolly, 'What has brought you here today, sir?' A rustle of dimity skirts was the only sound as she paced to and fro, waiting for his response. Suddenly she halted and frowned at his silence. 'If the answer is nothing in particular, then I must ask you to leave.'

'I think you know why I'm here,' Gavin returned mildly. 'I want my inheritance and I am prepared to comply with the spirit of Edward's will to get it. In short, Miss Marchant, I have no objection to protecting you in the way my brother intended I should.'

'You might have no objection, sir, but I do,' Sarah hissed once she had drawn sufficient breath to do so.

Chapter Five

'Perhaps if I tell you I am willing to improve on Edward's terms, that might help you overcome your objections.'

'You do not know what he gave me!' Sarah cried in muted anger. 'Besides, it is of no consequence for I want no more. What I had was adequate…I was satisfied.'

'Were you?'

The insinuation was subtly sensual and made Sarah's heart pound. But she managed to boldly hold his narrowed gaze as she murmured, 'I had no complaints.'

'I'll not disappoint you, either.'

His dulcet reassurance dried Sarah's throat.

In the interminable moment that followed she noticed how vivid blue were his eyes, and how earth-dark his hair. With her vision heightened by her awareness of his virility, she saw that the dissipation in his face was not so pronounced. In fact, he appeared more tired than debauched.

'There was obviously more to Edward than I knew.'

Her tongue tip wet her lips. 'Perhaps you didn't know your brother, sir, but he knew you very well, indeed.'

The bitterness in her voice caused Gavin to ironically smile. 'And how perceptive are you, Miss Marchant? Did you know Edward?'

Sarah's teeth closed on her ready retort. Gavin had a knack of touching on a very raw nerve. How well had she known Edward? It was a question that constantly tormented her.

Simply to occupy her fidgety hands, she busied herself with clattering cups on to saucers, forgetful of how inappropriate it was to offer one's tormentor hospitality. In a daze she set about pouring the tea.

Was her trepidation born of anger? Fear? Modesty? Was it a calculated sham? How genuine an ingénue was she? Gavin watched her ruthlessly. His eyes roved the curvaceous lines of her buttoned-up back whilst he pondered the mystery of Sarah's relationship with Edward.

His brother had obviously not seduced her with fake promises of marriage. Janet Stone's name had been mentioned several times during the will reading and Sarah had not displayed any surprise at the existence of her late lover's wife. So what had propelled such an exquisite beauty into Edward's bed? He'd had wealth, but from what Gavin saw around him, had not lavished it on his delectable young mistress. Sarah's home and her clothes looked serviceable rather than stylish, and if all her jewellery was contained within the box on the sofa she owned just a few modest pieces of gold and silver. Gavin was not surprised by his brother's parsimony. Edward had advocated constraint and his character, like his physical attributes, were at best described as pleasant. All that remained was the possibility that Sarah had been in love with his brother. That conclusion should have brought solace…but it didn't.

In a swirl of skirts Sarah turned about and held out his tea, a quantity of which now floated in the saucer. Gavin gripped her wrist to steady the clattering crockery before taking the offering. Having deposited it on a table, he slowly walked back to her. He stood quite still for a moment, gauging her reaction to his closeness. When she made no move to skitter away and her cool allure was too great a challenge to ignore, he raised a single finger, elevating her chin so she must look at him.

'I'm not a monster, Sarah,' he said softly. 'Whatever Edward has told you about my wickedness is sure to be exaggerated.'

Sarah gazed, as though entranced, into eyes grown black with desire. His long fingers had fanned to cradle her jaw in a touch that was gentle yet firm. His extreme proximity brought a scent of sandalwood to tempt her closer to its source. Involuntarily her head swayed forward. A shoulder to lean on would be so very nice.

Why should she not agree? Would her acceptance of a proposition from notorious Gavin Stone be so very wrong? She had no way of truly knowing the level of this man's licentiousness. Perhaps a natural jealousy of his handsome sibling might have led Edward to exaggerate Gavin's faults. There was nobody she might ask about his alleged debts and debauchery. Joseph Pratt might call him a licentious fellow, but how valid was the word of a hypocrite? The more she thought sensibly on it, the more she realised it was highly likely the lawyer had called on her hoping to take advantage of her predicament, not to ease it.

Sarah had had very little experience with men. She knew nothing about the rakish bachelors who frequented Mayfair. She had lived in London until she was fifteen but, in the latter years, far away from the best locations. She had been gently bred, but after a calamity destroyed her family, a début was out of the question. She had not been launched into society to attend the balls and soirées where she might meet such sophisticates.

She could recall occasions when she was about twelve and her mama would sit with her friends, sipping tea and talking in whispers. Sarah had been old enough to understand that their hushed gossip concerned illicit liaisons—often those in which her own father was entangled—but was too young to grasp the whole sordid tale.

Not five years later she had become a gentleman's

mistress. But Edward had not seduced her in the true sense. She had been glad to take the protection he offered, for how much worse might her life have been had she not? She had not loved him and he had known that. He had nevertheless told her that he was fond of her. He had seemed gentle and kind…and accepting of the scars she bore from her traumatic childhood.

Apprehension crept along her spine. How gentle… how kind would his brother be? The brother who had mocked and insulted her and called her a harlot? How important to him was her physical beauty? Would he settle for a pretty face? She was not perfect…not at all…

'I know you don't trust me, Sarah,' Gavin said softly.

Something akin to alarm jolted through Sarah for again it was as though she had spoken aloud what occupied her mind.

'Did you trust Edward?'

'Of course,' she breathed.

'Then why do you doubt the provision he has made for you? He wanted me to take over the role he played in your life. He did not intend you become my house-keeper. He intended you become my mistress.'

'And are you happy that your brother has organised your future?' she scoffed.

'Of course I'm not happy about it,' Gavin replied bluntly. 'But I am willing to accept it.'

'Because you want to claim your inheritance.' The statement was tinged with acrimony.

'Yes, I want my inheritance.'

Eyes that had become sleepy roved her figure.

'And I want you.'

Her honey-coloured eyes flowed over the hard planes of his face, hoping to detect something repulsive that might free her from his spell. He had said he wanted her in a voice that was enticingly gruff with need. How much did he want her? Enough to overlook her flaws?

'When first we learned of this madness in the lawyer's office, you boasted you did not coerce unwilling women to sleep with you.'

'I know,' he admitted and a corner of his mouth tugged upwards. 'So you must prove to me how very willing a partner you will be, Sarah, or I will be obliged to reject you simply to protect my integrity.'

Sarah gave him an exceedingly quizzical look.

'Well…that apart, there's also my vanity to consider.'

A spontaneous little laugh bubbled in her throat. It was stifled into the sound of a sob. It was a long while since she had shared a joke and somehow he could make her laugh with his self-deprecating humour. 'You are a most conceited and arrogant man,' she said with a half-hearted glower.

'I know…' His head drooped until barely a finger space separated their skin. 'But you could soon cure me of it,' he murmured.

'Please don't be flippant—' Sarah managed a mild

reproof before further words were stifled by a touch from his lips.

The light contact between them increased pressure as his mouth slid to mould to hers. She tasted warm and delicate and his male instinct was to immediately part her lips and plunge inside. But he felt the quiver of her uncertainty and knew it was no teasing response to inflame him. His wooing tongue tip began stroking the silky smoothness of her under lip, petitioning for entry.

Sarah felt blood surge through her veins. Edward had not kissed her in this way. In fact, Edward had not kissed her much at all. A peck on the cheek as a greeting, a perfunctory fusing together of mouths before the act of union; that was Sarah's experience of being kissed by a man.

This was so very different. It was pure pleasure that made her limbs feel boneless. His hands were sliding over the undulating contours of her back to her hips, easing them closer to his. They remained there, lightly massaging her flesh, but he didn't otherwise touch her intimately, although she'd expected he might.

Edward's fingers would by now have breached her bodice; he might have fondled and tasted her breasts, for, tender as he'd been with her, he'd always taken his pleasure quickly.

Gavin seemed to enjoy kissing for kissing's sake and Sarah realised with a sense of wonder that she did too. Her soft mouth clung to his, tracking its skilful movement until her lips were widely parted. Readily she accepted a caress from his tongue, tentatively she responded with a flick of her own.

Far from wanting this game to stop, Sarah desired more of the sultry heat that was coiling in her belly, urging her to press her pelvis harder to his. When his mouth became more demanding, she felt her whole being yield in response. Immediately he repositioned, taking advantage of her loosening limbs. A muscled thigh insinuated between hers, chafing lightly against the core of her femininity. Sarah gasped, and instinctively her back arched.

A dazed corner of her mind recalled that this was simply an experiment. He was testing her willingness to be his bed partner. A feeble moan in the back of her throat was her pride's protest, but she felt too languid to push him away.

Slowly he slid his mouth from hers, returning briefly in tender farewell as she tried to recapture the bliss. In consolation his lips touched the sensitive place at her throat, warming the pulse there before he put her from him.

Gavin had not been prepared for the force of the desire that had swamped him. His loins throbbed hard and thick with blood. It had been just a kiss…a simple, sweet kiss to persuade her to accept his protection. Now he felt like a callow youth unable to control his passion until a more suitable time and place.

One of Sarah's hands gripped the nearest chair to steady her balance. She felt oddly cheated. He had put an end to her delight too soon, and knowing how wanton he must think her made her voice querulous. 'Will I do?'

Gavin shot her a look from narrowed black eyes. He thought they had got past peevishness. 'I think you know you'll do very well.'

Sarah blinked, moistened her bruised mouth with a nervous flick from her tongue. What was she to do? Tell him now? Better by far to do so and avoid the humiliation of being rejected when stark naked. But the necessary words seemed to stick in her throat.

'Have I your permission to tell Joseph Pratt that we are in agreement on this?' Gavin asked softly.

There was barely a pause before she blurted, 'Yes, tell him he may release your money.' It was uttered in a faintly distracted tone, for chaotic thoughts still mired her mind.

'It's not just about the money, Sarah.' Gavin grimaced disbelief. 'God in Heaven! Don't you believe that I want you?'

'You don't know me,' Sarah whispered, and then repeated it with more vehemence.

'I know I want you. What else should I know?' Gavin asked, sensing something new was bothering her. When her ruby lips parted, but no sound issued, he took a step closer and repeated pitilessly, 'What else should I know?'

His intransigent attitude evoked in her a similar stubbornness. 'Nothing. Nothing else matters, does it?' She

saw that cool answer had not curbed his curiosity and
he was fast becoming impatient for an explanation.
She set about collecting the cups. 'I resent being passed
on to you like chattel.' It was true, if not at all the revelation she had been about to make.

'I don't think of you as such.'

'No?' A small bitter laugh preceded, 'You think of me
as a—' She broke off, unable to say the word, and
whipped about to look at him. Small fingers clutched at
mahogany behind her hips, the knuckles showing bone.
'I think you should go now.' Her chin was up, her pride
restored.

She'd wanted none of this. She didn't want a replace-
ment lover or improved conditions or anything different at all. She sought enough to get by, as she always
had, and, for the first time, she cursed Edward for not
allowing her that. If his womanising brother wanted to
persist in his pursuit of her, let him find out the hard way
that she might not live up to his lecherous expectations.

'I'll return tomorrow afternoon and let you know
what arrangements I have made.' Gavin watched her
face closely; apart from a tiny facial movement she
didn't react.

'Good day, sir.'

'Good day, Sarah.' He said her name with ironic
emphasis.

When he had gone she sped to the window and
peeped out to watch him lithely mount a large black

horse. He glanced towards the house and she whipped out of sight, flattening back against the cold wall of the Lodge. Slowly her eyes closed and she was filled with regrets. Her arms crossed over her waist and she curved forward. What had she done? She inwardly railed at herself. She could have finished this here today. Why had she not told him her secret? He might have agreed to her first suggestion that he use her in a different capacity. What had kept her silent? Vanity? She plunged away from the wall, exasperated with herself. Now what was she to do? Run after him like a fool and beg he listen to something she had forgotten to say? Wait until he came tomorrow and endure another pantomime of polite pretence whilst the atmosphere between them fizzed with friction? Would she ever find the courage to bring his attention to her ugliness?

Her eyes flew to the door and her heart leapt to her mouth as it opened. But it was Maude who came in and, having given her mistress a shrewd stare, made herself busy with the tea tray. 'The master didn't want no tea, then?' she said, eyeing the cups.

'Don't call him that.' It was a faint correction.

'Why not? Who is he, then?' Maude asked without looking away from the tray she was stacking with crockery.

'He's…he's Edward's brother, that's all he is.'

Maude slanted a look over a shoulder. Her wages had stopped when Edward Stone died. She and her husband had travelled from London with Sarah and her kin.

They'd been loyal to the family through good and very bad times. Over the years loyalty had been joined by love. Maude loved Sarah and treated her to the same affection and blunt advice she would her own daughter. Sarah felt reciprocal affection for the old retainers, but especially for Maude. More than once Maude had made known her opinion of Willowdene females who she knew were no better than they ought to be…and in their hearing.

'You'd better hope that this one treats you better than the first Mr Stone. What Edward done to you is nothing short of wicked.'

'He was good to me,' Sarah insisted with frustrated tears springing to prickle at her eyes. She knew that she sought to convince herself as well as Maude of that.

'He was good to himself, that one, if you ask me,' Maude returned pithily. 'Ruined you, he did, however he dressed it up, and him with another woman already on the go. And I don't mean his wife.' She planted her hands on her hips. 'As I see it, Edward Stone paid your bills, but he was no better nor worse than that lawyer feller who came by. I knew straight off what he wanted. Wait till his uppity wife finds out…'

'Promise me you won't say anything about Mr Pratt's visit to anyone, Maude,' Sarah quickly demanded. 'Rumours spread so quickly and he didn't say or do anything very inappropriate.'

Maude muttered to herself, but gave a little nod. As though just remembering something interesting, she clucked her tongue. 'Matthew saw Mrs Hayden's in town this morning. Her pa has passed on and has already been buried by all accounts. Still wouldn't have known about any of it, but for her being in Willowdene to sort out her pa's affairs with Mr Donaghue. Kept that quiet, didn't she?'

A little sound of mingled surprise and sympathy issued from Sarah. She knew that Mr Donaghue was Joseph Pratt's partner in the law firm in the town. She had not seen Ruth Hayden for some weeks, but when they did meet by chance in Willowdene, they exchanged a polite word or two. They were not friends, as such, but Ruth did not shun her as did the other townswomen. But then Ruth had been similarly stigmatised by past misfortune and her presence was only tolerated a mite more than was Sarah's.

Little was known about Ruth's background other than that her husband had been shot for desertion from the army when he served under Wellington. Sarah didn't know of the circumstances surrounding Captain Hayden's disgrace, but she certainly knew that it had destroyed his widow's standing in the community.

After that terrible incident had blighted her life Ruth had, several years ago now, returned to live with her widower father in the village of Fernlea. Sarah had known that Ruth's father was poorly, but she had thought it to be a minor ailment, not one likely to put him soon at death's door. If Ruth had not been expecting his demise, it must have come as a great shock to her to so suddenly find herself alone. She had lost her companion and her kin, for she had no other relative hereabouts as far as Sarah was aware.

'I shall call on Mrs Hayden to offer my condolences.' Sarah gave voice to her decision. She had never visited Ruth before; she had never received an invitation to do so. But she would go and hope to be welcomed. If she were not…at least she would have someone other than Gavin Stone troubling her peace of mind.

Chapter Six

The following afternoon Matthew Jackson collected Sarah from Elm Lodge and, having helped her to climb aboard the dogcart, they set off at a sedate pace to the village of Fernlea, where Ruth Hayden lived. It was a journey of about two miles and, jogging along beneath a fierce September sun, Sarah adjusted her bonnet brim and contemplated the likelihood of finding Ruth at home.

Concentrating on Mrs Hayden's misfortune helped suppress anxiety over her own situation. She had passed a restless night, wondering whether Aunt Bea and Timothy had enough provisions to last the week. She believed that their stock cupboards would not yet be empty, but undeniably merchants would want their payments before they made further deliveries. In the main, her tossing and turning had been caused by a bittersweet sensation of hot hard lips stroking on hers, and a sensation of masculine hands on her. It was not a yearning for Edward's body beside her that disturbed her sleep. Her phantom lover was Gavin Stone.

'Here we are then, miss,' Matthew growled.

The dogcart had come to a halt outside a white-washed cottage. It was a larger property than Sarah had imagined it to be. The front garden was wide and deep and prettily planted with colourful climbers and flowers that frothed over their angular beds. The house had a double front with four lattice-paned windows, all of which were open.

Matthew heaved himself off the cart and came round to help Sarah disembark. He tilted his head at a place unseen. 'The George Tavern be along the lane a bit.' He managed that past the pipe clamped in his teeth. It was removed so he could add gruffly, 'I'll be supping in there. Just come ter find me when you're ready ter go.'

A nod answered him, but Sarah was already wondering if she might, within a very short space of time, be interrupting her driver's imbibing. She had no idea what sort of reception her impromptu visit might get.

Having clambered aboard again, Matthew clicked at the old mare and got her clopping off along the track. Sarah gazed at the cottage whilst shaking creases from her skirts. Then, with a deep breath, she pushed open the wooden gate and walked confidently to the door. A hand was raised to knock when her bravado faltered. It was the first time in her life she had paid a call on a lady. Of course she went to see Aunt Bea but, that apart, her only experience of a social visit had been as a child when she accompanied her mama to see her friends.

Another snatched breath emboldened her to employ the black iron knocker. There was no response. She rapped a little harder; she could hear the noise of movement somewhere within and she would prefer to be turned away than ignored. Suddenly she heard footsteps rapidly approaching. The door was opened and Ruth was there, attired in black with a white apron to protect her mourning clothes. A basket of washing was under an arm. For a moment the young ladies looked startled at the appearance of one another.

'I…I'm sorry, I hope I have not called at a bad time for you. You are busy…' Sarah went rather pink and stepped back as though to leave.

'No…don't go.' Ruth snatched her cap from her thick dark hair. 'I'm not too busy to receive you, Miss Marchant.' She deposited the basket on the floor and wiped her hands on her pinafore. 'I was just pegging out. My maid does not come till Friday and there is much to do…life must go on…' She gave a wavering smile.

'I have only just heard about your father. I'm so very sorry,' Sarah said gently.

Ruth crushed the cotton cap in her hand and quickly undid the strings of her pinafore. 'You must think me rude.' She opened the door wider. 'Please do come in.'

Sarah stepped inside and followed Ruth as she led the way to a small sitting room.

'I'll just be a moment,' Ruth said quickly. 'I'll put the kettle on to boil for tea.' She spun back, her dark brown eyes shadowing doubtfully. 'Oh, that was rather presumptuous…you will stay and take tea?'

'Yes, I'd like to,' Sarah responded warmly.

Twenty minutes later Sarah and Ruth had settled in comfy chairs with a pot of tea on the table between them. A plate held slices of seed cake and Ruth offered it again to Sarah.

'It was delicious, thank you, but no more.' Sarah gestured that she had eaten her fill.

They had chatted about the fine weather and Sarah had paid formal condolences. Now she felt enough harmony was established between them to speak plainly.

'I had no idea that your father was so very poorly—'

'Oh, he was not,' Ruth interjected. 'It was not a horrible lingering disease and for that I thank God. Papa was active and happy to the last, despite being afflicted with gout and rheumatism for some years.' She paused before reminiscing, 'His garden was his passion and he would dig and hoe and grow all manner of things to his heart's content.'

'I noticed that the front garden has a wonderful mix of colours and plants.'

Sarah's comment drew from Ruth a reflective smile.

'That was where I found him. One of the ostlers

from the tavern quickly fetched Dr Bryant from Willowdene. He said the attack had been severe and death almost instant. Papa would not have known what happened or felt any pain.' She looked out of the window towards the verdant space that had taken her papa's body. 'He was one and seventy and said he'd had a good life…' She paused, rotated her cup on its saucer. 'There were only two incidents to upset his equable nature. The death of my mama and the injustice that caused him to lose his son-in-law.'

Sarah had wondered whether Ruth might divulge a little about her sad history. She was curious about Ruth's secrets, yet reluctant to reveal her own. 'It must have been a terrible time for you.'

A distracted nod answered her for Ruth's eyes seemed to watch events far in the distance. 'When my husband was buried I thought I would weep until my eyes were washed away. Now my father has been laid to rest next to my mama and I feel sad, but also quite serene. It was as fine a death as one can hope for.' She glanced at Sarah and smiled softly. 'The funeral was two weeks ago and a very quiet affair. He didn't like a fuss.'

Impulsively Sarah leaned forward to take one of Ruth's hands between her palms. She felt she had found a friend despite having talked with Ruth for less than an hour. Ruth squeezed her fingers in wordless gratitude for the comfort.

'Have you any relatives who share your loss?' Sarah asked.

Ruth shook her head, setting her thick dark curls bouncing on her shoulders. 'I have no brothers or sisters. I am quite alone.' A gruff little laugh ensued. 'I have made myself sound quite the helpless waif. I am not. I am capable and independent. I need no brother or uncle to sort out our affairs. When Papa was alive I would act as his factotum.' A rueful grimace preceded, 'A practical nature is essential for an ostracised woman.'

'As I am equally aware.' Sarah had adopted the conspiratorial tone Ruth had used. Placing down her cup, she said simply, 'I don't doubt your capability, but if there is anything at all I can do to help, I beg you will ask. I would like to be of service.'

'I appreciate the offer very much,' Ruth replied. 'And will not be too proud to remind you of it.' After an easy little quiet she raised the teapot and her delicate eyebrows in wordless question. A nod from Sarah and she poured. 'I could make an excuse that there has never been an opportunity before for us to have a proper conversation. But it won't do. Had I your courage, I might have approached you first. I might have called at Elm Lodge to say I was sorry to hear that your friend Edward Stone had died. I always found him a pleasant gentleman.' A humble look accompanied her speech. 'I wish now that I had come to see you. I thought to do so often then sought something more pressing to stop me.' Ruth proffered Sarah's tea. 'I know you were close to Mr Stone and I suspect, in its own way, your loss is as great as mine. You have kindly offered to be of assistance to me and I reciprocate…not from politeness but because I sincerely would like us to be friends.'

'So would I like that…I'd like it very much indeed.'

'May I visit you at Elm Lodge?'

Sarah's response was a vigorous nod. 'Will you stay in Fernlea? In this house?'

Ruth looked around the small neat sitting room before answering, 'Papa was not a wealthy man by any means, but if I am very prudent I can continue to live here without recourse to employment or borrowing.'

'That is very good,' Sarah said with a genuine gladness.

'And you?' Ruth asked. 'Have you family hereabouts?'

That unforeseen enquiry caused Sarah to blink and frown in confusion.

'Oh, I am sorry.' Ruth put down her cup. 'How ill mannered of me. I did not mean to pry.' Ruth knew as did most people that Sarah had been Edward Stone's mistress. Now she chided herself for being crass. It was obvious to all who met her that Sarah was a woman of gentle birth. Thus, it was natural to assume that her liaison with Edward Stone had resulted in her being cast out by any respectable family she had.

'Please do not apologise. I don't consider your question prying.' Sarah paused, wondered whether to divulge a little about her woeful history. Only Edward had known of the tragedy that had propelled her from London with what family remained to her.

Instinctively she knew she could trust Ruth to keep a secret. 'Edward knew that I have relatives living close by, but I think…hope nobody else is aware of it.' She paused. 'I should like to keep it a private matter, not because I am ashamed of them or they of me, but because it would be certain to give rise to probing questions.' She hesitated before continuing, 'And those questions would open old wounds.' Sarah gave Ruth a glance. Her new friend's expression was a study of concerned sympathy. 'My younger brother and my aunt live near Willowdene. My brother was involved in a horrible accident as a child and the scars on his body and in his mind have made him reclusive. My aunt cares for Tim, but she is five and sixty. Aunt Bea is still quite sprightly, but is finding it hard now to cope with his bitter moods.'

'And so you must live apart from them whilst you attempt to cope for all of you.' Ruth said softly.

Sarah gave an almost imperceptible nod. Briskly she put up her chin. 'But we have established, have we not, that we will not be cowed by fate?'

'Indeed we will not!' Ruth declared. 'I am conscious of the trust you have put in me telling me your secret. I will not let you down, I swear.' She sat back in her chair and gave a contented sigh. 'I am glad you have family hereabouts, for I am encouraged now to think you might stay despite your loss.'

'I will stay at Elm Lodge for as long as I am able,' Sarah said firmly.

'I saw Edward's brother in town,' Ruth commented. 'He is very handsome…very worldly, I imagine.' That last was accompanied by a puckish glance from under dusky lashes.

'Oh, yes,' Sarah readily agreed with a half smile. 'But handsome is as handsome does…' Sarah knew that Ruth was anticipating an explanation for her acid comment. But she felt she had disclosed enough for one day. Besides, her feelings towards Gavin Stone were annoyingly ambivalent; from one moment to the next her opinion of him differed.

In equal parts Gavin fascinated and infuriated her. She wanted to see him again, yet was apprehensive of his visit that afternoon. In anticipation of it her palms felt moist, her heartbeat strengthened by a mix of dread and excitement. Conscious of Ruth's attention, she simply explained, 'Gavin Stone is Edward's heir. I doubt he will be in Willowdene for long once he has received his inheritance. I understand he is keen to get back to London.'

Ruth grimaced her disappointment. 'We have too few personable gentlemen hereabouts to let him off the hook so easily. You must persuade him to stay a while.'

'I think Mr Stone will do as he pleases no matter what I say.' That sour retort was followed by a sigh of genuine regret. 'I must be on my way. Matthew Jackson brought me here and will be in no fit state to drive the cart if he is left to his own devices in the George Tavern.'

Having taken a fond farewell of Ruth, Sarah was soon walking the dirt track in the direction of the inn and her ride home. She glanced about at the hedgerows heavy with bramble fruit. The sound of birdsong and bumblebees accompanied her progress down the sultry dusty lane.

'Straight home?' Matthew grunted at Sarah once they were settled on the cart.

'Yes, please,' Sarah answered. As the vehicle rolled along Sarah reflected on her conversation with Ruth, savouring the wonderfully unexpected amity that had sprung up so easily between them. Had they not been united in being shunned by polite society she was sure they would have, in any case, been friends. They were kindred spirits.

She frowned pensively at a cliff of clouds on the horizon. She wanted to continue relishing her time spent with Ruth, but it was impossible to do so. Infiltrating her mind were thoughts and images of somebody else. Yesterday Gavin had arrived at about five of the clock in the afternoon. Probably he would do so at the same time today. She imagined him to be a creature of habit…not every one commendable.

With that thought lodged in her mind, she made the decision not to go straight home. Confronting her demons was preferable to dwelling on them for over an hour. She had made a friend and a sense of solidarity had given an exhilarating boost to her confidence.

Rather than wait for Gavin Stone to come to her she would seek him out and tell him what she should have revealed yesterday.

'I have changed my mind, Matthew.' Sarah spoke to the wisps of white scudding over blue sky. 'To Willowdene, if you please. I have a meeting with Mr Stone today and would see him immediately.'

Once they reached the town Sarah despatched Matthew to the Red Lion. She had no intention of causing tongues to wag by brazenly accosting him at his lodgings. Waiting on the cart, she again reflected on his character, for she found it irritatingly intriguing.

His reputation as a scoundrel was established; yet she had no proof it was more than hearsay. There were no specific instances of his wickedness to cite. She had been the butt of his anger and scorn, but not of deliberate malice or cruelty. Considering the shocking situation into which he had been unwittingly plunged by his brother, a fair assessment would be that so far his behaviour had been reasonable. He had acted the flirt and seducer...but at Edward's behest...and at her encouragement! Her skin tingled as she again sensed the sweep of his fingertips on her face, his mouth tasting hers with bewitching skill. She had wanted the bliss to continue and he had known that. She put up her face to the breeze to cool it. What did he think of her now? Was he confident that she would willingly succumb to all his sensual demands?

An exasperated sigh broke from her lips. She was

heartily sick of the man constantly preying on her mind. And where was he? She had despatched Matthew to fetch him some time ago. As he had an appointment with her this afternoon she had assumed he would not have gone out of town.

She peered about for a sighting of her driver. After waiting another several minutes, Sarah disembarked. Perhaps Matthew had got waylaid by a pint pot or a game of skittles and forgotten his errand.

The Red Lion was towards the far end of the High Street and, as she walked, she glanced at the shop displays. The haberdasher's window drew her to a halt. It was impossible to pass by without hesitating just for a moment to admire the variety of pretty wares. Caught by a movement her eyes were drawn from French lace to a reflection in the glass.

A colourful twirling parasol had attracted her attention. Sarah recognised at once the elegant woman employing it. She also knew the urbane-looking gentleman who was with her.

Christine Beauvoir and Gavin Stone appeared at ease in each other's company. Gavin had a hand braced idly on the black railings that enclosed the small green to one side of the market square. The other reposed in a pocket. A cosy chat seemed to be taking place, judging by the smiles and elegant gestures on Christine's part. More than once Sarah observed her gloved fingers briefly alight on to her companion's arm before again describing a pretty point.

A sudden thought occurred to Sarah that caused a sharp pang of emotion to tighten her belly. Perhaps they knew each other of old! Christine had been Edward's mistress for many years before Sarah came into his life. Despite the fact that the brothers were not close and rarely saw one another it was possible that Christine and Gavin were acquainted.

An undeniable need to properly observe them urged her to slowly turn around. Other people on the High Street were also finding it difficult to go about their business without casting inquisitive looks at the handsome couple.

Most of the townswomen cold-shouldered Sarah. Christine Beauvoir did not bother with any such demonstration. If Sarah passed her in the street, or they chose to enter the same shop, she might have been invisible. Christine made it plain she considered her rival less than nothing, not worthy even of her contempt. Sarah had long ago ceased to fret over it.

At the outset of their relationship Edward had told her he'd had an intimate lady friend for many years. Sarah had been grateful for his honesty. She had accepted his offer to care for her and the terms that went with it and not once had he or Sarah referred again to his other mistress.

For an incomprehensible reason Sarah felt vexed at seeing Gavin Stone with Mrs Beauvoir. Perhaps Christine had sought him out. Willowdene was a small town and new people were always the butt of avid attention. And Christine was certainly giving him that.

Perhaps sensing he was under observation, Gavin idly turned his head, still smiling at something his companion had said. His gaze swept the street scene, hesitated and returned to where Sarah stood.

A flush stole under Sarah's skin; she hated being caught blatantly watching him, but she curbed her instinct to turn tail. She had every right to window shop. And that is what she resumed doing. With her chin up, she turned about and gave her riveted attention to the haberdashery.

Fiercely she compared the leather gloves. Long or short? Embroidered or plain? Which colour would she choose from the rainbow display? Thus occupied, she nevertheless knew the instant he stopped close behind her.

'Are you in town in the hope you might avoid seeing me later?'

'No, sir, I'm in town to find you.'

'That's encouraging news.'

'Do you think so? Perhaps you ought to first discover what I have come to tell you.' Sarah gracefully pivoted on a heel to look up into vivid blue eyes.

A glance shot past him to see if they were under observation from Christine. They were, but after a moment the brunette swept on, her maid trailing behind her. Sarah felt a reckless need to comment on the intimate tableau she had just witnessed. 'You and Mrs Beauvoir appear well acquainted. Are you obliged by your brother's will to keep *all* his women, or only me?'

Chapter Seven

'Only you,' Gavin said, sardonically. Sarah had made him aware of something that should have been obvious to him. 'Thank you for enlightening me.'

Remorse raced hotly through Sarah's blood, dulling her mind to his self-mockery. She had just been shrill and impertinent because she'd seen him pay attention to another woman. It was the behaviour of a jealous shrew. When Edward had divided his affection between them she had not felt possessive. She was most certainly not jealous of the widow because Edward's disreputable brother might have taken a fancy to her. 'Please forgive me. I should not have spoken so—'

'I'm glad you did,' Gavin interrupted her. 'Mrs Beauvoir mentioned several times that she had been a dear friend of Edward's. I'm rarely quite so obtuse on these matters.' He gave her an indolent look. 'Perhaps if I were not constantly brooding on another woman, I might have paid more heed and comprehended her meaning.'

A warm glow to Sarah's cheeks betrayed she was conscious of being the female tormenting his mind. 'I'm sorry I've become a thorn in your side,' she said sharply. 'If it is any consolation, sir, I have had no peace of mind either since you arrived in Willowdene.'

'I think you have wilfully misunderstand my meaning, Sarah.' Gavin corrected. 'But let me phrase it another way: you frustrate me, my dear.'

'What I have come to tell you is sure to provide you with some relief,' Sarah returned, her complexion aflame. Oh, she understood his meaning now, but there had been no wilful misunderstanding on her part. How naïve of her! She had made it necessary for him to point out that lechery dominated his mind. Her major concern was how she and her family might live. 'Once I have said what I must, I expect Mrs Beauvoir might more easily hold your attention.' Again she had sounded petulant, in need of reassurance, and this time he didn't overlook it.

'Let me put your mind at rest, at least on this score. Should Christine Beauvoir aspire to be my dear friend now Edward is no more, I shall decline her offer.'

Bright tawny eyes flew at his face. 'I'm sure it doesn't matter to me if you accept.'

'Well, it does to me, Sarah,' he said with some ennui. 'Taking on both of my dead brother's mistresses would be extreme bad taste.'

'And does a libertine worry over such things?'

'It seems he does.'

Silver coat buttons were in her line of vision and for a moment she stared fixedly at them. She sought a suitable scathing comment. Unable to find one, she snatched her skirts in tight fists ready to walk on. An irrational annoyance at seeing Gavin and Christine together was making her insides writhe.

Gavin shifted slightly to block her way, but it was a casual movement that would not arouse interest from any observer. 'I met her in Joseph Pratt's office this morning. We met again by chance in the street. That's all there is to it.'

'You do not have to explain your actions to me,' Sarah retorted stiffly whilst showing him a perfect profile.

'I am aware of that,' Gavin replied levelly. 'Nevertheless, I want you to understand that I have no interest in my brother's affairs other than to satisfy the requirements of his will. I want to return to London at the earliest opportunity.'

'I'm glad we are in accord on that one thing,' Sarah muttered and endeavoured to ignore his amused smile. The heat in her cheeks remained maddeningly apparent. She felt as though she had received a rebuke, yet he had not changed the tenor of his voice and the warmth in his eyes was undiminished.

'What have you come to tell me, Sarah? Have you changed your mind about becoming my mistress?'

'I am here to say that *you* might want to reconsider the matter.' She glanced about. They had been conversing in discreet tones, but were none the less drawing attention. She would sooner they moved somewhere less conspicuous to conclude this business.

Many of the locals gained their livelihood from the Willowdene estate. Naturally, the new master would arouse immense interest in people, as would the women with whom he chose to spend time. Sarah imagined that rumours about the two of them were already gaining momentum. Joseph Pratt's profession might demand his discretion, but how rigorously would he adhere to that dictate? How long would it be before the whole sordid tale came out and it was common knowledge that she had been passed from one brother to the other like a chattel?

'Perhaps you would be good enough to escort me to my ride home.' Her voice was barely above a whisper and she indicated the position of the dogcart by glancing along the street. She had purposely directed Matthew to stop in a quiet spot past a bend in the track. It was shaded by oak trees and concealed from general view. She must soon reveal something very personal and she'd rather do it away from any snoopers.

Wordlessly they walked side by side with just the hum of summer as an accompaniment. It was a short distance to the cart and, as they rounded the bend in the track, Sarah was relieved to see that Matthew needed no telling to allow them privacy. He had returned to the cart to wait for her but, as soon as they hove into view, he disembarked and made off on his bowed legs, his only acknowledgement a tug of his greying forelock as he passed them.

'When we spoke yesterday you said you would not disappoint me,' Sarah blurted out almost before they came to a halt by the vehicle. She ran a nervous hand over the dappled coat of the elderly mare in harness whilst awaiting his response.

Gavin was silent for a judicial moment. He could have responded immediately with something subtly suggestive that hinted at his prowess. Usually he would have done so. But he could sense anguish penned behind her proud demeanour. Whatever was troubling her was no idle matter and he would not trivialise it with ribaldry. Eventually he enquired, 'Should I assume you think you might disappoint me?'

'Yes.'

'How so?'

'I am not as attractive as I seem.' She glanced at him, wishing he would probe for a better explanation. For a reason she didn't fully understand, she baulked at volunteering news of her ugliness. She willed him to say something, but he simply captured her eyes, locking their gazes. His quiet patience became unendurable and the admission burst from her. 'Only my face is pretty. My body is scarred.' The bald truth was out and the barrier to telling him more of it gone. But she could not face him as she revealed the worst of it. Swinging away, she fiddled with the mare's bridle. 'Edward knew, of course, and was kind and accepting of my disfigurement, but I cannot pretend it is a minor blemish. Part of my back is very red and the skin puckered…'

'How did it happen?'

'It was a long time ago,' Sarah said, tracing leather with a finger.

'That's not what I asked,' Gavin gently corrected. 'Were you born with the scar? Were you in an accident?'

Sarah gave a single nod and chin raised, turned back to him. 'An accident,' she murmured.

Gavin walked away a few steps. He hung his head and contemplated his boots as he tried to comprehend the courage it must have taken for her to come here and tell him that. She expected him to reject her as unsuitable because she was not an ideal specimen of womanhood. And what else would a jaded Mayfair rake want?

'I'm sorry…I should have told you straight away.'

'No…you shouldn't. You shouldn't have told me at all,' he said quietly, still grimly contemplating his shoe leather. 'But you did because you assume—quite understandably, I have to say—that I'm shallow and heartless and preoccupied with satisfying my carnal appetite…amongst other indulgences.' His saturnine face swung towards her and he directed at her a relentless stare. Her pale features were set in lines of strain, her slender figure was tense as a coiled spring, yet to him she had the appealing appearance of a melancholy goddess. He had marvelled before at her apparent innocence. Now he knew she was brave and honest too. A most unusual courtesan.

Sarah frowned in confusion, made to speak, then sank her teeth into her under lip. After a moment she demanded, 'What does that mean?' An agitated gesture illustrated her bewilderment. 'Are you willing now to reconsider my suggestion of employment? It is not absolute deceit and you will be able to claim your inheritance just the same—' She broke off suddenly as he strode towards her. So swiftly did he approach that she skittered backwards in alarm until her heels hit a cart wheel.

A moment ago she had not known how to converse with him. The searching expression on his face betrayed that now he had no idea what to say to her. In wonder she realised he looked quite vulnerable and oddly she regretted causing him to lose his confidence. She had no time to decide whether it might be his disappointment rather than her disfigurement that had upset him, for over his shoulder she spied Matthew hovering at the bend in the track. He was still some distance away, but might decide to approach if he sensed her uneasiness.

'I understand, sir, that you would want to reconsider…perhaps a little time is needed before a decision…' Her words drifted away and she shifted slightly sideways to escape his closeness, for only a few inches separated their bodies. A hand immediately braced against the cart, blocking her escape, but deep in his eyes she read a tortured apology for imprisoning her. Then his other hand moved too, towards her face as though to soothe or caress, and with bated breath she watched, waited.

Abruptly he pushed away and went to stand in the shade of one of the mighty oaks. His eyes slanted upwards as though examining the clear sky through the leafy canopy. 'I've told Joseph Pratt that we shall fulfil the terms of Edward's will. Nothing has changed for me. And you?'

'Do you think I am lying about my injury?'

'Are you going to disrobe and show me that you are not?' he softly challenged and brought his gaze back to her.

Sarah gasped in outrage. 'Of course not.'

'Then I must believe you, Sarah, until I see for myself.'

'Perhaps you will not. You are too sure of yourself, sir,' she returned with an edge of bitter accusation and a stony glare.

'But you are not sure of me at all, are you?' he countered. 'Whereas I am quite certain of many things about you.'

Sarah bristled. Was she about to again hear her character attacked? 'Please explain,' she invited icily.

'Thoughts of you have dominated my mind since I met you in Joseph's office. Some bad…but most…' he hesitated and his smile hinted at self-deprecation '…most have been good. As a result I've resisted temptation from a tavern wench and from Mrs Beauvoir.' He came slowly back towards her, till he stood just in front of her. After a moment a long dark finger elevated her chin. 'It seems you improve my character, Sarah… nevertheless, I deserve a kiss for constancy. At the very least you owe me that and right now.'

It wasn't at all what Sarah had expected to hear and for a moment she simply gazed up at him with limpid amber eyes. Was he informing her that her scarred body would not hinder his lust? Or was he hinting, in as gallant a fashion as he could manage, that he'd simply settle for her, having recently forgone the services of other prospective bed partners?

He barely knew her, so no fine emotion—other than pity—could be stirring him to overlook her flaws. And she certainly did not want his pity or his charity. Perhaps the mundane yet pressing need to fulfil the terms of his brother's will still drove him. She needed to know.

'Why do you still want me after what I have told you?'

'I feared you might ask me that.'

'Why?' The demand was replete with suspicion.

'Because it proves to me—more clearly than any insults might have—just what you think of my character,' he replied quietly. 'I'm no angel, but neither am I the callous fornicator Edward has doubtless painted me.

If you're intent on having a reason: you fire my blood. I could take you right now on that cart…but as I said, I'm no callous fornicator. I have manners and self-control. I know how to behave even if I don't always do so.'

Sarah gulped in a ragged breath at such plain speaking.

Reading her embarrassment, Gavin said softly, 'If you don't want to know, Sarah, don't ask. I want no lies or deceit between us. And, from your honesty, I gather you want the same. I admire and appreciate your courage in telling me, but it was unnecessary; it makes no difference.'

Sarah dropped her eyes from his, searching for some-thing to say. Her thoughts were more turbulent now than prior to his explanation. Aware that he was awaiting a comment from her, she quickly moistened her lips and murmured huskily, 'If that's what you want, sir, so be it.'

'What I want is a kiss…and for you to stop calling me sir. You know my name, say it.'

For a moment Sarah was tempted to do so. But, as she hesitated, a mocking glint fired his eyes, making her swallow the single word. Instead she blurted, 'I must go. My driver is waiting to travel home.' She peered around a broad shoulder to see that Matthew had disappeared.

'I want you to kiss me,' Gavin repeated in an exceed-ingly obstinate tone.

Sarah's eyes raked his face. 'It is broad daylight and someone might see,' she hissed in shock. 'Besides, I thought I had already passed that test.' They were prim reminders, yet she could not quite pull away from the cool finger soothing her flushed complexion.

'With flying colours,' Gavin praised wryly, but his eyes remained a little solemn. With a sigh, his head lowered very slowly, allowing her the chance to avoid him. Gently his lips began moulding on hers; a moment later they moved with urgent passion as though he hoped his desire might convince her if his words did not.

After a dazed moment Sarah surrendered to the warmth flooding her body. Her hands travelled upwards of their own volition. Small fingers locked about his neck, twined into the soft hair at his nape. Her mouth yielded beneath the ardent onslaught as she dragged his head down, increasing the bruising pressure on her parted mouth. His tongue teased over the silky interior, drawing a little pant from her throat. Her small, slender frame surged up on to tiptoe in the circle of his arms so she might taste more of him.

A growl resonated deep in Gavin's throat. He grabbed her up against him as though she were feather-light and strode the two paces to the cart. With wood at her back and his hard sinewy body at her front, she felt firm hands slipping beneath her thighs, easing them up and apart so his body might wedge between them.

Her head angled to allow his stroking lips to find the

sensitive places on her neck, behind a small ear. Another kiss widened her parted mouth, lavished attention upon it until her head was pressed far back against his supporting arm. Long firm fingers forked into her silky blonde hair, cupping her scalp.

'I think you're beautiful and I'm going mad with desire for you. Do you think that's a lie? Tell me!'

Sarah moved her head in his hand. 'No,' she moaned and tempted him again with her parted mouth.

He obliged her with a sweet, drugging kiss that was abruptly curtailed. 'I want to visit you later. I want to properly make love to you tonight, Sarah.'

Sarah raised her sensually weighted lids to look at him. 'Of course, if you want,' she murmured.

'And what do you want?'

Sarah closed her eyes. What did she want? She hated him for asking, for focusing her mind. The delightful sensation was receding already and she knew she should push him away. She should act outraged and decorously draw together her thighs. She should put her feet to the floor and her skirts over her knees and immediately go home instead of acting the harlot.

So what did she want? Was she about to embrace her shame or, worse still, put all the blame on him? Would she pretend that this man did not arouse her and she was no victim to his practised seduction? She could no more resist him than she could heal her scars. She wanted him to kiss her again, open her clothes and touch her aching breasts and it was not just because her life and that of

Timothy and Aunt Bea would once more be secure and comfortable. With that thought came another…she must ask for her allowance, for her money was severely depleted. She had received nothing since Edward died. 'I want my allowance, please,' she whispered unsteadily. 'I need some money to pay my bills.'

'Of course you do.' Gavin's mouth swooped, taking hers in a short savage kiss.

A moment later he'd released her and turned away, leaving her stumbling, grabbing at the cart for support.

'I'll find your driver and send him to you,' he said without losing pace or turning around.

Sarah watched him stride lithely to the bend in the road, then disappear from sight. Her heartbeat was still erratic and her breathing laboured when a few minutes later Matthew came into view.

Chapter Eight

'Gav!'

Gavin had almost reached the Red Lion when he heard his name bellowed out. He halted and looked up. He had been striding along with his eyes devouring the baked earth and his loins throbbing with every hard step. He frowned apathetically at the astonishing sight of his friend, Sir Clayton Powell, about to spring down from his racing curricle. A little crowd had clustered about the vehicle to goggle at the dashing traveller, but Gavin's Mayfair chum seemed impervious to the attention. With his brash good looks and ready cash Clayton was accustomed to drawing an audience wherever he went. He threw the reins in the direction of his tiger and a handful of coins into the dust for the children.

Gavin shifted aimlessly whilst waiting for Clayton to reach him. Despite the incongruous sight of his friend in all his sartorial splendour, abandoning his expensive equipage to the rural urchins' grubby fingers, Gavin's mind and body remained obstinately in thrall to Sarah.

Outwardly his tension began to slowly ease and he wordlessly welcomed his friend with a grin. Inwardly Sarah was still haunting his thoughts. He was angry with her for reminding him so bluntly that she had agreed to sleep with him from necessity. Yet had he not a short while ago praised her honesty and pledged his own? In truth, he was angrier with himself than he was with her. He felt selfish and mean for making it necessary for her to bring her financial difficulties to his notice.

As Edward's mistress she had been provided with a roof over her head and sustenance. Now she was relying on him for her keep and it had not occurred to him that she would require money for essentials. Gavin's routine with mistresses was thus: they had his authority to buy on his accounts whatever they desired and he settled their bills when they arrived. An allowance was provided as petty cash, so a paramour might enjoy social outings with her friends, gambling at the tables and so on. Gavin was unfailingly generous, for he liked a mistress to be independent and have her own interests and social circle. Nothing was surer to extinguish his desire than a woman who expected him to be at her beck and call and to account to her for his absences.

Gavin knew of his brother's frugality. He should have realised that Edward's method of keeping a mistress would have differed to his own. At Elm Lodge he'd noticed signs that Sarah had not been used to generosity. Edward would not have kept even his wife in luxury. Now he'd considered the matter, he realised Edward would most likely have periodically given Sarah a fixed sum and expected her to budget accordingly. He blew a sigh through his lips. Had he not been so bent on chasing Sarah's consent, he might have considered her needs rather than his own.

'Where in damnation have you been?' Sir Clayton halted close by and planted his manicured hands on his hips.

Gavin narrowed his eyes at his friend's surly tone. 'Surely you know where I've been; you've tracked me here,' he mildly pointed out.

'God's teeth!' The oath was uttered in irritation. 'Had you forgot we were off to Newhaven today?'

'Yes,' Gavin admitted and started to walk on.

Sir Clayton stared after him with an expression that veered between bewilderment and exasperation. He had expected at the very least an apology: their excursion to Newhaven and then on to France with a few friends had been planned for some while. With a hopeless shrug, he started after Gavin. 'You've a devil of a nerve, you know.' When that complaint drew no response, he slapped a conciliatory palm on the closest of Gavin's shoulders. 'Didn't much fancy a trip on Warrington's yacht in any case. Paris and so on is overrated, if you ask me. The ladies like it, of course; all that cloth and scent…' Noticing that his friend seemed totally uninterested in his conversation, he asked shrewdly, 'What's occurring in this backwater to keep you here?' He took a judicious look around and raised a fastidious eyebrow. 'Ain't exactly the liveliest place I've seen.'

'You know the way back, don't you?'

'That's nice,' Clayton protested, but on a chuckle. 'So what's keeping you here?' he insisted on knowing. 'You reckoned you'd settle with the lawyer the same day and be back in town by nightfall.' He shot an astute look at his friend's pensive profile. After walking on in silence for a moment Clayton opined, 'You're not ill, so it must be money or women.'

'Edward's will and my inheritance,' Gavin returned succinctly. 'The procedure is not as straightforward as I'd hoped…expected.'

Edward had deliberately shackled him to Sarah Marchant. But he was coming to accept that the idea of being with her, not just as bedfellows but as companions, perhaps friends, no longer seemed absurd or repellent. It held a certain appeal that transcended his understanding. They had known each other such a short while that there was no logic to explain the mellowness flooding him or the feeling she'd cast invisible bonds about him. Gavin had never believed in *coup de foudre* and scorned fools who did. But something in Sarah's quiet grace and dignity, in the fresh look and scent of her, beguiled him like no other woman ever had.

Inwardly he reviled himself as a hypocrite. Was he attempting to convince himself that his relentless pursuit had little to do with the subdued passion in her he sensed he could liberate and enjoy? Whatever she said or did to deter him, she could not deny the lust that flared between them. Her instinctive response to his kiss, his touch, told him more than any words could that eventually they would scale the heights of sensual pleasure together. He dug the toe of a boot irritably into solid ground and swore beneath his breath at his lewdly fanciful ideas.

He was by nature predatory with women, certainly no lapdog to be kicked and return for more. Ordinarily he would by now be done with chasing and wooing and have moved on. If he were in control of his sanity, he would give Sarah Elm Lodge and an annuity, then hotfoot it back to Mayfair with Clayton before he embarrassed himself by acting like a moonstruck swain. He could still join his friends in France. They could roister away a month or two with good cognac and a few *jolies mademoiselles* at Edward's expense.

'Your brother has drawn it all up tight as a miser's purse, I suppose,' Clayton observed morbidly. 'I reckon he never wanted you to have it all in any case.'

'Perhaps,' Gavin said with a reflective smile. 'But it's too late now.'

Clayton flashed him a grin. 'It might be too late for another fellow too. I know you didn't know him, so won't be grieving to discover your uncle was thrown off his horse. It doesn't look good for him. He landed on his head and is still unconscious. As Edward is gone, you could be in line for another visit to a lawyer, this time to hear something of benefit concerning the late Viscount Tremayne.'

Mild interest shaped Gavin's features. At one time, knowing that two hefty inheritances were in the offing would have overjoyed him. He would have already been planning how to spend the blunt. His lack of enthusiasm was dismissed with the explanation that, despite never liking his brother or knowing his uncle, he had not wished them harm either.

Their family had never been harmonious. His uncle, Jack Stone, Viscount Tremayne, was his father's brother and they had loathed one another. At the age of twenty-five the Viscount had lost his betrothed to his younger brother Joshua. Joshua Stone had lost his beloved wife to his second son. Gillian Stone had died giving Gavin life and from infancy Gavin had been reared beneath his father's forceful resentment. All of Joshua Stone's attention and affection had been lavished on his firstborn. On his death, Gavin had received nothing but a gold watch he knew his father had not liked or worn. He promptly sold it and gambled the cash at Newmarket. It was his first big win.

As they reached the Red Lion Gavin ceased to quietly ponder on his desolate childhood. He glanced up to notice the young maidservant he now knew to be Molly watching him with a pout on her full mouth.

'Not bad at all,' Sir Clayton remarked in a low tone. He gave the saucy girl a smile. 'But hardly in Mrs Warren's class.' He slid a look at Gavin. 'And that reminds me. Elizabeth is getting restless. She wants you to come back to London. She said I must tell you so and that you must be home in time for her friend Moira Greene's little bacchanalian extravaganza.'

'And you may tell her that I'll be back when I'm ready,' Gavin responded tersely. Clayton had just reminded him that he had a mistress waiting for him in London. Elizabeth Warren was an accomplished lover and an amusing and attentive companion. Yet he'd forgotten her since he arrived in Willowdene. It was hardly fair—Elizabeth worked hard to keep her pampered position in his life; the least he could do was cast a thought her way once in a while.

Would his neglect of Elizabeth continue once he'd bedded Sarah? Was it the chase or the woman keeping him here in Willowdene? It would be despicably selfish behaviour to uproot Sarah and take her with him to London, then despatch her back to the countryside when he grew bored with his sweet conquest. But how long would she hold his attention once Elizabeth or one of her ilk lured him with their sophisticated tricks?

'Are you lodging here?'

Gavin frowned at his friend in incomprehension. He knew Clayton had said something, but hadn't the vaguest idea what.

'Are you lodging at the Red Lion?' Clayton repeated

with more volume. 'What in damnation is up with you?' he demanded in frustration. 'You've been acting awful strange, you know.' It was an observation given emphasis by a shake of Clayton's fair head. 'This thing with the will and the inheritance…it's nothing serious, is it?'

Gavin focused on Clayton's concerned expression. 'I'm not sure, that's why I'm preoccupied,' he ruefully made his excuses. 'I'm staying here for the time being,' he finally answered his friend's question.

'Then I'll take a room.'

Clayton's decision caused Gavin's dark brows to again draw together, but his friend was already surging through the entrance to the tavern to find the landlord.

'Go home.'

When Clayton appeared to be deaf to his dismissal Gavin followed him inside. 'There's nothing here to occupy you.'

Clayton shrugged carelessly.

'Go home,' Gavin repeated more forcefully. 'You'll be bored stiff within a couple of hours and driving me mad with your complaints.'

'There's an assembly room. I saw it as I came into town.' Clayton cursed as the dim interior caused his head to come into contact with a low beam.

'I don't think a country dance will satisfy you,' Gavin jeered softly, ducking his lofty frame beneath the oak.

'I'll try anything once…as you know. Besides, if

there's nothing else going on, I'll learn to like it.' Clayton turned round whilst rubbing vigorously at his forehead. 'Good of me, ain't it, to come and keep you company?'

'Exceedingly…' Gavin muttered at his friend's broad back as Clayton disappeared into the snug.

Gavin and Clayton had been friends for more than two decades. They were closer than kin. But he wanted his friend to be on his way. He would have great difficulty extricating himself from Clayton's company to visit Sarah this evening without running into a barrage of questions as to where he was off to. For some reason he felt compelled to protect Sarah's privacy and her reputation, sullied though it undoubtedly was.

'I've made your supper and left it on the stove.'

Maude settled her shawl over her plain work dress, for the late afternoon air had a chill to it. She gave Sarah a penetrating look. 'Did you see Mrs Hayden?'

'Oh…yes…' Sarah managed a smile. 'She is very pleasant and friendly. We had quite a long chat. I'm pleased I went to visit her.'

'So…it's not her that's put that look on your face,' Maude bluntly remarked.

'How do I look?' Sarah darted her housekeeper a sharp glance and raised a hand to touch a cheek as though her fingers might divine her appearance. Was she scarlet still from her shame at acting like the veriest trollop, and in broad daylight too?

'You look…a bit sad…a bit guilty…' Maude candidly told her. 'I thought when you was late back that you might have asked Matthew to take you into town. Is that where you've been?'

'Yes…I went to town. How did you guess?'

'Cupboards are empty.' Maude jerked her head in the direction of the larder. 'You've not got much for supper. I made a hotpot with the last of the mutton and peas. And there's a fresh baked loaf.' Maude paused. 'I don't suppose your brother has much left to put in his belly either. That's why I thought you might go and see Mr Stone.'

'I did.'

A silence settled over the two women for a moment.

'All settled then, is it?' Maude eventually asked.

'Yes, it's settled.'

'I like him,' Maude said. 'And it's not just because he's the handsomest man to stop in Willowdene in a long while. I think he acts like a gentleman and a lot of people in town say the same.' She paused near the door to add, 'He's paid up all the back wages up at the Manor even though he don't seem to want to live there. So long as he does right by us he can do what he pleases in London.'

Sarah's small answering smile had soon faded to nothing. 'I told him about my scars in case it might make a difference. I thought he ought to know…'

'And did it make a difference to him?'

'He said not; but by tomorrow he might have changed his mind.'

'Ah…' Maude said knowingly. 'Well, your supper might stretch to two. But if it don't…well, he'll know what to do about it, won't he?'

Sarah whipped off her bonnet and combed unsteady fingers through a tumble of blonde hair.

'I'll be off. I'll come by in the afternoon tomorrow.'

Sarah followed Maude to the door and gave her a spontaneous hug.

Maude clucked her tongue. 'There's nothing to worry about,' she gruffly soothed. One of her rough hands slipped over Sarah's shoulder, lay heavy and warm against the place where fabric hid skin that was ridged and red. Gently she patted her, then put Sarah away from her. 'I like him,' she said flatly and went to join her husband on the dogcart stationed by the gate.

Left alone, Sarah wandered aimlessly from room to room, trying to quell her chaotic thoughts and concentrate on making ready for her gentleman visitor. Would he want to eat with her? Edward had often done so, but over several years a routine had developed between them and Sarah had learned what was expected of her. A light supper had been followed by a little conversation and then, when Edward had finished his bottle of wine, it was her cue to go to her bedchamber and get into bed. By midnight at the latest he would be on his way home.

Unless she was indisposed, or he was ill or from home on business, Edward had visited her twice a week, on Wednesday and Sunday. He always came at about nine of the clock. During the summer months he would arrive a little later. Sarah was aware that he timed his arrival to coincide with the dusk. Whether that was for her sensibility, or for his, she had never decided. But he had only ever seen her naked in half-light or candlelight and, when in bed, if his fingers accidentally nudged her scars, they would shy away to fondle smoother flesh. Despite having told him that her injury no longer hurt, Sarah had liked to imagine it was not his revulsion, but the fear of causing her pain that had made him recoil as though scalded.

She halted her pacing and drew in a determined breath. There was no time now to reminisce about Edward's habits or the routine they had followed. His brother might decide to arrive at eight of the clock…or midnight. He might stay an hour…or till morning. He might like to dine…or consider it peculiar that she would suggest it. She didn't know Gavin Stone other than by reputation.

That wasn't true, a little voice in her head whispered mockingly. She might not know his preferences, but she knew much about him that she shouldn't. She knew the scent and taste of him. She knew his sound and his touch. She would know him instinctively in blackest night and couple with him. Sarah closed her eyes and slipped back an hour or so in time. Her lips parted beneath phantom pressure and she swayed on the spot as her arousal reignited, sending blood, hot and thick as molten honey, pouring through her veins.

With a frustrated little moan her eyes sprang open and she banished the memory of Gavin Stone from her consciousness. She must busy her mind and protect her reason. The last thing she wanted was to fall prey to an infatuation with a practised womaniser. He had openly told her that his intention was to return to his life in London at the earliest opportunity. She might, after tonight, only see him sporadically when business brought him to the countryside to check on his estate. And the less she saw him the less complicated her life would be, she impressed on herself. And now she must get on; she needed to wash and change and prepare a table to dine before his arrival.

Before she changed her clothes she would dearly love a bath, she decided. The day had been hot and humid and she felt mucky from her constant journeying on the dogcart.

Having set two large pots of water to boil on the stove, she brought inside the small tin bath from the outhouse. She put it down on the rush mat in the kitchen and briskly busied herself finding towels, soap, and some lavender oil. She neatly ranged the things she'd collected on the kitchen table and then checked the water pots. She watched the bubbles slowly rising from heavy bases and the vapour curling away from the iron vessels to merge with the atmosphere.

A tempting aroma teased her nostrils, reminding her that the pan at the back contained her dinner. She lifted the lid an inch or so and peered at the mutton and peas simmering within. Indeed, it looked a tasty if rather meagre meal, filling as it did just half the pan. If Gavin accepted her invitation to dine, he might not eat his fill, but he would taste no better fare. Maude was a fine cook. The hiss and spit of boiling water focused her mind. Carefully she lifted the first cumbersome pan and emptied it into the tin bath. She returned for the other and repeated the procedure before cooling the bath with cold water from a china pitcher. A finger gingerly tested the temperature by twirling about. It felt just right and she quickly dropped in some oil before disrobing in a heady aura of steamy scent.

Having lowered her body into the shallow bath, she relaxed with a sigh. The water lapped softly against her skin as she soaped herself all over, then scooped up double handfuls of lavender water to rinse away the lather. Wearily she closed her eyes and sank into the soothing warmth.

She did not immediately respond to the knock at the door. When it came again, louder and more insistent, she shot up to a sitting position, blinking in a misty daze, then grabbed the towel from the table. She found her feet rather unsteadily and concealed her nudity with white cotton.

Maude had her own key, but perhaps she had returned for some reason and was wary of barging straight in lest Gavin Stone was already with her. It certainly would not be him. She had every faith in Mr Stone's vast experience in conducting a liaison. It would be extremely ill behaved to turn up before six-thirty after he had arranged with her to visit in the evening. By no stretch of the imagination was it yet evening; the sun was still shining.

Gavin had said he possessed good manners; he had also said he didn't always employ them, she reminded herself with a pang of alarm. Quickly she secured the large towel about herself and flew silently to the door. She edged it open an inch and froze. For a moment blue and amber eyes locked, before his were lured to the milky swell of bosom thrust above a tightly furled fist.

After what seemed an eternity, but was probably no more than a minute, she gasped, 'You're too early, sir! I'm not ready to receive you.'

'Open the door, Sarah,' he said in a voice that was so harsh with authority it made her shiver more than the breeze blowing through the aperture and drying her skin.

A slight shake of her head answered him.

'Open the door,' he repeated in the same fiercely per-suasive tone. One of his palms spontaneously flattened against the wood panels. A look of panic in her eyes was followed by an unmistakable sheen that had him inwardly cursing himself for an oaf. He removed the hand and shoved it in a pocket. 'Please…open the door. I just want to talk to you.'

Furiously Sarah dashed the moisture from her lashes. What was she so upset about? She inwardly scoffed at herself. That he had interrupted her bathing?

That the good manners with which she had credited him were sadly lacking? Or was it that the sunshine was beaming its golden warmth directly through the kitchen window and on to her naked, scarred back?

Chapter Nine

'What do you want to say?'

'Let me in and I'll tell you.'

The rough demand was gone. Instead he was using gentle coaxing to get his way. Without understanding why she would succumb to his velvet-voiced cunning, she abruptly let go of the handle and backed away. She faced him by the bath, with admirable poise considering her stripped state.

Gavin closed the door and turned to take in the charming domestic scene set out before him. He knew some men liked to watch their women bathe; some liked to make the experience an erotic game and bathe with them. It had never appealed to him. Bathing, like sleeping, was best appreciated alone…so he'd always thought. The room had a steamy somnolent scent, the beautiful woman in front of him an ethereal gracefulness. A halo of flaxen curls framed her flushed face and, exquisitely self-conscious, she swept away a few that had stuck to her damp cheeks. Her golden eyes were wide and watchful and his first tentative movement closer made her fist tighten on the towel covering the figure igniting his imagination and further tormenting him.

He watched her slowly blink away the tears, watched disillusionment settle on her features. She thought the rampaging heathen had breached the door.

'I'll wait while you get dressed,' he heard himself say.

'Get dressed?' Sarah echoed hoarsely, her eyes widening in surprise.

'You don't have to. It was just a suggestion,' he said, softly ironic, and then fell deliberately silent.

Sarah hesitated and frowned. How she would love to dash to her chamber and pull on some garments, for she felt at a severe disadvantage with just a cloth covering her body. He looked quite immaculately attired as usual in black tailcoat and biscuit-coloured breeches that enhanced the athletic lines of his body. Only his topboots were less than perfection—a dusty fog marred their polish, betraying that he had arrived on horseback.

If she turned about and went to her chamber to dress, she would present him with an abrupt introduction to her disfigurement. The heat from the bath would have made it yet more unsightly. The florid stain that stretched from one shoulder blade almost to her waist was probably now purplish. If she backed away from him, he would know how desperately she wanted to conceal from him her ugly scars. Yet if she stayed where she was, stark naked beneath a scrap of cotton, it was likely that he would eventually see…and touch. She swallowed the lump in her throat. If it were to be his intention to visit her during daylight hours, she would want fair warning of it. She might then set the stage with closed curtains to shade the light and a negligee to veil her blemished back. Suddenly she felt cheated that he had denied her the chance to appear at her best. Despite her nerves feeling raw and every fibre of her being tingling with mortification, she must collect herself and send him away to return at a more appropriate time.

'I don't want to seem rude or inhospitable, sir, but I would like to finish my bath,' she uttered in a low breath. 'You may return in an hour, but not before.'

'Thank you,' Gavin said with studied politeness. 'But I've actually come by to tell you I cannot visit later as planned…much to my regret.'

It was several silent moments later that Sarah grasped she was being rejected. Immediately heat bled into her cheeks. So violently did her complexion glow that one of her hands sprang from the towel to soothe it. She averted her face, hoping to shield the worst of her reaction from his piercing sapphire gaze.

So his reason for arriving early was not prompted by ungovernable lust. He had decided to extricate himself from their arrangement…as she had earlier suggested he might.

'I see,' she whispered. 'Thank you for informing me.' She frowned, feeling awkward. Why thank him for what was tantamount to an insult? 'Please leave.'

'Have you no interest in knowing my reason?'

'I can guess at it,' she said in a voice that was barely audible.

'I know you can, but I doubt you will be correct. Whereas I would wager a lot of money that I'm right when I say that what I told you this afternoon didn't alter your opinion of me one bit. I'm still a callous swine, aren't I?'

Tawny feline eyes sprang to his face. 'I am not about to squabble over something so trivial. Please go; you can see, in any case, I was not ready to receive you.'

'On the contrary—I would say my timing was perfect,' Gavin said with a slow smile.

Anger and entreaty were mingled in the look she gave him. 'And that is why my opinion of you has not altered, sir,' she retorted in a trembling tone. 'What of your boasts of your good manners? Is this mannerly behaviour?'

'I think so.'

Sarah choked a harsh laugh and her scornful gaze raked him from top to toe. 'Well, I do not.'

'That's because you have no idea what prompted me to come early to speak to you.' He moved a step closer, then stopped where he was when he saw what effect that wrought. He could tell from her flashing amber eyes and tightening fists that she was prepared to fight for her dignity.

'I'll tell you my reason, Sarah, and you may believe it or not as you choose.' A long finger traced his lower lip as though he was pausing from indecision; when he spoke, he kept his eyes from her. 'A good friend of mine has arrived unexpectedly in Willowdene. I've tried to send him on his way back to Mayfair, but he seems intent on employing his thick skin and remaining where he's not wanted.' He ceded to the need to again look at her and was tormented by regret at having made such an uncharacteristic sacrifice. Temptation again gnawed at him, refreshing the blood storming his loins. Had Clayton been within reach, he might have throttled him on the spot.

'A friend?' she murmured, frowning in confusion.

He forced his eyes to keep steady on her entrancing heart-shaped face, but then she took in a breath that forced her breasts upwards, tantalising his vision, and his aching fingers, with a glimpse of dusky rose crescents.

'I won't manage to shake him off.' His voice was harsh with frustration. 'He's like a shadow. I've escaped for a short while because he's famished after his journey. He's let me alone only so he might enjoy a hearty dinner at the Red Lion.'

Sarah's expression was a study of suspicion.

'Sir Clayton Powell,' Gavin abruptly introduced his absent friend to her. 'If I go out this evening, he'll want either to know where I'm bound, or to accompany me. At some time you'll meet him, but I guessed you'd not want us both here tonight.'

'Indeed not!'

Slowly Gavin tilted back his head and a grimace of regret skewed his features. Her horrified whisper had betrayed that she now suspected him to be a deviant, too. An expulsion of breath whistled through set teeth. Never in his life had he acted such a bumbling fool with a woman. It was time to go before he made matters yet worse, for he could sense his self-control eroding. He was within a hair's breadth of reaching for her, proving in no uncertain terms that he was the uncouth lecher she'd feared. He strode to the door, jerked the handle with such force he heard the screws loosen. 'I've made arrangements through Joseph Pratt for you to buy what you will from the shops. I'll settle with the merchants. You may also collect from the lawyer's office a cash allowance to cover any incidentals you require in the short time you remain here—'

'But…what…?' Sarah quickly interrupted him, having heard something she found extremely perturbing. But already he had the door open as though impatient to get away.

'When we arrive in London, things will be simpler and you may buy everything you want on my accounts.' With that and a brusque farewell, he was gone.

Sarah stood stock still with her jaw dropping open. London? She was not going to London. What had led him to believe she would? Gathering her senses, she sped barefoot to the door and flung it open, still clutching the towel to her breasts with rigid fingers. But already he was some way away. She watched in despair as, having cleared the copse in front of the Lodge, he kicked his mount into a gallop. She stood shivering on the threshold, watching him disappear from sight. Far from wanting him gone, she now wanted him back so he might immediately explain what he meant. She was not leaving Willowdene. Abandon Tim and Aunt Bea? Return to town and perhaps be recognised and risk reviving all the horrible scandal surrounding her papa's death? It was unthinkable. And why on earth would he want her to go with him? Perhaps he was not the inveterate philanderer of his brother's reports; nevertheless, she would wager a tidy sum that he already had a lady friend in Mayfair who pandered to his needs.

When the dawn light peeped through a gap in the curtains, Sarah gladly arose from bed. She had slept but fitfully whilst she waited for a new day. She padded to the washstand and poured water from the china pitcher into the bowl. Her weary eyes were bathed to freshen them, then, still in her nightdress, she went to set the kettle to boil for tea. As she spooned tea into the pot, she wished she had been able to slumber on for a while. She must kick her heels for some hours before it was time to set off for town and an explanation from Gavin Stone. Turning up at the Red Lion and demanding an audience with him before the sun was high would cast grave doubts on *her* good manners. But, of course, the townspeople had already decided what sort of woman she was. Such behaviour would simply confirm their prejudices.

Sarah sat down at the scrubbed pine table and sipped at her tea. The new loaf was still temptingly fragrant and she drew it towards her on the board. She cut a crust, quickly spread it with butter from the dish and nibbled. Her light breakfast did little to settle the queasy feeling in her stomach.

Maude had expected Gavin Stone to become her lover last night. She thus had diplomatically offered to come to do chores later than usual, obviously to give the gentleman plenty of time to take his leave. Matthew always brought Maude to work on the dogcart. But Sarah could not wait that long for a ride into Willowdene. The need to confront Gavin was a constant nag in her mind. She was now as uncertain of her future as she had been the day Edward's will had been read.

She would walk into town this morning. She had done so before and, in truth, she was glad that she might use up some time on the journey. It was no more than a few miles across country and the weather seemed clement. Her shadowed eyes stared out of the kitchen window to distractedly appreciate the glorious September morning.

By the time the wall clock in her parlour chimed ten, Sarah had made Maude's prospective visit unnecessary. She had swept out the grates, set the fires and tidied every room in the Lodge simply to keep busy and use up nervous energy. Having finally attained the hour she'd appointed to set off, she checked her appearance in the glass in her chamber. She had on her finest walking dress. It was of royal blue material and quite stylish. She slipped on her pelisse, then calmly collected her bonnet and gloves.

Within five minutes she had quit the Lodge and reached the spot on the track where she had watched Gavin Stone disappear from sight yesterday. But she would not think of him, she told herself as she marched. She was not going anywhere with him; she was staying in Willowdene and fretting over what might or might not be was pointless. She would banish him to the back of her mind, she decided, and instead appreciate the benefits of an unexpected constitutional. The ground was dry and hard underfoot, but she had donned her sturdy shoes. The air was clean and lightly scented with ripening fruit and mown hay. Having scanned the sky for clouds, she was pleased that there was no suggestion of rain on its way. At least her gown would remain reasonably unstained, she cheered herself. Had it been wet recently, she might have arrived in Willowdene looking quite a mud-spattered fright after clambering about the hedgerows.

Despite the risk to her appearance, she took a short cut through a meadow, scrambling down a drainage ditch and up the other side. As she unsteadily found her feet on the opposite bank, a frisson of guilt passed through her, for her mind had been incessantly churning over recent events. She had not visited her aunt and brother for some days. Usually she would visit several times a week. Worse yet, she had not missed seeing them, or given much consideration to their predicament. Gavin Stone had dominated her concentration and, if she were to be honest, thoughts of him had not been wholly unpleasant.

She had allowed Edward to take her virginity and, over three years, lain with him as a wife. Their physical intimacy had certainly not been unpleasant although, if she were truthful, she had been glad at times that it was soon over. Never had he stoked deep within her feminine core the craving that Gavin could with a kiss. She brushed down her dress, and leaned against a tree trunk to recover. It was not simply exertion that was robbing her of breath. Damn the man. She would not think of him, she told herself severely. Whipping about, she gathered up her skirts in her fingers and started to run through long prickly grass, down towards the track that wound into Willowdene.

Fifteen minutes later, and rather bedraggled from negotiating briars and ruts and other obstacles that had hampered her progress, the noise of an advancing vehicle prompted Sarah to stop and turn around. She could not yet see who or what was approaching, but she moved to the grass verge to give it room to pass. Finally a pony and trap hove into view. A delighted smile widened Sarah's mouth and she waved.

Ruth Hayden was capably steering the small con-
veyance towards her. She immediately returned Sarah's
salute and drew the wiry little beast to a halt close by.

'My, you're up early.'

'So are you,' Sarah returned.

'Are you walking in to town?' Ruth asked with an
amount of surprise.

Sarah nodded. 'Matthew Jackson usually gives me
a ride, but today he and Maude are not due to call till
this afternoon. I cannot wait. I have some pressing
business to attend to.'

'Well, hop on,' Ruth urged. 'I was planning to come
to visit you soon, so now I can combine two trips.' She
wrinkled her small nose. 'Actually, I was looking
forward to making a proper occasion of my first visit
to Elm Lodge.' She tucked strands of chestnut hair back
from her brow with a black-gloved hand. 'I suppose
that admission would be enough to give Willowdene's
gracious ladies an attack of the vapours, should they
hear of it.' A rueful look was slanted at Sarah. 'I know
I'm in mourning and should be confined to the house
rather than planning a social call. But Papa would be
cross to think of me moping. On the other hand, he
would be delighted to know I have found a friend.'

Having settled herself on the seat next to Ruth, Sarah
immediately turned to look at her. 'The town tabbies
will not hear of your visit from me. They do not speak
to me for a start.' A wry smile followed that declaration. 'I will be most glad to receive you at any time.'

Sarah squeezed one of Ruth's hands in emphasis. She looked about at the countryside she had just traversed and huffed a little exhausted breath. 'I am very happy to accept a lift. Hoisting oneself over stiles and turning an ankle over in a ditch is not the best start to the day!' Her seed-studded skirts received a cursory brush with the back of a hand.

Ruth picked an autumn-tinted leaf from the top of Sarah's bonnet and handed it to her with a chuckle. 'I was raised in these parts. I recall quite clearly skipping through the meadows, fishing with sapling stem and string in the stream.' She nodded to the left, indicating where the silent water ran. 'Oh, to be a tomboy of twelve once more.'

'Indeed,' Sarah agreed wistfully as she allowed her memory to dwell on her own childhood. It had been mainly spent in London but, before her father had squandered all the family's money, they had enjoyed an annual sojourn at a small countryside retreat. She could recall similar times to those Ruth was describing. 'We had a large pear tree with a swing. It was huge…far above thirty feet high. I could almost reach the top of it. Did you like to climb trees?'

'Of course,' Ruth emphasised with a nod. 'And I was very good at scrumping too, which was just as well as my cousin, Jake, was no use at all in picking the fruit. But he could field what I dropped down to him. Little got bruised.'

'Your cousin?' Sarah asked curiously. 'Does he still

live close by?' She recalled that Ruth had said she had no close relations.

'Jake was just eighteen when he was killed in the Peninsular War. He was an only child, like me. After he died my uncle and aunt moved to the continent to live…to be close to him, I think.'

'Oh, I'm so sorry…'

Ruth flicked the reins over the little pony and set the cart once more in motion. She gave Sarah a bright smile that conveyed more clearly than any words could that no apology was necessary. 'So, what brings you out so early?'

'I might ask you the same thing,' Sarah countered with strained joviality. The bond between her and Ruth seemed a little stronger, a little more intimate; she did not want to jeopardise it by shocking her friend, or by lying. And she feared she must do one or the other if they conversed about her need to see Gavin Stone.

Ruth knew that she had been Edward Stone's mistress. But how would she react to knowing that she was on the verge of sleeping with Edward's brother, too, to earn her keep? Sarah's pensiveness was abruptly curtailed by a heavy sigh from Ruth.

'I'm off to town early as I have to see a gentleman on a delicate matter and I'd sooner do it than dwell on it.'

Sarah shot Ruth a sympathetic glance. Her friend could have been describing her own reason for being abroad so early.

'I hope I am not mistaken in what I am thinking,' Ruth said. 'Or I will seem very foolish and conceited.'

Sarah's amber gaze begged a better explanation from Ruth.

After a quiet moment Ruth blurted, 'I know we are only just become friends, but you confided in me about your family and the private troubles you have. May I confide in you, Sarah, about the private troubles I have?'

'Of course,' Sarah said quickly, emphasising her agreement by giving her friend's arm a squeeze.

Ruth sighed, looked heavenward as though seeking divine guidance. 'Doctor Bryant may, I think, have misconstrued my heartfelt appreciation for his swift attendance on my dying papa, and his subsequent support.' She frowned and made a little gesture. 'He did much to try to ease my grief and was a great help with the funeral arrangements and so on in the following weeks.' She explained quickly, 'I was quite distraught and a little hysterical at times and felt unable to cope with much at all.' She paused. 'I admit I did lean on him…in the literal sense. I needed a little human comfort and he offered it. He held me. We embraced.' Her frown deepened. 'But, for my part, there was no significance in it.'

'And for him?' Sarah probed quietly.

Ruth shrugged helplessly. 'I have received a note from him. Judging from its content…well…not to put too fine a point on it…I think I have been propositioned.' Ruth gave Sarah a long look from earth-brown eyes. 'In one respect I hope I am wrong and he is innocently offering me his unconditional friendship. Yet that would mean I have thought ill of him and I *am* affected with conceit.' She pulled on the reins again, stopping the cart. Turning to Sarah, she said gravely, 'I know we said we would be of assistance to one another. I am afraid I would like to already impose on your kind offer. Would you read the letter and give me your honest opinion to its intention? If you think I am being too sensitive, please say so. I would far sooner you tell me than he.'

'Of course,' Sarah said quietly. 'I'd like to help you if I can.' A few moments later she handed back the single sheet of paper covered in a bold masculine script that Ruth had given to her to read. 'It's very polite… very respectful…and he stresses he does not want to diminish your grief or end it too soon, but I think you are right. Doctor Bryant is hinting he wishes to become much more than your friend.'

Ruth folded the paper. 'I imagine I have given him the wrong impression. He is a kind fellow. As I'm sure his wife would agree,' she said ruefully. 'He probably thinks I am in need of a man's protection. Even had Papa left me without funds, I would not resort to—' She broke off and looked at Sarah. 'That was thoughtless. I'm sorry.'

Sarah managed a gruff laugh. She gestured the apology was unnecessary.

'What I meant to say was that I don't feel any attraction to him in that way. Perhaps if it had been someone else…' She twisted a smile at Sarah. 'Oh, I know I shall be lonely. Even when Papa was alive I hungered for the company of a younger man.' Her cheeks bloomed faintly. 'I have made myself sound quite a hussy. But there is more to the relationship between a man and a woman than what occurs in a bedchamber. Companionship is what I miss, I suppose, and a family. I should like children but, of course, for that a husband rather than a lover would be ideal.'

As she listened to her friend quietly describing private yearnings that struck a chord deep within her own soul, Sarah's eyes prickled with empathy.

'What I am trying to say is that I miss Paul dreadfully. He was my first love but…I hope he will not be my last.' Ruth tilted back her head to gaze at the sky.

'I'm sure you will again find someone very special,' Sarah stated quietly.

'I hope you do too,' Ruth said.

That kind comment made Sarah turn her face away. At that moment she ached with envy; at least her friend had known what it was to love and be loved. Edward's *fondness*, as he'd termed it, she now knew had been simple desire. In his own way she believed he had felt some affection for her, as she had for him, but now she accepted that she had stirred no greater emotion in him. At least Gavin did not attempt to cloak his lust in deceitful words. For that she supposed she ought to be grateful.

'I'm going to see Gavin Stone this morning,' Sarah suddenly told Ruth. 'Edward has left me nothing but his brother's protection.' She watched anxiously for Ruth's reaction to that bald shocking admission.

'I imagined something of the sort had occurred,' Ruth said gently. 'What will you do?'

Sarah frowned at the horizon. 'I know what I will *not* do. I will not go to London with him. I am on my way now to Willowdene to tell him so.'

Chapter Ten

As soon as Sarah caught sight of the elegant gentleman lounging against a racing curricle, she accepted that Gavin had not fabricated the tale about his friend's arrival in Willowdene. Sir Clayton Powell—she had remembered his name—had about him the same air of insouciant worldliness as Gavin. If that were not sufficient to betray his Mayfair pedigree, his stylish clothes and expensive transport were further clues to his recent arrival from the metropolis.

Ruth had noticed the charismatic stranger too. 'It seems we are graced with another member of the *haut ton*,' she whispered to Sarah as she drew the trap to a halt in Willowdene's High Street.

'I believe he is Gavin Stone's friend. Sir Clayton Powell is his name,' Sarah informed in a similar hushed tone to Ruth's, for the gentleman's eyes were tracking the vehicle as it slowed to a standstill.

'That name seems familiar.' Ruth frowned. 'Perhaps I'd heard my father mention him. At one time he was acquainted with a lot of well-to-do families when he worked in the City.'

The words withered on Sarah's lips as she was about to make a comment. Her eyes had been drawn to the Red Lion by a well-recognised tall figure. Gavin had emerged from the inn and was striding to join his friend by the smart black carriage. Other than a crisp determination in his step, there was no indication that the appearance of the two attractive young women interested him.

Less appreciative eyes were also watching the arrival of the pony and trap. Joseph Pratt's wife, Rosamund, poked her head out of the haberdasher's doorway to get a clearer view of the two brazen hussies. She nudged the woman next to her and whispered before they both peered over raised shoulders. A good deal of what irked them sprang from seeing Miss Marchant and Mrs Hayden together. They did not want those they ostracised joining forces, for it might dilute the ignominy of their rightful place as outcasts. When Rosamund spied the two distinguished gentlemen start to approach the young women, her lips pinched into a knot of resentful outrage. So far her attempts to arrange a proper introduction to Willowdene's fêted visitors had been thwarted by her inconsiderate husband's refusal to carry out his duty.

'I will not delay you,' Sarah murmured to Ruth, aware of Gavin's proximity. 'I know you have an ordeal before you too.' With an restorative breath she gathered her skirts in her fists in readiness to alight from the vehicle. Her heartbeat strengthened mercilessly, making her ribs ache. Why was it that just a glimpse of the dratted man was enough to make her become light-headed? Never had a chance meeting in town with Edward elicited this fluttery faint feeling. She clenched her insides in an attempt to control them and focused her unruly mind on the task ahead. Somehow, whilst under scrutiny, she must once again discreetly convey to Gavin that she needed to speak to him privately.

A bronzed hand appeared in her line of vision. Her amber eyes travelled along a muscular limb sleeved in fine charcoal cloth until she was looking into strong satiric features. Aware of their increasing audience, Sarah lightly placed her slender fingers in his and allowed him to help her on to solid ground. 'Thank you, sir, for your assistance, and a good morning to you,' she said with admirable aplomb.

'And to you, Miss Marchant,' Gavin returned easily.

After he had introduced her to his friend, and Sarah had received Sir Clayton's warm greeting and amiable remark on the fine weather, Gavin turned his attention to Ruth. A staying hand was placed on the side of the vehicle, causing her to lower the reins.

'Are you not going to introduce me to your companion, Miss Marchant?'

'Oh…yes, of course.' She quickly did so and was pleased that Ruth responded with just enough cool courtesy to make it evident she was not overwhelmed by the honour.

Sir Clayton stepped forward and tilted his fair head to venture, 'You are in mourning, Mrs Hayden?'

'I am, sir. My father has recently passed away.'

'My sincere condolences, ma'am,' he replied gently. Now his long patrician fingers were on the trap, delaying its departure. 'Are you by any chance related to the Derbyshire Haydens who reside at Croxley House? Colonel Hayden was once my senior officer.'

Ruth blenched and her lips compressed to conceal their wobble before she made a concise reply. 'I am related only by marriage.' She barely paused before adding, 'I have some pressing business to attend to, sir.' A flash of dark eyes indicated his restraining hand.

Clayton removed it and, as the vehicle set in motion, he followed it two steps. He halted, turned about, and frowned back at Gavin. 'I've a few things to do,' he said and wandered off in the general direction Ruth had taken.

Gavin narrowed amused eyes on his friend's departing figure. 'I know now how to get rid of him. It's a pity he wasn't introduced to Mrs Hayden yesterday. He might have sought her company whilst I enjoyed yours. It seems he finds her intriguing.'

Sarah darted a startled look after Sir Clayton. 'Mrs Hayden is recently bereaved. She is still upset and vulnerable...'

'And you think Clayton might upset her further or take advantage of her vulnerability?'

The hint of mordant humour in his tone made Sarah bristle and narrow on him a reproving look.

'He is probably simply interested in the family connection,' Gavin soothed. 'He no doubt wants to reminisce about army life. As he knows Colonel Hayden, he is probably also acquainted with her husband.'

'Ruth is a widow,' Sarah informed him sharply.

'Ah…' he muttered in a way that made words unnecessary.

'*Ah,* indeed!' Sarah mimicked with a mingling of alarm and anger. 'Make him come back at once,' she ordered and spontaneously gave one of his elbows a push to send him on her errand. When he didn't budge a small hand again surreptitiously found his sleeve and waggled it.

Gavin removed the fierce fingers ruining the elegant line of his jacket and held them concealed between their bodies. He levelled a steady look on Sarah. 'Rest assured my friend also knows how to behave.'

'But does not always do so, I'm sure, just like you.'

An exceedingly sardonic laugh rolled in Gavin's throat. 'My behaviour with you has been irreproachable…wouldn't you say, Sarah?'

His self-mockery put Sarah immediately to the blush, for she knew which incident had prompted it, and that he was entitled to praise his restraint. Yesterday, when he had disturbed her bathing, she had been naked and at his mercy. He could have taken advantage of the situation and taken his pleasure speedily. Had he done so, he might have returned to the Red Lion before his friend properly noticed his absence. But he had not. Why not? For the best part of a restless night Sarah had pondered that conundrum.

Puzzlement furrowed her pale brow as she again reflected on it. The only answer she'd so far found was that he had not wanted to embarrass either of them by being confronted for the first time, in broad daylight, with her disfigurement. In common with his brother, he would probably choose to lie with her after dusk and feign ignorance of it. She twisted her fingers to try to free them, but he wouldn't allow it.

'Are you in town to shop?'

'Yes…I need groceries, but…'

'But…?' Gavin prompted after a long pause.

'I must first speak to you on a matter.' She took a quick glance about and noticed they were drawing much attention from passers-by. She again wriggled her fingers in his to release them, despite being oddly loath to relinquish the comfort of his warm hand cradling hers.

'I imagine you will not want to take breakfast with me in one of the inn's private rooms.' Gavin imperceptibly returned her hand to her side.

'Of course not.' Sarah gulped. 'Heaven only knows what rumours that would start.'

'Rumours that you are my mistress?' Gavin mooted with gentle irony.

'Well, I am not,' she hissed back.

'Are you not?' he queried in a voice of silken steel that sent a tremor through Sarah. He glanced along the street. 'Shall we go for a drive?' Gavin nodded at the impressive carriage close by.

'Is it yours?' Sarah asked in awe. She had never ridden in such a sleek contraption and the animal in harness looked to be a splendid thoroughbred.

'It's Clayton's, but I have a similar curricle in Lansdowne Crescent.'

At the mention of the prestigious London address, Sarah stole a look at him. So he had a mansion as well. No doubt he had all the trappings of opulent living. He also now had the means to keep them safe from seizure by his creditors. But she would not be swayed by hints of luxury and reflected glory. Such was not for her and never would be. She was here with him now to tell him that she was staying where she was…in Willowdene… with mean people who despised her, and enough assistance from him to get by.

'I will go for a drive with you, sir,' she agreed. 'But not too far. I must be back shortly as I have much to attend to today.' And that was the truth. She would go to see her aunt and brother without further delay. Now she had Gavin's permission to buy from the town's merchants, she would take provisions with her on Matthew Jackson's dogcart.

They had travelled many miles, she guessed, but at a sedate pace. She was rather pleased that he had not immediately taken the curricle off at full pelt. She slanted a glance at his lean angular profile, softened by glossy ribbons of dark hair, and felt a twinge of unidentifiable emotion contract her heart. She frowned, quickly looked at her hands held neatly in her lap, and determinedly returned her thoughts to his driving skill. If he chose to impress her with his daring prowess, he could, she just knew it. Just as she knew that he had perfected every other dubious art associated with a rackety existence.

Not a word had been spoken since she thanked him for helping her into the curricle, but the quiet between them was as mellow as the balmy atmosphere. The condition she had laid down, that they must not go far, or be away from town for long, seemed hollow. She realised, with a placid astonishment, that she was enjoying his company and would have liked to travel with him along autumnal lanes till nightfall forced them to a stop.

It was a simple pleasure, being taken for a ride in a plush vehicle by an urbane escort. Yet it was one she had never experienced before. She knew young ladies of class and refinement—amongst whose numbers she might have figured had fate been kinder—enjoyed outings with their beaux to pleasure gardens or to the shops. How many débutantes had Gavin squired to Hyde Park, or to Regent Street? Or did he prefer to devote his time to ladies of a different stamp?

Sarah sank small teeth into her under lip, chased

wistfulness from her mind, and resigned herself to attending to business.

As though he'd sensed the magical harmony evaporating, Gavin drew the curricle off the road and brought it to rest in a small clearing beneath a huge oak.

He turned towards her, leaning back against the side of the vehicle, the reins loosely crossing a broad palm. He waited with his relentless gaze directed at her delicately colouring profile.

'Yesterday you said something odd.' She had immediately grasped the nettle and commenced proceedings. 'You mentioned my buying things on your account in London. I won't be taken to London…if indeed that is what you intended for me,' Sarah blurted, still looking straight ahead.

'I intended we become lovers.'

'I know…and I have agreed to that,' Sarah returned, darting a glance at him.

'Yet it is going to be rather difficult if I am in London and you are over fifty miles away,' he commented drily.

'I will be here when you come to supervise your property and estates and so on,' Sarah reasoned.

He smiled until his amusement strengthened into a low chuckle. 'You really believe that I'll settle for that, don't you?'

'Of course,' Sarah replied, a little prickly at being mocked. 'Why would I not? I live here, and I'm sure you have…a lady friend in London. Perhaps someone of whom you are fond…' She hesitated fractionally, but he volunteered no information.

'You might think it odd,' she speedily continued, lest he imagined she was keen to discover if he had given his affections elsewhere, 'but I assure you it had not once occurred to me before you mentioned it yesterday that you would expect me to go there with you.'

'That is exactly what I expect.'

'Well, I shan't go.'

Her mutinous tawny eyes grappled with his, then dropped warily to the long fingers that had started drumming in irritated rhythm on the side of the curricle.

'Why not?'

'I have already said.'

'You're annoyed that I might be fond of another woman?'

'No, of course not,' she burst out, horrified that he might believe she was jealous. But, try as she might to further convince him she couldn't care less how many women he kept, no words would pass the ache in her throat.

'Edward divided his time between you and Christine Beauvoir. I imagine his wife, too, on rare occasions.'

Sarah fluttered a little gesture she hoped might convey she'd held a blasé attitude to their permissive arrangement. Still speech eluded her, but an awful thought did not. Did Gavin have a wife? Her widening eyes flicked to him. Why had the possibility not previously occurred to her? Edward had never commented on his brother's marital status, just on his immoral character. Had she assumed Gavin's reputation as a rake indicated he was a bachelor? Her papa had been a married man and one of the *ton*'s most prolific adulterers. Startled eyes searched his face as though she might read there what she felt suddenly compelled to know.

'Does it make a difference if I'm married?'

Heat suffused her face at his ironic tone, and because he'd so accurately assessed her anxiety. 'Yes,' she whispered, immediately discrediting her previous pretence at worldliness.

'Your scruples don't seem to have troubled you at sixteen when Edward first took you on. Did he lie? Pretend he was unattached?'

Sarah shook her head, setting her blond curls rippling. 'He was honest at the outset. He told me his wife was ill and that they had long lived apart. He also told me about Mrs Beauvoir and that my becoming his mistress would not affect their relationship.'

'If you accepted an indiscriminate affair with him, why not with me?'

'Edward's marriage was already a sham. He was not a hypocrite. He told me the truth: that Janet was frail and resided in Brighton. He said they were amicable and he visited her there on occasion and provided for her needs.' She wrenched her eyes from his, for something far back in their smouldering sapphire depths unsettled her. What was it he *really* wanted to know? Was he trying to determine if she might attempt to cling or interfere in his life?

'Edward's wife lost nothing because of me. Neither did Mrs Beauvoir. I was never a threat to his other women.'

'But you think you are a threat to my other women?'

Gavin cynically noted the concerns she'd cited. If she were genuinely conscience-stricken at the idea of beguiling an attached gentleman, she'd be the first courtesan of his acquaintance who was.

'You may scoff if you like,' Sarah said in a shaking voice, slashes of indignant colour highlighting her cheek-bones, 'but I have my own codes. If you *are* married, and a hypocrite, it will certainly not be me who causes your wife pain and humiliation. Neither would it be right to blame your legion of paramours. It would be your doing.'

'It would be Edward's doing, and you know it,' he mildly corrected.

'It would be *your* doing, for you are aware there is an alternative,' she insisted fiercely. 'There is no need for you to be unfaithful to any woman—wife or mistress—because of me.'

Gavin turned his head, tilted his face skywards. A tic leaped in the lean cheek presented to her. 'Well, you may trust that I'm no hypocrite...leastways where wedded bliss is concerned. I've always given that blessed union a wide berth.'

Involuntarily Sarah's features relaxed and a light sigh betrayed her relief that he was at least single.

A corner of Gavin's mouth tugged in to a smile. She was a beautiful enigma and every further moment he spent with her he risked her stealing a little deeper beneath his skin. Never before had he submitted to any paramour's interrogation over her likely rivals. But never before had he known a courtesan like this one.

'Will I cause hurt to any other woman?'

As the tense quiet protracted, Sarah looked away and fidgeted on the seat. 'I did not mean to be impertinent, or to pry into your private affairs—'

'I avoid women likely to be possessive,' he interrupted with carefully chosen words.

'I see…' Sarah murmured. And she did see. He was subtly warning her to mind her own business.

'Will you now come with me?' he demanded huskily.

Sarah firmly shook her head and repeated her flat refusal.

'You'll have everything and anything you want in London…anything at all.'

'I don't want anything at all…' she cried reflexively and then clamped together her soft lips to suppress and silence her anguish. He was wooing her with generous terms and she should not forget for one moment that he considered her no more than a rather irksome, if desirable, Cyprian. She stared into the trees, composing herself. 'Thank you for your generosity, but it is unnecessary. I just want to stay here in Willowdene.'

'Have you family hereabouts?' Gavin asked as a hint of what might be troubling her occurred to him.

Sarah's complexion turned chalky. Swiftly she turned further away from him to study the cool quiet glade to one side of her. She moved her head.

'Was that a yes or a no?' he asked, watching her closely.

'My parents are dead,' she whispered hoarsely. Briskly she turned to him and put an end to the perilous pause. 'It seems we will not agree on this. It would be a great shame if you lost your bequest because of a silly battle over where I reside. There is a way we can close this awkward episode and both quickly resume the life we know. Why do you not reconsider my first suggestion and employ me?'

'You know why,' Gavin ejected through his teeth. His eyes were twin black slits fixed pitilessly on her face. 'God knows I've shown you enough times how you affect me without the satisfaction of finishing what I've started. What is it you want, Sarah? More proof? Another chance to tease me?'

'Of course not. I've not teased you,' she vehemently defended herself. With stricken countenance she stared at him, stunned momentarily by the bitter emotion she'd detected in his voice. Surely he did not believe she'd been deliberately scheming to torment him? To what purpose? Immediately she knew the answer and it caused her to inwardly wince. He'd offered her anything she wanted because he considered her a mercenary harlot, and one base enough to intentionally aggravate his desire for coin before capitulating.

He'd probably not believed a word she'd said about her principles; her loathing to usurp another woman's rightful position, yet they were as truthful, as important to her now, as they had been at a tender sixteen. 'I'm sorry, but I have no more suggestions as to how we might resolve this,' she said with a quivering finality. Swiftly her gaze was averted from the dangerous glint in his eyes. 'Please turn about now and take me back. I don't want anything at all from you. I cannot leave Willowdene and will lie with you here or not at all, and so you may take it or leave it.'

'In that case I'll take it. Now.'

Chapter Eleven

In shock, Sarah twisted about on the seat and her golden eyes scanned his harsh features. He surely could not mean…

There was nothing ambiguous in his ravening gaze or the imperious hand that shot towards her. Yet he didn't touch, merely turned up his palm in challenge, and waited.

Why not? The phrase sighed over and over in her mind, bringing a peculiar enervating release. If they sealed their contract in the way they had agreed, it would allow both of them a little peace. They might then pick up the threads of the lives they had known before Edward Stone had taken it in to his head to shackle them together. Gavin would return to the city and enjoy his fortune. In a week or two, when again surrounded by his friends and lovers, he would forget that he had ever wanted her with him. She would continue her life at Elm Lodge, near her family, and on occasion be startled to learn that the master was paying a visit to Willowdene Manor.

Her gaze darted from tree to quiet lane to the canopy of quivering leaves overhead as though to detect a place where voyeurs might lurk. But they were quite isolated. He had taken the precaution of stopping the vehicle a good distance from the lane and out of sight of any passing traffic. There was nothing to disturb them, no sound or movement besides that created by nature. A pastoral melody of birdsong and whispering greenery would accompany their first coupling, she realised. The seat was compact, but she rather supposed he would be accomplished in carrying off impromptu amorous escapades. She parted her lips to murmur her agreement, but no words came. To conceal that she was thoroughly daunted, thoroughly dumbfounded, she showed willing by sliding towards him until his mouth was a mere inch away from her forehead.

For a moment she thought he might embrace her, for the hand that had taunted her to accept his outrageous proposal had moved to rest on the seatback, close to her shoulder. Abruptly he stood, pulling her up with him and, before she realised his intention, had swung her up into his arms. With little respect for Clayton's property, he leaped from the glossy coachwork on to peat. A moment later he was into the wood with her pinned against his chest and she was dragging in air to pant outrage at such buccaneering behaviour.

'Put me down,' she demanded in a suffocated shriek whilst wriggling in his grasp. When her lungs had breath enough to eject the edict, it was repeated shrilly through gritted pearly teeth.

And he did; as soon as he'd found a suitable clearing beneath an umbrella of branches, he let her feet drop to soft soil.

Within a few seconds he'd stripped off his jacket and dropped it to the leaf-littered ground. His silver silk cravat followed and then dark fingers were undoing his pristine lawn shirt.

Not once did his low-lidded gaze quit her face. A sardonic smile and a flick of his dark head indicated her buttoned-up figure. 'Do you want me to undress you?'

'No!' Sarah gasped.

'Pity…' he said and gave her a devastatingly wicked smile.

He tugged the shirt out of his breeches and the edges parted, revealing a broad tanned torso lightly meshed with dark hair. At that point his ruthlessly efficient hands were planted on his narrow hips, and he waited.

Sarah wrenched her eyes from the awesome sight of him. Never had the difference between the two brothers seemed so pronounced. Edward had been rather paunchy about the middle and his skin quite pallid. This man did not have a spare ounce of flesh on his muscled ribs and his burnished olive skin was in stark contrast with the gaping snowy shirt.

Unable to bear the scorching heat in his hard-eyed

stare, Sarah turned away to fumble at her buttons. Quickly she stripped off her pelisse and took a moment to look for somewhere to put it. She resorted to neatly laying it on the ground by his carelessly discarded coat. As efficiently as quaking fingers would allow, she removed her shoes and clothing until just her undergarments remained. She was acutely conscious of him watching her whilst supporting his back against bark and jerking off his boots. She heard first one, then the other being negligently lobbed aside.

'Is your injury painful?'

Sarah shook her head, her fingers plucking at, but not loosening, the laces on her chemise. 'It need not concern you…' she answered whilst her eyes and fingers concentrated on ivory ribbon. The shadows cast by a million leaves dappled her cambric-clad body; still, she did not want to strip naked before him. It was not just the wish to keep her scars veiled. Harboured within her soul was the ghost of a virginal teenager who had, against every principle she'd possessed, bared her body to a stranger.

The fastenings were ferociously pulled apart as she drove such memories from her mind. It was a little late to rue four years of sin. Her chin came up and she brazenly locked her eyes with his as she parted the chemise. Cool air flowed over her breasts, bringing the nipples to soft peaks under cotton.

There was something in his absolute stillness, in the way his unwavering eyes engulfed hers, that calmed

Sarah. The breath that had been dizzyingly blocking her throat was at last expelled.

Gavin walked towards her slowly, stretching out a hand that vibrated slightly. It skimmed over her tense jaw, feather-light, before sliding to cup her nape. His fingers stroked soothingly against her sensitive skin, easing her closer until their partially clothed bodies came together.

She could sense the crisp hair on his torso chafing her breasts to an aching sensitivity and her cool quaking figure warmed by his.

'Come to London with me.' It was an uncompromising statement.

The rough demand stirred loose tendrils on her brow, accelerating the tremor stalking her spine. Her answer was immediate and wordless. She swayed her head and tried to step away for she'd sensed him stiffen at her defiance. But the fingers splayed on her nape were unyielding. They shot upwards to anchor in luxuriant silky hair, tilting back her head to a perfect angle to receive his mouth. Silently he studied her.

For a moment she drowned in the stormy emotion in his eyes…waiting for the first crucial indication of whether he was angry enough at her recalcitrance to want to punish her for it. Within a second she knew the answer and something tender trapped within her heart shrivelled.

It was the first kiss he'd given her that was brutal enough to make her flinch. But she allowed him to manoeuvre apart her jaw with an artful hand so his tongue could immediately plunge within. Slow erotic thrusts parted her lips further and, despite her yearning for a little of the honeyed wooing he'd used before, a coil of treacherous heat unfurled low in her belly. Ten fingers spanned her narrow ribcage beneath the flimsy chemise, thrust up until her breasts were high on his hands. Heavy thumbs swept arcs of heat against swelling flesh a hair's breadth from the tiny buds that were beginning to darken and engorge.

He lowered his head, touched his fiery mouth to a pale column of throat whilst his hands started a fluid exploration. They lingered at rounded abdomen and curvaceous hips before cupping her buttocks. Through her flimsy drawers she felt long fingers draw her pelvis to the potent proof of his ardour.

'I want your consent, Sarah…your proper consent. Withholding your refusal isn't the same thing.'

The urgent words steamed against her naked cleavage, causing her to part dusky-fringed lids and reveal her eyes as slits of misty gold. A detached part of her mind cringed on acknowledging she was succumbing to him with shameful alacrity. He was now aware that seducing her was insolently easy to achieve and, despite her knowing that he was unlikely to be kind, a single nod gave him the answer he wanted.

'Say it.' The demand was raggedly ejected through his teeth.

'Yes,' she murmured, instinctively sliding against

him to use his powerful physique as lee from the gusting breeze. She watched his mouth, her breathing momentarily suspended as she wondered where next it would plunge to torment her. His lips looked narrow, his eyes a flinty shade of blue. Why had she not before noticed those cruel traits? Yet no observation was threatening enough to stir her to flee his mesmerising presence.

'Don't be frightened of me, Sarah.'

Again he had read her thoughts. He also seemed to rue his brutal kiss, for a thumb traced soothingly on her scarlet lips.

'I'm not.' A tiny break in the denial betrayed her.

'I swear I won't hurt you.' As though to reinforce that hoarse promise a hand travelled gently over the fragile contours of her back. If puckered skin was palpable beneath the flimsy covering of cambric, he gave no sign, yet as his touch ascended in a leisurely massage from buttock to shoulder he attentively smoothed every plain and hollow whilst urging her so close she felt her body melding to his.

Sarah felt a sob swell in her chest, not because of his unexpected concern for her injury but because she knew now that he could hurt her. The pain might come soon, swiftly and unstoppable, to wound her heart, not her body, and perhaps endure till she died.

To dispel the heat needling her eyes she craved that other drenching warmth. She needed the narcotic of his mouth on hers, his hands on those parts of her that were so excitingly sensitive to his touch. She tipped back her head and offered him her parted lips. When he seemed to hesitate and his searing gaze became too much to bear, she surged up on to tiptoe and slammed her soft mouth on to his. Her tongue flicked on his lips, forced inexpertly between, tempting him, begging for the sweet release she sensed was hauntingly almost hers.

He gave her what she wanted: a kiss of courtship spiced with a passion that was fractionally curbed. Harder strokes brought milky flesh to swell and fill his palms and the play of skilful fingers on her breasts drew little delighted moans from deep in Sarah's throat. Yet mingling with the fire in her blood was a welcome peacefulness. As she wound her arms about him, an avid accomplice in her own seduction, a little reason still hovered in a corner of her mind.

When Edward had rolled away to get dressed after their lovemaking, and the warmth blossoming inside her had died to ashes, wistfulness had filled the void. Sarah had sensed that something vital was lacking. Now, the thrill within was heightening rapidly, gripping at her more fiercely than she ever imagined was possible. A primitive sense told her she was about to discover why she had always felt disappointed.

Gavin heard the rasp in her throat, encouraged the bow to her back by increasing the pressure of his kiss. The sinuous angle of her body parted the chemise to allow his gaze to feast upon a lush white bosom. He lowered his face to the scented sweetness of her, suckling, until he heard an anguished gasp that warned him the line between pain and pleasure was finely drawn. Still she craved more, her fingers curving over his scalp to keep him close to her throbbing breasts.

With a groan Gavin dropped lithely to the musky earth, tipping her off balance so she fell with him. Her fragile figure was cushioned by his brawny width, but as he hauled her atop him Sarah wriggled away on to her back, her arms covering her nudity in instinctive modesty.

Her eyes remained closed, her breathing ragged although she was aware he was removing what remained of his clothing. He did not come down on her as she expected, but snatched her up against his muscular torso.

A deep sweet kiss followed, then Gavin turned them both sideways, an arm beneath her protecting her tender flesh from scratches. His fingers brushed away the twigs that clung to the cotton covering her scars, an unnecessary solicitude, as a moment later he had her out of her chemise. With practised ease the garment had been slipped from her arms and Sarah's objection was stifled as his fingers began smoothing over exposed ribbed skin on her shoulder blade. She tensed, arching her back as she tried to shrink her disfigurement clear of his touch. The strings on her drawers were loosened by a single pull, an encompassing caress working the material to her knees. So sinuously did Sarah react to his hands stroking on her buttocks that she unwarily abetted in the loss of her last piece of clothing.

Gavin pressed close to her again, but not before he had taken a hungry stare at her naked beauty. A detached part of him acknowledged his sorrow; the injury his fingertips had encountered was no minor blemish. But it didn't detract from her allure or dampen his desire in any way. The skin he was looking at was pure and pale, her breasts and hips roundly accentuating the valley at her waist that was made to take the curve of a man's hand. He felt the increased buoyancy at his groin; the throb of blood now so violent it seemed to resonate through his whole being. Far back in his mind a tiny voice told him that he would greatly rue this madness…and so would she. Never before had he treated a gently bred woman to such insulting behaviour. But he couldn't go back, and his only redemption lay in his certainty that neither could she. But it wouldn't stop her hating him afterwards.

With a rough oath of sheer torment grazing his throat, he rolled them over so she lay atop him with her legs secured beneath the brawny length of his.

Sarah tried to scramble away on to her back, for she knew the position to adopt for a man to couple with her. Gavin's chest slipped beneath her small palms like satin-coated steel. Her fingers curled into crisp hair, her knuckles innocently abrading his nipples as she shoved at him. A spasm of pleasure jacked his back from peaty ground with her still astride him. He remained resistant to her silent fight to turn over and, guessing it was a novel experience for her to be on top, his hand drew her head to his and a kiss of profound mellifluousness lured her into acceptance of the position. Calculated caresses soon had her legs widened so the apex of her thighs grazed his belly. The backs of slow fingers smoothed up and down in bewitching rhythm on the satiny skin of her inner thighs. When finally they teased the dewy core of her, she gasped as the tiny bud flowered beneath his thumb.

Gavin looked up at the beautifully taut features above his. Her honey-coloured hair had escaped its prim pleat and now tumbled in tangled abandonment about her face and shoulders. As she started a shy, almost reluctant rocking against him and he heard her soft choked moans, he realised she could be there before he was. With swift sure hands he guided her down.

Gavin closed his eyes, his features still, as he felt the hot slick velvet of her femininity mould about him. She fitted him perfectly, but then he'd feared she would. He'd feared a lot of things about her would suit him too damned well since he'd first clapped eyes on her.

As Sarah felt him smoothly impale her she instinctively relaxed to ease the bittersweet pain straining her pelvis. She folded forwards to rest on his chest, waiting for him to roll over and finish.

Gavin smoothed a hand over the crumpled silk of her hair. He knew she expected him now to put her on her back and drive to his own release. His brother's generosity as a lover had probably matched his financial protection: the mean, selfish bastard had given her as little as possible. But then Edward, as far as he knew, had not tumbled his virginal young mistress on a forest floor. He'd had the gallantry to take her to bed. He'd also had her full permission to do so, not a whispered word of assent given under duress. And, more importantly, Sarah had been fond of Edward.

Gavin felt the blaze in his blood heighten, not altogether pleasantly. It had been wrong to think of his brother at such a time; he sensed an intense frustration hardening his mind and body and it was not just caused by the torturous image of an innocent temptress swaying, enraptured, with her plundered mouth a beckoning pillow of scarlet in her adorable face.

It was a fantasy too far. Edward had nominated him to have her. But what if it had been the lawyer, or any other man who'd shown willing to take her on? Would this angelic-looking blonde have writhed and sighed for Joseph Pratt as she was for him?

Abruptly his hands girdled her waist and he lifted her, then fully rammed her home. With crude intention he tugged forward her thighs to bring her torso closer so he could again feed on her lips, her ripe breasts. Her knees were widened with his until she'd dropped so low over him her belly grazed his chest and every movement he thrust against her wrung from her a low moan. He rammed his weight up, pinning her down hard against him until he felt her convulsing peak and the involuntary cries stealing her breath were pleas for mercy. Swiftly he took her sideways with him and drove towards his own release.

Savage breath hissed through Gavin's teeth as he felt the savagery of her climax undulate around him and with a final plunge he joined her in Heaven.

Drained, Sarah lay within the circle of his arms trying to hold on to the languor that had numbed her mind and body. It was receding too fast, as was the exquisite pleasure. Now she knew what she had sensed, but never before experienced. It was wonderful, quite excruciatingly so, and yet…it wasn't enough. A small lonely part of her still yearned for more.

He had said he would not hurt her, and he had not, yet she had been subjected to deliberate torment. He had caressed her back as though he would melt away her scars, yet at times his anger had burned her as fiercely as his lust.

Edward might not have mastered such clever sensual skill as his rakish brother, but when they had lain together she had been responsive to Edward's trust and affection and respect. And because of it she had felt satisfied that there was nothing sordid in their relationship.

Now she had lain with a stranger who she felt did not trust her or like her, or respect her. Her pride was shattering painfully into pieces. Yet she could not wholly condemn him for wounding her self-esteem.

She had agreed, at every turn, to participate in her own degradation.

Her eyelids fluttered up to a shady square chin. His expression was inscrutable, but one of his hands lay splayed over his eyes, shielding them, as though he too had private regrets. She swallowed jerkily, making a tentative movement to pull away. The ache between her thighs made her breath catch in her throat.

'Are you all right?'

It was a toneless enquiry as though he were belatedly acting the gentleman. She glanced up to see his hand still shielding half his face. Perhaps he had sensed her wince and thought he had hurt her. He had, but not in the way he thought...

'I am fine, thank you.'

She pushed at his arms, determinedly wriggling free when he would have stayed her. She heard the low, gritted oath beneath his breath as she scrambled away on her knees towards her clothes.

Sarah cast him a quick glance and was glad to see that, despite him swearing, he'd not altered position. His hand was all that had moved. Instead of concealing his eyes, it now pinched between them as though to ease strain. She hurriedly grabbed up her undergarments and skipped out of sight behind the tree to scramble into them. Her dress was thankfully close by, and she crouched down and dragged it by the hem until she could grab it up against her. Immediately she stepped into it and was fumbling, clumsy-fingered, at the fastenings when she saw his boots come into her line of vision.

Obliquely she marvelled at the speed with which he'd dressed himself. A slanting peek at him told her that he didn't look nearly as immaculate as he had when they had set out on this fateful journey. His silk cravat had been stuffed into a pocket and he'd not fully buttoned his shirt. Her fingers flew down her bodice as she raised her chin to boldly meet his eyes. She might feel deeply ashamed of allowing herself to be used, in daylight and on the ground, like a tavern harlot, but he would never know of it. Neither would he ever know how wounded she was by his calculated expertise.

At least there would be no more negotiation, no more cat-and-mouse game, she told herself. She had become his mistress, however base the manner in which it had been achieved. And that silly notion that had crept into her mind that she might pine for him when he went away, it would not be. He was a sophisticated rogue, she had first-hand knowledge of it, and would now do well to remember it.

To distract his steady sapphire gaze she started to search for something amongst the peat, stirring the soil with the toe of a shoe. 'My hair's a dreadful mess.' It was a regret emphasised by a little cluck of the tongue. A handful of thick honey-coloured hair was attacked as nervous fingers raked into it. 'I've lost the pins.' Sarah again shifted soil.

'I don't think you'll find them there,' Gavin said with gentle amusement.

And she knew what he meant. Her hair had been quite neat up until the time she'd sank to the ground with him and his hands had begun divesting her of every scrap of decorousness she'd possessed. She turned away to conceal the fizz of blood in her cheeks, winding her hair with her fingers into a neat bun and savagely plunging the single pin she had into it in the hope it might secure it.

'Sarah…come here…' His words sounded hoarse and the hands that arrested her seemed less confident than they had been when holding her naked.

Again she snatched herself free of his restraint, but pivoted about to look at him. 'I am quite able to walk back, sir,' she said with a fake smile and immediately set off to do so. The leaf- and twig-cracking ground was a blur of russet beneath her swift feet as she headed towards the sun and the silhouette of a sleek carriage.

Chapter Twelve

'Miss Marchant!'

Sarah turned to identify who had hailed her. She sighed beneath her breath as she saw Joseph Pratt determinedly approaching. Again a disappointed huff parted her soft lips, for she had no wish to speak to the man. She had very nearly got all she needed from the general store. Another moment or two and she would have been away with Matthew on his cart. As Matthew loaded the last sacks, Sarah took a few quick steps towards the lawyer.

'Good day, sir.'

In response to her greeting, Sarah received a rather impertinent look. Joseph then tilted his head to stare meaningfully at the laden cart. 'I'm pleased to see that you and Mr Stone have settled your differences.' It was conveyed in a way that hinted a reverse sentiment to be true.

Sarah felt her colour rise. She gave a neutral nod and made to step away.

'He has also provided a cash allowance for you, you know. Would you like to collect that also while you are in town?' The lawyer had come rather too close to her again and his expression, his tone of voice, betrayed that he was bitterly reluctant to have to distribute such largesse. Sarah turned sharply to confront him. 'I would prefer my private business not to be discussed in the street, sir,' she stiffly murmured. 'And I am astonished that I need to bring that to the attention of a gentleman in your profession.'

A smirk writhed over Joseph's fleshy mouth, but her rebuke was justified and turned florid his plump cheeks. 'Well, if you can spare the time, Miss Marchant, come along to my office. There is a small matter remaining that concerns you and the deceased's will.'

Sarah hesitated. She had no wish to go anywhere with this pompous oaf but, if there was something to be discussed, she would sooner deal with it now than have him again visit her at home. He was obviously more resentful than she had realised at having made a fruitless visit to proposition her.

When settled in the same chair she had used once before in his office, she glanced at the vacant seat close by. It seemed an age had passed since she had first met Gavin Stone in this very place and had her relative contentment whipped away from her. Collecting her thoughts, she concentrated on the lawyer and the paper he was pushing towards her.

'I require your signature on this document. Mr Gavin Stone has informed me that…umm…all is as it should be between the two of you for the matter to be finalised.'

He had paused to leer speculatively and Sarah knew that the beast was waiting for her to confirm that she had become Gavin's mistress. The gleam of lewd amusement in his eyes strengthened and she felt tempted to leap up and rip the paper to shreds. She said nothing, but reached for the pen, dipped for ink, and put her name to it.

Joseph stabbed a finger on the paper and drew it towards him before rising and going to unlock a safe. He extracted what looked to Sarah like an enormous amount of money.

Joseph wagged the cash at her. He would make the little hussy abase herself and tell him what he wanted to hear before he handed it over. He'd always known he'd little chance of success with her whilst that handsome devil was around. But when his hopes had been thoroughly dashed he, illogically, could not accept being thwarted. The fact that Gavin Stone was a phi-landering scoundrel encouraged him to hope he might, at some time, have her. But for now he would settle for a little salacious snippet to whet his appetite and stoke his resentment of the fellow's damnable luck. 'I appreciate that it is a delicate situation, Miss Marchant, but you must properly confirm that you are entitled to take this.'

Sarah shot to her feet. 'Know this, sir, and make of it what you will,' she bit out icily, 'I do not accept charity.' She barely paused before adding in the same freezing tone, 'And know this too: it is all I shall ever say on the matter.'

Thoroughly taken aback by the violent anger in her voice, in her whole demeanour, Joseph again flapped the cash. 'Would you like to take it with you now?'

Sarah's eyes were momentarily transfixed on the notes bunched in his paw-like hand. She could not remember ever having seen, at one time, such a sum of money. 'Yes,' she said clearly, although her insides were writhing in mortification. She would take it, although she had no immediate need for it. She had no intention of coming back another time to ask this vile man to give it to her.

'He is a very generous fellow.' An edge of acrimony coarsened Joseph's opinion as he relinquished a small fortune. 'But I imagine he is unused to our modest country ways. No doubt, in Mayfair, *ladies* such as yourself are tempted to frivolous spending by all the finery on offer.'

'No doubt,' Sarah returned in a snap. She had understood the emphasis he put on the word ladies. She had also recognised his delight in letting her know that Gavin was sure to have more than just one woman to keep.

There was nothing in his spite that could hurt her, nothing she did not already know. Swiftly she plunged the cash into her reticule before turning for the door.

'You may have more if you want,' he called after her. 'As yet he has put no limit on his generosity. But, I imagine, that ought to suffice until he comes back. Unless, of course, he does not come back....'

Sarah felt her face tighten and whiten. She turned sharply on the threshold. 'Come back?' she echoed in a whisper.

Joseph gave her a malicious grin. 'Ah...I see...he did not tell you. He has gone. He left the Red Lion quite early yesterday morning, with his friend. I saw them load up and set off. I believe some of the young serving maids were quite sad to see their raffish guests go. Obviously your new gentleman friend has had his fill of Willowdene and what it has to offer.'

Sarah blinked, parted her lips, but no ready retort would come to her aid. She swished about and exited the room, speeding down the stairs and out into sunlight. Her heart was racing and she swallowed jerkily to remove the clog of humiliation in her throat. It was not just the lawyer's blatant insolence that had caused her face to burn—his bold hint that Gavin had taken what he wanted from her and immediately headed back to London would not have wounded her so deeply had she not feared it was true.

She had not seen him for several days; not since he'd taken her home after they had lain together in the woods.

That journey had passed in silence and Sarah had been glad he had not tried to make light of it all and press conversation on her. The few times she had slid a glance his way he'd seemed to be lost in introspection and grateful for the quiet. She had slipped immediately from the curricle without allowing him time to assist her, and with just a murmur of farewell. Once inside the sanctuary of Elm Lodge, she had watched him for a moment from behind a screen of curtain. He had not immediately set off again. He had found a cigar from somewhere and lit it, drawn on it several times with it barely quitting his lips, before turning in the general direction of Willowdene. But now he was gone and, oddly, she wished she had said something to him to alleviate the unbearably tense atmosphere that had wedged awkwardly between them and might be her final memory of their time together.

Her eyes were drawn instinctively to the Red Lion a way along the street. Young Molly seemed to be sulkily going about her business cleaning windows. She recalled Gavin had told her that he had rebuffed the advances of a tavern wench when keen to secure her consent and his inheritance. Joseph Pratt had just hinted at an attraction of some sort. Perhaps it had become more than a flirtation and that was why the girl looked so downcast.

Sarah briskly got up on to the cart next to Matthew. He gave her a steady look from his beady old eyes. He missed none of her moods…neither did Maude. She was glad. Despite not wanting to worry them it was a comfort to have around her people who were loyal, and who cared. She flashed him a smile. 'Off we go, then. 'Twill take us a while to reach Aunt Bea's.' It was a bright announcement, but her levity was unmatched by the look in her eyes. She lifted her face to the heavens. 'It looks like rain is on the way,' she cheerily observed as her gaze followed heavy grey clouds traversing the horizon.

She had what she wanted, she told herself, as they proceeded along the High Street. She had all the material things that Edward had given her, but in greater abundance. She had now more than enough to get by. And, as for a gentleman companion with whom to share a meal…as she had done with Edward…or to share pleasant conversation…as she had done with Edward… she might not have had that at all with Gavin. He had never shown any interest in sharing anything with her…other than a bed. Tears prickled her eyes and she blinked down at her hands. And, of course, in the event, they had not even done that.

'I'm not sure I understand any of this,' Aunt Bea said whilst she happily stacked flour and sugar and dried fruit and pulses in the larder. She emerged from the cool recess to add, 'You say that Edward's brother is now to help us, but he lives in London and is happy to stay there. So why would he…?'

'Because he'll be back when he wants to tumble her again,' a rough voice interjected from the threshold.

Sarah spun about to see her brother, Tim, in the kitchen doorway.

Aunt Bea flung a hand at her throat. 'What a thing for a boy to say,' she gasped in shock. 'And to his own sister.'

Tim gave an unpleasant sneering laugh. 'I'm not a boy; I'm a man. And I might be blind, but I'm not stupid. I know how she feeds us and keeps the rent paid.'

Blood suffused Sarah's face, but she said nothing as her brother used his grasping fingers on a cupboard, then on the table, to guide him into the room. He dropped his frail body down into the chair by the cooking range.

'It's nice to see you up today,' she told him. 'Lazing in bed will do you no good at all. A little exercise is what you need.'

'A pair of eyes is what I need,' he snarled and then swung aside his head towards the warmth of the black iron range.

Sarah felt, as she always did, a wrenching sadness as she gazed upon the blemish that ran from his temple to disappear beneath his collar. It was dreadfully ugly, and whenever she was presented with it she felt ashamed that her scars, easily shielded from view, should sometimes make her despondent. If there was any small consolation, it was that Tim had never seen his vivid disfigurement mirrored back at him. The fire that had burned their bodies and made Aunt Bea's hands gnarled had destroyed Tim's eyes too.

'Have you brought my dope?'

'No.'

Tim turned fiercely towards her and Sarah gazed again on the beautiful visage he might have had. Face to face, little of his injury was discernible—it appeared as just a one-sided silhouette of high colour. His hazel eyes were open, if vacant, and his strong handsome features only coarsened a little from constant pain. And the pain that tormented him most now was in his mind, not in his body. He was seventeen, an intelligent young man, who had no way of expressing the grief and frustration he felt at his life and who thus numbed it into oblivion with laudanum.

'You go back and get me some,' he bellowed, pushing himself to his feet and standing with his hands clawing the arms of the chair. 'I need it…you go and get it.'

Aunt Bea took a startled gawp at her niece. 'You should have brought it, you know, Sarah. Did you forget? How on earth am I to cope with him when he's like this?' she fretted with a despairing look at her enraged nephew. He was swinging his blond head back and forth in mute frustration.

'I'll stay here tonight with you,' Sarah promised quietly. She took a few steps towards Tim and stretched out a hand to gently press his arm. He slapped away her comfort with surprising strength, considering the wasted look of his limbs. 'You must try to manage without it, at least for a few days in the week. It is dangerous to take so much. I have heard of cases where people have not woken from the coma and—'

Tim threw back his head and rattled with laughter. 'What can it do to me? Kill me?' He again swung toward her the shrivelled side of his face. 'It is what I want...what I dream of,' he spat bitterly. Pushing past her, he stamped back towards the door, colliding heavily with the table in his haste. He would have stumbled but for Sarah springing to steady him. He shoved her away and in a moment she could hear his tread on the stairs and then his bedroom door crashing shut.

Sarah and her aunt exchanged a bleak look.

'I cannot go on like this,' Aunt Bea said tearfully, wringing together her gloved hands.

'I know,' Sarah said. 'And there should be no need for you to cope alone any longer. While Edward was alive we could not all live together. He expected me to stay at the Lodge.' She paused. 'Edward's brother has gone back to London, but if he visits Willowdene from time to time I should have fair warning of it and will return to the Lodge for a few days.'

'The Lodge is a little bigger,' Aunt Bea pointed out. 'Could we not all move there?'

Sarah shook her head. 'It would not do to uproot Tim. I have no proper lease or entitlement to Elm Lodge. And if Gavin Stone did come back and stay a while, it would mean you both must move back here again.'

'You have not told him about us?' Aunt Bea ventured.

'I have told nobody…' Sarah hesitated, remembering unburdening her soul to her friend, Ruth. 'I have told nobody who might recall the scandal and betray us. Gavin Stone has always lived in London and is of the right age to have been about in society when the scandal broke. He might recall it.'

'But Edward knew…'

'Yes, Edward knew,' Sarah echoed. 'It was unfortunate that he recognised you straight away.' She glanced at her aunt and gave her a small smile of reassurance. 'Of course, I meant to say it was fortunate for, indeed, he was our saviour.'

A day later, as Sarah was packing up a few things to take with her when she moved to stay with Tim and Aunt Bea, Ruth paid a visit. Sarah was very glad to welcome in her friend.

Once she had taken Ruth on a little tour of the Lodge and its neat appointments, they settled in the small sitting room with a pot of tea. Maude poured and distributed warm honey biscuits she'd only an hour before taken from the oven.

'I'll be off in a little while. I won't come back and disturb you young ladies when I'm ready to go. I'll leave your dinner in the oven, miss. Beef and potato pie, so it won't spoil so long as you take it out in about an hour.'

Sarah smiled her gratitude and, as Maude withdrew, the two young women exchanged a look. They had not seen one another since Ruth had given Sarah a lift into town on a day when they both had most dramatic business to attend to.

As soon as they were private Ruth announced lightly, 'Doctor Bryant, I fear, is no longer my friend.'

Sarah replaced her cup on its saucer. 'From that I take it he was not pleased to hear what you had to say.'

Ruth gave a little laugh. 'He was most *displeased*, and made sure I knew it.' She paused and fiddled with the handle to her cup. 'But he did not deny wanting to take me as his mistress. What annoyed him was his certainty that I had been trifling with his affections. I wish now that I had not sought comfort from him in the way I did.'

'You did nothing wrong and must not blame yourself.' Sarah gave her friend an inspiriting smile. 'If anything, it was inappropriate of him to have sent that letter so soon after your father's funeral.'

'Gentlemen can be most arrogant and impatient when they see a woman they fancy,' Ruth said meaningfully.

'Oh, indeed…'

The acerbity in Sarah's tone did not go unnoticed by Ruth. She took a glance at the cases by the walls. 'Are you moving out?'

Sarah nodded. 'I am going to stay with my brother and aunt. Tim is being very difficult and is too much for Beatrice to cope with alone.'

'I suspect that your meeting that day we went to town did not proceed well either. Will Gavin Stone not allow you to stay here as you have refused to move to London with him?'

Sarah lifted her limpid golden gaze to her friend's face. 'Oh, I may stay here, I think. He has not said I must leave. I have cash and the provisions I need…'

'But still something is not right,' Ruth observed quietly.

'It will be soon, when I have forgotten about him.' Sarah smiled wistfully at Ruth. 'He has already returned to London with his friend.'

For a moment Ruth was silent but her eyes were solemn with sympathy. She understood very well what Sarah had left unspoken: that he had taken his pleasure then taken himself off. 'As well as being arrogant and impatient, gentlemen can be selfish brutes.' She added cheerfully, 'I have to say I'm glad they've gone.'

A frown from Sarah met that bold opinion.

'Oh, I had no objection to Mr Stone. He *seemed* perfectly charming and polite…' She paused and laughed lightly at the wry expression that observation elicited from her friend. 'But I am relieved that Sir Clayton Powell has gone. I recall now how I knew his name. The Powells knew my husband's family. Sir Clayton might recall Paul's court-martial and execution.' Ruth's voice throbbed with tears as she concluded, 'I would hate to have someone pick open that scar.'

Sarah quietly allowed Ruth to dab at her eyes before

she drew her hands into her own to press them in comfort. 'Did he speak to you?' she eventually asked softly. 'He seemed to follow you that morning.' Sarah recalled how she had tried to make Gavin intercept his friend in case he had improper designs on Ruth.

'He did appear to be loitering about in the High Street, but I gave him no opportunity to again speak to me. I was so overset after my meeting with Dr Bryant that I must have looked quite grim-faced and unapproachable, in any case. I returned home straight away.'

The two young women finished their tea and sat chatting amicably for a little while. The savoury aroma of meat and potato pie made Sarah jump to her feet. 'Heavens! What is the time? I must make sure my dinner is not burnt.'

'I should go.' Ruth quickly stood up. 'I had not realised either how the time has passed.' She glanced through the sitting-room window at the sun on its downward path to the horizon.

'Please stay and dine.' The invitation was spontaneous, but heartfelt. 'Maude is a wonderful cook and she always makes me more than I can eat in one sitting.' Before Ruth could decline politely, Sarah urged again, 'Please do stay. You will be home before dusk and I should so enjoy having a dinner companion.'

'So would I,' Ruth said. 'So, I thank you, and shall be delighted to eat some of your beef-and-potato pie.'

Chapter Thirteen

The following morning, having spent a thoroughly pleasant few hours with Ruth over dinner the previous evening, Sarah was humming as she stacked some books in a packing case.

Several volumes had been removed from the bureau yesterday when she and Ruth had discussed their favourite authors. She had been pleased to discover that Ruth shared her passion for Jane Austen's works and that *Gulliver's Travels* was another that found favour with her.

A reverential hand smoothed the jacket of that particular novel. Tim had loved the story of Lilliput as a child. Sarah wondered now if he might like her to read it to him. Or would it simply make her angry because he could no longer see the printed pages he once had independently enjoyed?

* * *

By six o'clock, when Maude had again left her dinner simmering in the oven and gone home, Sarah was satisfied that everything was ready for her move. Matthew was to come at about noon the next day to take her to Bea's.

Sarah went to her chamber to wash the dust from her hands and freshen herself before she sat down to dine. She gazed through the window at the sun close to the horizon as she pulled a brush through her boisterous shiny tresses. Having found a few hairpins, she shrugged and abandoned them on the dresser. She would leave her hair unbound as the day was almost done. Slipping a light shawl about her shoulders, she wandered out of doors to enjoy the mellow evening sunset.

When she had first moved to the Lodge she had planted a small physic garden. The herbs had thrived to form several sturdy bushes about the perimeter. She brushed her fingers through lavender and rosemary and dill and drank in the mingling scent lingering on her fingers. On reaching the small vegetable plot, she stooped to pull out a few rogue dandelions amongst the carrots and onions. Fetching a pannier from the small outhouse, she began picking the plump blackberries that remained on the bramble, taking care to keep the thorns from nipping her skin. Tim had always enjoyed eating blackberries. As children enjoying a sojourn in the countryside, they had often come home with their mouths purple with berry juice. There was more than enough fruit to make him a jelly tomorrow.

A jackdaw screeched raucously close by, making Sarah start. Maude's cat flew out from his hiding place beneath the lavender to leap at it. Felix was a superb mouser and slept in the outhouse. He also preyed on songbirds and that annoyed Sarah. More than once the ginger tom had dropped a lifeless little feathered body by her kitchen door. Basket in hand, she sprinted to shoo the cat away. She had no wish to see the clacking crow ripped asunder before her eyes. So occupied, she sensed, fractionally before she saw, that somebody was close.

'He'll catch it another time.' The amused voice was masculine and its owner had obviously observed her dashing heroics.

With her hair flying out in a shimmering flag of gold, Sarah spun about. Her heart leapt to her mouth as she saw Gavin strolling towards her. He looped the reins of a black hunter over the branch of a tree and stopped where he was, watching her.

Sarah was rooted to the spot, staring at him ashen-faced, as though he were an apparition. She felt light-headed and a hand sought the flint wall of the outhouse to steady her. After a moment, when she realised he wasn't a figment of her febrile imagination but virile flesh and blood, her emotions were in turmoil. She wanted to fly at him and lash out…but she also wanted to lay hands on him for a different reason entirely. She knew her consternation was apparent: the colour had fled from her complexion, leaving it icily tingling, and the handle of the pannier was so tightly gripped it was vibrating against her skirt.

Gavin was very aware of her stricken reaction to his arrival. He would have liked to think it was simply that he had startled her, but he knew it wasn't. She was white and trembling because she was still angry and hurt and hating him. And more than that, she thought he was here to re-offend.

'Do you want me to go away again?' he asked hoarsely.

'No,' Sarah blurted. She flushed and looked down at the basket in her hand. The single word had been replete with yearning and quickly she sought conversation to cover her heartfelt outburst. 'I've been picking blackberries.' She lifted the basket to show him.

'I can see,' Gavin said gently. He walked a little closer. 'It's a fine evening.'

'It is, indeed,' Sarah croakily agreed. Her gaze flowed over him. He looked…he sounded the epitome of elegant civility, yet she knew what crude passion was cloaked by expensive tailoring and courteous words. 'I did not expect to see you again so soon. Why have you come back?' The phrases rotating dizzily in her head were blurted out.

'Come back?' He stopped in front of her, close enough to touch, but his hands remained rooted in his pockets. He simply gazed down at a crown of honey-gold hair burnished to brilliance by the setting sun. When she seemed to be fighting to regiment her thoughts, he asked softly, 'Where do you think I've been?'

'In London.'

'I've moved into the Manor,' he said. 'That's where I've been.'

'Why?' Her eyes had whipped to his in astonishment.

'I've been asking myself the very same thing,' he said with mordant self-mockery. He took a casual step closer so his chest was mere inches from her pert quivering bosom. 'Perhaps I thought I should stay until I found the courage to apologise to you.'

A haughty tilt to her head brought eyes that were suspiciously glossy up to clash with his. 'If I thought an apology was due to me, sir, I would have already demanded you give it.' She stepped away from him. 'So, if that is all that is keeping you in the vicinity, you have tarried unnecessarily and may head for home with a clear conscience.'

She would have swept past, but he arrested her with a firm grip on her arms. Relentlessly he positioned her in front of him. 'So, I'm forgiven, then,' he said sardonically.

A spontaneous blockage sprang to her throat, denying her the satisfaction of flaying him with caustic words.

'I thought not.' Gavin muttered.

Sarah tried to break free of his restraint whilst protecting Tim's blackberries from spilling by cautiously dropping the basket. Her faked nonchalance had not fooled him for one moment. She was outmatched in this mercenary game Edward had devised for them. Of course she wanted an apology. Pretending that she was careless of what he thought of her, of how he treated her, was impossible. Her lack of sophistication was mortifying and perilous, for she felt needled to reck-lessness. A small hand flew up and cracked against his cheek and, when he simply turned his head with the blow and made no sound, she hit him again. The oath exploding beneath his breath was enough reaction to satisfy her and a terrified exhilaration constricted her chest as she struggled against him.

For an instant Gavin's fingers became vices on her upper arms, then just as swiftly they were gone.

Sarah backed away from him, her eyes darting to the vivid colour she'd put on his bronzed cheek. She in-stantly regretted her vulgar behaviour. It seemed she knew no other way to conduct herself when with him. He must think her the commonest doxy alive. 'Now it is my turn to offer an apology, sir,' she said shakily. 'I should not have done that, but I am afraid you can incite me to act in a most shameful way.' Immediately she wished she had chosen her words more carefully. A gleam of dark humour was firing the back of his eyes as he raised a few fingers to press to his jaw as he flexed it.

'There was no shame in it, Sarah,' he said softly. 'But I won't make you act so again…I swear.'

'*No,* you won't,' Sarah choked. 'Never again. *I* swear.'

As she retreated from him, Gavin stalked her with that deceptively leisurely pace of his. When the wall of the Lodge was at her back he halted too, stretched out a hand. She flicked him off, but he persevered until finally she allowed his fingers to touch her face. He drew her against him and enfolded her in his arms. 'I'm sorry.' he murmured.

After a gruff little sob, Sarah shot her arms about him, hugged at him, greedily accepting the comfort he was offering.

'Are you going to invite me in?' When she did not respond, Gavin tipped up her chin with a finger and repeated his question. His tone was deceptively light, his eyes dangerously sultry.

A nod sanctioned his request, although Sarah knew she had no right to deny him access to his own property. She could tell simply from the way he was looking at her that he would soon make clear his intention to take her to bed. The thrill of anticipation was muted by apprehensiveness. Desire could lead to exquisite pleasure, she was no longer ignorant of that, but without a little affection and respect between lovers it was tawdry fornication for her.

He had said he was sorry. But did he want a stronger bond to exist between them than that created by their entwined limbs? Perhaps it was foolish and arrogant of her to suppose that a philandering rogue might feel tenderness for a woman who had been summarily foisted on to him by his dead brother. Nevertheless, she could not dismiss from her mind that, on a few occasions when they had talked together, or shared a joke, a tender rapport had been present.

When setting out on their quiet drive into the countryside Sarah had sensed real warmth between them. For a short time her problems had been submerged beneath an enveloping sweet tranquillity. She had forgotten about Tim and Aunt Bea; she had forgotten that Ruth had to cope with a prickly situation with Dr Bryant. She had been lost in her contentment with the man at her side. As the sun had beamed down on their steady progress she had believed it possible they might at least come to like one another. Of course her hopes had all been dashed. Every scrap of harmony had disappeared to be replaced with an atmosphere so heavy she would not have been surprised had thunderclaps accompanied them on their return journey.

Once inside the Lodge, Sarah led the way to the sitting room. Momentarily she stood before him, unsure whether he expected her to be hostess or mistress. Her chin tipped up and a militant look from her beautiful amber eyes dared him to gainsay her choice.

With an indulgent look Gavin took the chair Sarah had politely insisted he use. He watched her as she darted in a tumble of honey-gold hair and swaying skirts towards the kitchen to fetch the tea she had decided he must have. He settled back in the comfy chair and raised a boot to rest on a knee. It was then he noticed the packing cases by the walls. His hooded eyes lingered on the unmistakable signs that Sarah had been about to leave the Lodge as soon as she thought he'd quit the neighbourhood.

As boiling water was streaming on to tea, the same disquieting thought occurred to Sarah. He would notice her things packed away. What was she to say? She could be truthful, say she was going to stay with family who lived close by…but then that would lead to questions, and she did not trust him enough to give honest answers. He wanted her still, but should he discover the shocking tale of swindle and greed in her background, how would he feel then? She had quit London with her aunt and her brother—there were no other kith and kin left to them. They had been despised and shunned by people they had thought were their friends, people they might have expected to offer succour and aid. And despite it seeming that decades must have since passed, it was not so long ago, only five years, and some of those people, especially those who had been affected by her father's fraud, would not have forgotten or forgiven what went on.

Edward had known, but not from information she had volunteered. He had recognised Aunt Beatrice as her father's sister, and from there it had been easy enough for him to fit together the puzzle of their impoverished state, and their flight from London to a place where they hoped nobody knew them.

Sarah carried the tea tray to the sitting room and carefully put it down. She knew he was watching her above the dark fingers curled against his mouth. She knew he was waiting to see if she would volunteer information, or whether he would have to first broach the subject of why her possessions were in boxes.

'Were you planning to follow me to London?'

So. That's what he imagined. That she had been so distraught to discover that he had left her that she would humble herself and follow him.

She poured his tea and put it on the table close to him. 'I haven't been to London for a long while.' It was honest prevarication.

'And now you want to go? What made you change your mind?'

Sarah turned away from him, and put her cup to her lips to take a dainty sip. 'I have not changed my mind. I'd sooner stay here.'

'And where would you rather I was? Here? There? Out of your life for good?'

A silence ensued until Gavin prompted softly, 'Are you going to give me an answer, Sarah?'

'Why do you need one?' Sarah angrily responded and suddenly put her tea down on the table with enough force to make the crockery rattle. 'We both know it makes no difference what I want. You will go or stay as you please. Just as you will remain in my life or remove yourself from it when it suits you.' She clasped her agitated fingers together to still them. She had not meant to sound so shrewish.

Gavin lithely gained his feet and took a few determined paces towards her before abruptly diverting to the window. He braced a hand on the frame, his features set in lines of savage frustration. He stared out through glass as he started to speak. 'You have no idea how much I want that to be true.' A fierce look was slanted at her. 'I admit I want to be in London, and I admit I want to be away from you when it suits me. That's what I want. Yet still I'm here.'

'Well you may go…right now,' Sarah whispered in a shaking tone. 'If you are fretting over legalities, you need not. I saw Joseph Pratt in town and went to his office with him. I signed a document. I have the money you left for me. I must thank you for it. And now it is all done.'

Gavin turned and leaned back against the glass. His hands swept back his jacket to plant on his hips and he regarded her with relentless leisure. 'But it's not all done, Sarah, is it? That's why I've moved to a manor house in a rural backwater instead of a townhouse in Mayfair.'

'I want you to go now.'

'Tell me why and then perhaps I will.'

'Because…' Sarah twirled to face the table and her hands gripped the edge till the knuckles resembled ivory. Her pale, taut features suddenly tilted to the ceiling. 'Because what we did was sordid. And I won't do it again.' She darted a glance at his hard inscrutable features before continuing quickly, 'I understand now Edward had no great attachment to me or he would have ensured I was properly cared for after his death. But there was some fondness between us, and trust. I was very young and naïve when we met and if I had my time again…' Momentarily she faltered before resuming vehemently, 'But Edward did not make me feel that I was simply an opportunity he was entitled to take.'

'That's how I make you feel?'

An almost imperceptible nod answered him.

'I can't blame you for thinking it. To start with that was an accurate assessment of my attitude. But don't solely condemn me. Edward made you an opportunity I was entitled to take. Why do you constantly defend him?'

'Because…' Sarah whirled about in mute frustration before bursting out impetuously, 'Because if I don't have a single fond memory of Edward, then I have nothing.'

'You have me,' Gavin said quietly. 'And if you think I have failed in caring properly for you, tell me in what way I might improve on it.'

Sarah choked a sad giggle, spreading her fingers to mask tears that sprang simultaneously to her eyes. 'Yes…I have you…and as I said, it was sordid and I won't do it again, no matter how much money you give me.'

'It wasn't sordid, Sarah,' he gently corrected. 'It wasn't wholesome either, I'll agree. Some of it might have been different to what you've been used to—'

'I've certainly not been used to rolling on the ground like…like a dockside whore, if that's what you mean,' she squeaked with her face aflame. 'And I won't discuss it for your titillation either.'

'You started it,' he reminded her and bit his lip to suppress a smile.

Sarah felt her indignation rising dangerously. He thought he was so clever, backing her into a corner with his slick answers and his hot, steady looks. But she'd known from the start she was no match for this man. The ladies of Willowdene thought her a jade. Most of them were probably more worldly-wise than was she. In truth, Sarah Marchant was simply a silly girl who had, at sixteen, succumbed unwisely to persuasion on a way to keep her family, and who had experienced very little…until Gavin Stone came along….

Her fists tightened at her sides as she sensed a writhing in the pit of her stomach. She wanted him gone…yet knew if he moved towards the door she might spontaneously launch herself at him to stop him. Damn him. She had been reconciled to the idea of going to live with Tim and Beatrice. Now she felt confused and as raw as she had when Joseph Pratt had told her he had gone away. She wished he *had* gone back to London. The longer he stayed, the worse it would be for her when finally the novelty of bedding a quaint ingénue palled and he went home.

'Would you like to go out somewhere?'

Sarah started from her distressful reverie. 'Out?' she echoed as though unsure what he meant.

'Yes…out,' he said with a smile at her bemused expression. 'Would you like to go to town? We could have dinner at the Red Lion, or I believe Clayton said there's some sort of dance at the Upper Assembly Rooms. He was hoping Mrs Hayden might attend, but knows it's highly unlikely as she is in mourning. Would you care to go?'

Sarah felt her jaw slackening in astonishment. It was the first time in her life a gentleman had asked her to accompany him to a social function and she felt flustered but also inordinately pleased. Abruptly she pressed together her lips as sobering thoughts crowded her mind. 'Thank you…but I never socialise.'

'Why not?'

'I have told you, the townspeople don't like me,' she said and elevated her chin to a proud angle. 'You must have noticed that they stare at me…shun me. It does not matter. I am used to it now.'

'Mrs Hayden seems to like you.'

An involuntary little smile touched Sarah's lips. 'Yes…I'm lucky to have such a good friend.'

'I should like us to be friends, Sarah.'

A golden glance flitted to his face, but she could discern no irony in his eyes, nor had she detected any in his voice.

'But I doubt you consider me anything of the sort.' Gavin came closer to her and raised a hand to smooth a finger on her face. 'Do you hate me, Sarah?'

A shake of the head was his answer. A hint of sandalwood cologne was discernible on the warmth emanating from his body and she swayed involuntarily closer to him.

Gavin dipped his head and warm lips replaced his caressing fingers on her cheek. 'I'm sorry for acting like a barbarian. It'll be sweeter next time, I swear.'

'There will be no next—'

His lips slid swiftly to cover hers, stifling her breathy refusal before it was fully given.

Sarah tensed for no more than a moment. The kiss was gentle, hesitant, and rebuffing it would have seemed unnecessary. She relaxed against him, gave herself up to the honeyed caress moistening and parting her lips. Her hands slid to his shoulders, crept further so small fingers could tangle in the soft hair at his nape.

'What's cooking?' Gavin suddenly asked against her lips. He felt her mouth curve beneath his, for the savoury aroma of her dinner had been steadily spreading throughout the room.

'Lamb hotpot.' She pulled back a little and looked up into warm blue eyes. 'Are you hungry?' she asked, feeling rather mean for not enquiring sooner whether he might care for something to eat.

'I am very hungry, Sarah,' he said. 'I'd like it very much if you invited me to stay.'

Chapter Fourteen

'Did someone tell you I had returned to London?'

Sarah put down her cutlery and employed her napkin whilst considering her answer. She could not in good conscience wholly blame Joseph Pratt for misleading her. She had suspected that Gavin had abandoned her before receiving the first smirking hint at it from the lawyer. 'Joseph Pratt told me you had left the Red Lion. I assumed you had returned to town.'

She had been proved wrong and she was glad. He was still here in Willowdene, and her yearning to spend a pleasant few hours with him, dining and talking, was close to being fulfilled. Contentedly she watched from beneath curved lashes as he enthusiastically set about clearing his plate. She felt hugely pleased that he was enjoying their humble dinner. It was no fancy meal but good, honest fare and, as usual, Maude had made plenty of it.

Sarah had set the table in the dining room with great care: new candles had been set in the sticks and her best china and glassware had been placed on its polished oak surface. Whilst she had attended to the necessary preparations she had given Gavin a glass and the decanter of ruby wine last used by his brother. She'd also found him a rather out-of-date gazette to thumb through to keep him occupied. But he had not bothered her whilst she flitted to and fro. She had been glad that he seemed aware of her need to appear a competent hostess. When finally she had stood on the threshold, flushed from the heat of the kitchen, and looked expectantly at him, he had risen, grazed his wine-scented lips on hers in a wordless sign of gratitude for her efforts, then seated himself at the table.

Now, as she gazed through wavering candlelight at her suave companion, she felt a familiar poignant wrench tilting her insides. It had assailed her the day they had driven through country lanes in amicable quiet and she had felt a flicker of optimism burn in her breast.

He looked now, as he did then, strong and youthful and heartbreakingly handsome—nothing like a libertine who squandered money and seduced women. But that rogue did exist. He had tumbled her to the ground in the woods and provided her with an indecent amount of his cash to fritter on what she would.

Gavin picked up his glass, twirled it by the stem and sank what remained in it in a single swallow. He reached for the decanter and, sensing Sarah watching him, a private smile quirked his mouth and he left it alone.

'You may tell your Maude that she is a fine cook.'

'I will, sir.'

Their eyes clashed and Sarah frowned and flushed beneath the extremely quizzical look she received. The name Gavin would still not roll off her tongue, even though she knew it was absurd to continue being so formal after what they had done together.

'So...Joseph Pratt made it his business to let you know I'd gone away. No doubt he hoped I had returned to London and left the way clear for him to again come calling.'

'I hope you are mistaken in that,' Sarah replied. 'I find him quite obnoxious and his wife is probably the woman who most openly shows me her dislike.'

'Perhaps she has guessed her husband has a *tendresse* for you,' Gavin said in a tone that made Sarah dart a wary look at him.

'I doubt Mr Pratt has any *fine* feelings for me,' she announced with asperity.

'It matters little whether he has or has not—if he approaches you again at any time he will have me to deal with.'

Again he sounded annoyed and Sarah deemed it wise to immediately change the subject. She had not believed him a man inclined to be jealous. Perhaps the notion of having a rival was troubling his ego. 'Maude will be greatly flattered by your praise. She is proud of her cooking skills and fêted for them hereabouts. She works as a cook for other households as well.'

'If you intend passing on my compliment she obviously knows that you are my mistress.' A hint of surprise modulated his voice.

'Yes…she and her husband know. They knew about Edward, too, of course.'

'From that I take it the Jacksons are trustworthy and have been in your employ a long time.'

'They are very fine people. From before I was born they have served our family…' Her words faded into silence.

'And where is your family, Sarah?' The question was silkily insistent as though for some time Gavin had been brooding on finding a suitable opening into which to slide it.

Sarah plucked up her glass with clumsy fingers and sipped from it. Inwardly she railed at herself for being careless enough to lead the conversation to this. 'I think I said, sir, that my parents are dead.'

'Have you any brothers or sisters?'

Was she to deny her brother's existence? Sarah moistened her lips with a dart of a tongue tip and slid a glance at him from beneath fans of dusky lashes. He was watching her with that ruthlessly steady look, as though he could guess at all her squalid secrets.

'I have told you…there was an accident…a fire,' she said huskily. She fiddled with her fork, pushing it this way and that. 'My brother was more badly injured than I.

Please do not ask more; it is very distressing to speak of it.'

'Did you speak about it to Edward?'

'Would you like something else?' Abruptly she stood up. 'I believe Maude left a lemon tart in the larder.' She carried her plate to the sideboard, then collected his and would have taken that away, too, but dark fingers lightly manacled her wrist, preventing her leaving. The dinner plate was removed from her grasp and replaced on oak.

Shoving back his chair from the table, Gavin drew Sarah towards him with gentle insistence until she stood between his spaced feet. 'I don't expect you to trust me, or like me yet. I hope in time you will, because I'm ready to trust you, and I like you…very much…though it might not always seem to you that I do.' Gavin captured her other wrist, passed his thumbs over satiny skin in a casual caress whilst bringing her down to sit on his knee. A large hand spanned her face and turned it up so she must look at him. 'I expect you'll think I'm lying, but I've known no other woman like you, Sarah.'

'You are very perceptive, sir.' Sarah's tone was witheringly ironic and she immediately made to spring up.

'Why do you assume it's a lie?' Gavin easily thwarted her efforts to escape.

Sarah flicked her face from his. 'I may be unsophisticated and live in a backwater, but I have now scraped together enough experience to recognise when a man has had many mistresses.'

'I'm not denying I've had many mistresses, but it's more than a decade since I dallied with a horde of petticoat, whatever Edward might have told you.' He paused, swept a tickling finger on her chin to lighten the mood. 'I know I'm supposed to be a man in my prime, but I've no longer the stamina for such sport.'

Despite not wanting to, Sarah's prim look collapsed and a smile curved on her lips. She curbed it and gave him an old-fashioned look. She remembered well enough the energy he'd had, and some to spare.

His eyes meshed with hers, heating her to the core, but he sounded touchingly diffident as he added, 'I swear there has never been anyone like you. You're quite unique.'

'Do I take comfort from it, or is a subtle complaint?' she asked with sweet acerbity.

'It is high praise, Sarah,' he replied gravely. 'Who knows…had I met you sooner…' The words he had been about to utter were replaced by sardonic laughter. He leaned back in the chair and regarded her from beneath long low lashes. 'I think what I mean is I'm aware you exert a civilising influence over me.' He smiled wryly at her sceptical expression. 'Except of course on those occasions when I need you so much that sanity deserts me.' Abruptly he straightened, curving a barring hand about her nape as she strained backwards. 'But I'm rational now, I promise.' It was a throaty reassurance uttered moments before his lips touched, scalding the pulse bobbing crazily at the base of her throat.

It was impossible to remain indignant with such treacherous sensations battering at her defences. She sighed in defeat, angled her head up and sideways to allow his stroking lips better access to the sensitive spots they seemed so easily to locate. Finally when he raised his head to look at her, she gazed candidly into his lazy gaze. Her hands slid along the front of his jacket to link quite naturally behind his neck. Her small fingers played with curling dark locks as she said meditatively, 'When first we met, and the terms of Edward's bequest were made known to us, I thought never would we be able to stay together within the same room, let alone enjoy each other's company for an evening.'

'The evening's far from over yet, sweet.' A glint of wolfishness in his eyes and voice was controlled as he noted her shy reaction. 'It was not an auspicious start.' he said solemnly, ceding to her need to retrace the rocky path of their relationship. 'But now we are better acquainted, and coming to be friends, I should like to know more about your background.' A hand smoothed her cheek, following on to gather hair like molten gold into a dark fist.

'Will you tell me more about your background?' Sarah countered, her heart starting a thumping tattoo beneath her bodice. 'I know, of course that you had a brother. Have you any other siblings? And what of your parents? Are they in London? Or do they also prefer the country?' As the genial questions streamed out, she slipped determinedly from his lap. Having removed his plate to the sideboard, she returned to her chair and sat down.

'I imagine if your parents are still alive, they must have reached good ages.' She cocked her head to gaze past the candelabra, interest animating her lovely features.

'Are you implying that I'm old?'

Despite the hint of teasing in his voice, Sarah blurted guiltily, 'No…not at all. I imagine you to be some years younger than Edward who, I know was approaching his thirty-eighth birthday.'

'I'm thirty-two and my parents have been dead for a long time. There are no other siblings that I'm aware of.' Gavin lounged back in his chair. 'Did Edward not tell you about his life in London?'

'No…' Sarah said with a pensive frown as she digested that fact. But it was hardly surprising she knew so little about the Stones. She had never probed for details as, in turn, she did not want to discuss her own early years. It had been a tacit agreement between them that their conversation would avoid touching on the tragedy in her past. 'I knew that Edward had acquired the manor about ten years ago and that he had a brother. He mentioned you but rarely, and then only to…' She hesitated, reluctant to betray Edward or wound Gavin by repeating the criticisms.

'And then only to slander me,' Gavin finished for her. A laconic gesture displayed his indifference. 'It's of no consequence. I had little good to say about him either. Now I know more about him, and what he got up to, I like him even less.'

Disgust was apparent in his voice and Sarah knew what caused it. Gavin thought his brother a hypocrite for taking a sixteen-year old girl as his mistress whilst naming him a degenerate. She felt some of his censure was directed at her easy virtue and she involuntarily cringed. Not so long ago she might not have cared a jot what he thought of her…but now she did. 'Might we not speak of our families? It is bound to lead to a squabble between us.'

'Still you defend him,' Gavin stated softly.

'No, it's not that…oh, what does it matter about your brother…my brother?' Her chair was sent back from the table and she sprang to her feet. 'We were having a nice time…why rake over past hurts and spoil it?'

'Because if we are not honest with one another there will be no real trust or intimacy between us. And I thought that was what you wanted, Sarah.'

'It is what I want,' Sarah murmured huskily.

Gavin placed his palms on the table and pushed himself upright. He smiled slowly, deliberately, as his burning gaze flowed over her, warming her to the core. 'But you're right; we were having a nice time, and why spoil it talking about vexing relatives?'

'Please do sit down again,' she speedily invited. 'I shall fetch the lemon tart.' Sarah noted at once the rueful amusement that skewed his mouth. He knew exactly why she wanted to prolong their meal and seemed unwilling to comply. A deceptively lazy pace brought him determinedly closer to her.

'I've had enough to eat, sweetheart.'

The silence between them strained expectantly and Sarah wound a silky blonde tress nervously about a finger. 'I have some cards,' she suddenly burst out in inspiration. 'We could play a hand or two of piquet, or there is a chess set that belonged to your brother—' She bit her lip. Edward again. It seemed the atmosphere was haunted by his presence. And never once had he agreed to play a game of chess with her. Now she considered it impartially, it seemed Edward had allocated a certain amount of time to visit her and once it was spent he was gone.

'I thought you said you don't play cards,' Gavin reminded her, ignoring the reference to his vexing relative.

'Well, I'm no good at whist or faro or anything like that, but I should warn you I play a mean hand of piquet.'

'Perhaps we should play chess then,' Gavin said with exaggerated alarm.

'I'm good at that, too,' she warned with a giggle.

'So am I,' Gavin said gently, following her through to the sitting room.

When the cards were on the small table positioned between two comfortable chairs, Sarah felt happy and relaxed again. 'I know you think you're a better player than me.' She leaned forward and put her sharp little

chin on a fist. 'But perhaps I'll surprise you and give
you a run for your money.' Ignorant of the fact she was
sitting opposite a cardplayer *par excellence,* she
believed she might. On several occasions, she had
trounced her Aunt Bea at piquet. By Bea's account she
had been something of a dab hand in her day and had
frequently quit Almack's tables with a clutch of
sovereigns reposing in her reticule.

Gavin idly inspected the pack. 'How much?' he
asked as his dexterous fingers cut, shuffled and flicked
twelve cards in front of them both.

'Oh, I see…stakes…' Her fair brow pleated. It
wasn't as though she couldn't afford to pitch high. She
had a wad of his banknotes in a drawer in her bureau.
'Opening bet…a crown…' she declared, hoping he
wouldn't think her dreadfully wasteful. When she'd
played with Aunt Bea, they'd used halfpennies. And
when those were precious, counters instead.

'A crown it is,' Gavin said, straight-faced, and picked
up his hand.

Sarah nibbled the side of a fingernail, deliberating
on whether to discard the jack of hearts. They had been
playing for almost an hour, during which time dusk had
settled on the sitting room. She had moments ago left
her seat to light the sconces whilst Gavin dealt a new
hand. Now wavering yellow flames complemented the
mellow ambience in the quiet room.

She glanced at him over the top of a clutch of cards

and smiled with spontaneous amity and not a little jauntiness. She felt confident that this pot might be hers. So far she had not won a single hand and her pride demanded she beat him at least once. She decided to keep the jack and pushed a spill that represented a crown to join the pile in the centre of the table.

Gavin discarded a card, took one, then palmed his hand into a semi-circle on the table for her to inspect.

Her frown of annoyance at having lost again lifted as she digested the significance of his winning hand. It was devoid of royalty, known as a *carte blanche*, and it was positioned facing her as though it were an offering. Slowly her eyes were raised from the cards to merge with his. One side of his rugged face was softened by candlelight; the other was shrouded in shadow and looked harsh and inscrutable. A tiny, lopsided smile preceded him suggesting, 'Shall we play something else?'

Slender white fingers swept over the table, scattering the cards. She didn't imagine he was hinting he'd like the chessboard brought out. Slowly she sucked in a silent breath, determined to calm the violent thud of her heart. She knew what he wanted…why he had come here this evening. It wasn't to eat dinner or play cards, although he had politely indulged her in doing both.

She had agreed to be his mistress; had already lain with him once. He had every right to be here. Never in her life had she acted craven and tried to renege on a deal. He had apologised for rough handling her, and treating her disrespectfully. Soon he might grow impatient with her constant prevarication and their fragile friendship would be in jeopardy. And more than anything she wanted to foster closeness between them. She sent him a bright smile as she neatly collected the cards and stacked them.

'You're a very good piquet player.' It sounded magnanimous, almost flattering. Swiftly she reserved judgement. 'Either that or I didn't notice you cheat.'

A grunt of laughter met her observation. 'I've demanded satisfaction at dawn for less than that, Sarah.'

'You've fought a duel?'

'A few times.'

'Over a card game?' A look of shocked interest was levelled on him.

'On at least one occasion, if my memory serves me correctly.'

'You *are* a reprobate,' she said with a sorry shake of her head, and her lips pressed together to repress a scandalised smile. 'In that case I suppose I must be a good loser and allow you…' she leaned forward and counted out spills '…five pounds of your money back.' Gracefully she rose in a rustle of dimity skirts and a ripple of wavy honey-coloured hair.

Gavin watched her figure as she walked away from him and instinctively his hands pulsed as the memory of her curves beneath his palms shot heat through his veins. The urgent throb in his loins was a constant torment, yet using subtle coercion to make love to her, as he'd done before, was out of the question.

He'd remained in Willowdene for longer than he cared to accurately recall. Most of that time he'd been in a state of unrelieved sexual arousal…because Sarah Marchant was constantly in his lustful thoughts. For a reason he didn't care to fathom, he had rebuffed women who were quite clearly attracted to him enough to give him release. Christine Beauvoir had coyly told him she would soon be pleased to receive his visits in Mayfair, when she thought that was the direction in which he was heading. The tavern wench had become tiresomely flirtatious. Yet under normal circumstances he might have succumbed to a dalliance with both women without his conscience bothering him.

But this was the only place he wanted to be. And he had every right to be here. It was his property; he'd paid for the food they'd eaten, and then she'd gambled with his money. More pertinently, Sarah had consented to be his paramour and they'd instantly become passionate and compatible lovers. Yet he knew if she asked him to leave, he would. He accepted now that she had him hooked in more ways than one. He hadn't lied when he'd said he liked her a lot, but it wasn't wholly correct that he was coming to trust her.

She was at times intriguingly evasive and aloof and instinct told him it wasn't just born out of a loyalty to Edward's memory or an understandable self-consciousness about her scars. She wanted to keep her family background private and he didn't want to upset her by demanding answers to questions that were bound to revive dreadful memories. There had been a fire, she had been scarred and her brother, he guessed, had been mortally injured. Perhaps she had been orphaned at the same time. Only a heartless inquisitor would force her to supply the agonising details. But in time…

Over many years he'd been regaled with countless pathetic tales from poor virtuous maids orphaned and forced on the streets to earn a crust. This time he believed the tragedy was genuine and the details were probably more harrowing than he could imagine. In any event, there was no comparison between the courtesans he had known and Sarah Marchant. He hadn't lied when he'd said he thought her unique. He could have added to his praise: she was astonishingly beautiful, courageous, amusing and a heavenly blend of knowing innocence. In fact she was all he wanted. For the first time in his life he was paying court to a woman and even the fact that she had been his pompous brother's mistress would not dull the tender feelings that held his lust in check. He hadn't fallen in love, of course. And he didn't want to. Gentlemen of his acquaintance who'd been prey to un-requited love had tended to act like damnable fools.

His lowered eyes tracked her lissom movements as she turned a key, plunged a hand into a drawer, then pivoted about with cash crushed in a hand. His lips twitched ruefully. Elizabeth Warren would have cleared her debt by treating him to a few erotic tricks. However, he knew his unimaginative brother had not schooled Sarah in any, and for that he was peculiarly grateful.

Sarah slipped back on her seat and placed the banknote in the centre of the table…where it remained. After a moment she said, 'Please take it. I know you might have let me win a hand or two. I'm glad you didn't. There is no triumph in being patronised or treated like a child.'

A soundless laugh revealed Gavin's even white teeth. 'Rest assured I've no intention of patronising you or treating you like a child, Sarah. And as for letting you win at cards…it never entered my head to cede that victory, not when you've come out on top in everything else…figuratively speaking…'

An embarrassed blush stained Sarah's complexion, making her grateful for the shadows in the room. The note was pushed closer to him. She couldn't be certain he had deliberately used imagery that would thrust thrilling memories in to her mind. Her thoughts tended to readily hark back to them without any prompting from him. No doubt he would be glad to know her wantonness was so encompassing. Again she took cover in conversation. 'So…if I were to accuse you of cheating me of five pounds, I must expect you to challenge me to a duel at dawn.'

'I can think of sweeter things to do with you at dawn,' he said softly. 'And that, Sarah, begs the question…do you want me to go or stay?'

Chapter Fifteen

'I'm not expecting you to go.'

Sarah felt her tension peak, then ebb away. The uncertainty was over and she was glad of that but sad that their lighthearted game was at an end. She had enjoyed their conversation whilst they played cards. It was the sort of casual amusement in which friends indulged. Now all was again serious. Her breasts were becoming heavy with anticipation, her heart beating erratically as pleasure of a different kind dominated her mind.

'Do you want me to stay, Sarah?' he pitilessly demanded to know.

There was but a tiny hesitation before she answered quite clearly, 'Yes.' She wrenched her eyes from his and rose from her chair. 'If you would allow me a short while alone to prepare to retire…' She made quickly for the door. 'The bedchamber is situated at the end of the corridor on the right-hand side,' she graciously informed him, then felt silly for having done so. A Lothario such as he was doubtless able to locate a woman's bed wearing a blindfold.

She was not prepared for this, she thought wildly as she quickly stripped and yanked open her chest of drawers to find a pretty nightdress. She tossed the confection of lawn and lace over her head. It was held together at the front by laces and simultaneously she began struggling to tie the ribbons and drag a brush through her stubbornly resilient locks. Next she sped to the washstand and employed the jug and bowl and washing cloth. The water was cold, sending a shiver along her spine, but moments later, with her face and body clean, and still damp from her rushed bathing, she slid between cool crisp cotton and lay back. Immediately her head came up off the feather pillow and she blew out the candle by the bed.

As though he had been waiting for such a signal, she heard the click of the door opening and closing and saw a wavering flame approach. The light descended to the dresser and she heard the familiar noise of a gentleman removing his clothes in her bedroom. She closed her eyes tight and listened past the beat of blood in her ears. It didn't sound like Edward; he would sometimes mutter to himself if a boot would not easily release a foot or a button stubbornly stayed in its hook. Gavin was silent…and swift.

The bed dipped beneath his weight as he lay down beside her with a low exhalation of breath. It was how she retired sometimes when particularly weary or careworn, but he didn't look either of those things when, a moment later, he was braced on an elbow and his preposterously long-lashed eyes were fixed on her face. Through shadow she met his gaze steadily, in no way betraying that her heart was attacking her ribs quite painfully.

A few slow fingers moved a stray curl back from her brow before his fingers forked into a mass of luxuriant hair that showed auburn against the snowy pillow. 'Would you like to go for a carriage drive tomorrow?'

A wide-eyed look met his invitation. She had expected a kiss not conversation. She resorted to nodding.

'Cambridge is not far. We could spend the day there.'

Oh, how she would love to. But her joy was fading before it was properly tasted. What of Aunt Bea and Timothy? When last she had visited them they both had been in very low spirits. Aunt Bea was tomorrow expecting her to move in with them to help her cope with Tim. Her aunt and brother had no idea a change of plan was in the offing because they must again play second fiddle to this man. Bea had no laudanum to offer Tim to mellow his moods and it was her fault. She had decided, in her wisdom, that Tim must curb his addiction to his only comfort in case it harmed him. She was the most selfish person alive to even think of enjoying a day's excursion with her lover when her relatives had such troubles. 'I'd sooner not travel so far,' she whispered. 'But a short drive would be very nice indeed.'

'Have you something pressing to attend to tomorrow?' His head dipped closer to her as a small hand slipped naturally to his shoulder, then absently skittered to and fro as she meditated on how to deflect his questions. He pressed his mouth fleetingly to hers in thanks for the touch; he knew it was the closest to a caress he was likely to get. 'Are you planning to spend the time unpacking your boxes now you have no need to pursue me to London?'

'Yes...I expect I shall unpack my boxes.' Her lashes fell over her eyes. His sardonic tone made her realise he had not sincerely believed she would chase after him.

'I don't think you should. I still want you to accompany me there.'

Her eyes clashed on his, sparking defiance.

'If I'd gone away, would you have eventually sought me in town?'

'No,' Sarah said, too honestly.

As he turned his head and gazed at something unseen, Sarah wanted to put a finger to the fleshless plane of his jaw to soften her rebuff. The need to soothe him withered as he swung back to study her with narrowed glittering eyes. 'That's not what I hoped to hear, Sarah.'

'Shall I lie to please you?'

A soundless laugh shaped his mouth. 'Why not?' he

drawled. 'And while you're doing so, tell me again that you want me.'

A glint of some unfathomable emotion smouldered in his eyes but in a second his head lowered and his mouth slanted over hers preventing her saying anything at all.

It was as sweet as he'd promised; an unhurried salute that parted her lips gently. His tongue touched, teased, withdrew before fully entering the silken recess to caress and tempt a response from her.

It was impossible to resist the intoxicating heat that was seeping through her veins. Sarah wound slender arms about him, parting her mouth as sensual pressure from his urged her to do so. Her back arched a little from the bed as his fingers flowed skilfully over her skin, lingering, then artfully straying away when she would have them stay.

His hands traced her silhouette, enclosed her breasts through cotton whilst subtly loosening the bows on her nightgown. He lowered his head, kissed one breast then the other before circling moist fire with his tongue. A gasp of pure pleasure was wrung from Sarah and his mouth plunged to a nipple to tantalise the tiny nub until a protracted whimper signalled her delight, her surrender to him. Firm fingers dug beneath her buttocks to lift her against the solid pressure throbbing in his loins. Instinctively her body recalled recent ecstasy and her thighs parted, her pelvis ground against him, flushing with moist heat.

'Slowly…' Gavin muttered in a raw whisper as his hands pressed her thrusting hips down and away to the mattress. She felt his mouth curve into a smile against hers. 'There's no rush,' he murmured. 'I promise I'll stay with you till morning.'

A sob of a laugh clogged her throat and she tried to twist her face away from his mockery. A ruthless hand plunged into her hair, curved beneath her scalp to lift her face up to his. The kiss this time was tender savagery, the hands at her nightdress efficient, intent on its removal. Only momentarily did he lift his mouth from hers to achieve his aim of having her naked. She felt a shimmy of lace on her warm face as the nightgown was whisked up and off, then his lips reclaimed hers.

'What time is the master arriving?'

'At two of the clock.' Sarah shifted her frown from Maude to the wall clock. It was just after noon. 'I'd be obliged if Matthew would take me into Willowdene now. There is time to go to the apocothery and visit Bea and Tim before Mr Stone is due to take me out.'

Maude gave Sarah a long assessing look. 'You've not told him about your relatives, have you?'

Sarah shook her head and avoided Maude's eye. She could sense the woman's disapproval. 'Our acquaintance is too short to disclose something so delicate. I hardly know him.' But I'm coming to know him, she thought. I'm coming to like him, as well…far too much.

'I think you know him well enough,' Maude opined with an old-fashioned look. 'And that brother of his knew all about everything straight off. Put it to use he did, too.'

'He did not,' Sarah said quickly, but with less conviction than might have sharpened her tone a short while ago. 'Besides, I didn't betray us. Edward learned nothing about our misfortunes from me,' she added fiercely. 'And neither will Gavin Stone. He wants to return to town and I expect soon that is what he will do. It would be awful if the scandal started up again.'

Maude plonked her hands on her hips. 'Mr Stone don't seem like a gossip or a mischief-maker to me.'

'Or to me,' Sarah agreed softly, 'But it only takes an unguarded word or two…and I imagine he and his friends are serious revellers when in their cups. It was a scandal that hurt many people. There are sure to be those who would still like retribution. No money is to be had, so mayhap they might settle on hounding us from our home…if they discover its whereabouts.'

Maude shook her head to herself and looked contrite. 'I wouldn't want that; but no good ever come of deceiving decent folk. The master's treated you more'n fair, yet that's sure to change if he finds out you been less than fair back. Don't do to gull a gentleman like that. Gavin Stone don't seem to me to be a fellow who'd take kindly to being made a fool of.'

If Gavin had not, on approaching the Lodge, heard his name spoken, he might have used the knocker and made known his presence. But he'd caught part of Maude Jackson's cautionary advice and it made him hesitate by the half-open door. He never eavesdropped. He despised people who did; but as his name and a fool had been uttered in the same sentence, he felt he had every right to know why that was.

Had he not used the back road that led here from the manor, the phaeton would have been positioned in full view in front of the Lodge. As it was, the cumbersome old vehicle he had found in Edward's coach house was not mobile enough to bring closer and neither were the nags in harness, so he had left the contraption some distance away and walked. He'd come early, hoping to persuade Sarah to have a picnic luncheon with him. So confident had he been of her acceptance of the idea, after the wonderfully pleasurable evening they had spent together, that he had with him a wicker box full to the brim with a selection of good things prepared by the Manor's cook. Now he knew his hankering to spend a lazy day in her company was in vain and he was about to discover why.

'I have not made a fool of Mr Stone,' Sarah answered Maude crisply. 'What he does not know will not hurt him. He has said he intends to go home to Mayfair. Perhaps I might not see much of him at all in the future. Tim will always be here in my life.'

'Yes, always here, and always trouble for you, too. I've seen the temper on him. I know he's not had things easy, but neither have you. It's time he bucked up his ideas.'

'That's enough,' Sarah said sharply. 'I love Tim and I know he loves me. Nothing will ever change that, no matter how badly he behaves towards me, or which gentleman pays for our keep.'

'See how much he loves you when his belly's empty and the rent's due to be paid and there's nothing left,' Maude roughly warned. 'If Mr Stone finds out you have secretly been keeping this place and another household too on his accounts he's likely to be angrier than you know. You'll end up on the parish, 'cos no man 'ud put up with it, I tell you!'

Sarah's hands gripped together in agitation. She knew that Maude was bringing potential pitfalls to her attention for her own good. 'There's no point in going over it all. I have made up my mind. Now please tell Matthew I should like a ride on the dogcart so I may go to Willowdene and buy what Tim needs.'

By the time the conversation between the two women had come to a frosty close, Gavin was just a score or so paces from the phaeton. He'd quit listening when he'd heard all he needed to. He halted, close to a docile bay cropping grass, with a thin self-mocking smile on his lips. He'd come here because he couldn't keep away from her for even a few more hours. He wished he was still in blissful ignorance of it all…but he wasn't. And his pride wouldn't allow him to do nothing.

Maude Jackson was quite correct—he was a man who didn't like to think himself a fool, and the unpalatable truth was that he'd been acting like a love-struck simpleton. Puzzling facts that had been rotating in his mind were swiftly brought into focus and finally he saw the full picture. The reason for Sarah's refusal to leave the area, or to supply details about her background, suddenly became crystal clear. His first instinct about her circumstances had been correct—she was a young woman of gentle birth ruined by a feckless swain.

She had a lover; an idle good for nothing from Maude's description, who was content to act the ponce and let her provide for him. Now he knew why she had had her boxes packed and ready to move out. As soon as she'd believed him to be travelling south, she had intended to use his money to set up home with the man she truly wanted.

Perhaps Edward had not deflowered the innocent Miss Marchant after all. Gavin was now more inclined to believe that, by the time Edward took her on, she'd already lost her virginity to Tim, the man she would always love as she'd vehemently declared. White-hot jealousy raged through Gavin, a novel and extremely unpleasant experience.

Rarely had he for long been captivated into monogamy by the women in his life. When a few mistresses had reciprocated and taken a lover as well, he'd accepted they had a right to a discreet dalliance. Sarah had been different, or so he'd thought. He'd battled his cynicism and come to consider her sweet and pure and poignantly principled.

He'd told her she was unique and he'd meant every word. How twisted an epithet it had come to be. She was unique in being the most perfidious harlot he'd ever encountered. His fists tightened at his side and one was punched against the phaeton's coachwork in violent frustration. What else was false? Had her parents disowned her rather than died? Had she been ill treated by her pimp and come by her scars that way? He'd overheard that Tim behaved badly towards her. For a moment he felt an overwhelming urge to seek out the bastard and beat the truth out of him.

He turned as he heard the dogcart set off towards Willowdene with Sarah next to Maude's husband on the seat. For a demented few seconds he moved forward, on the brink of racing towards it and demanding Sarah give an immediate explanation for all he'd heard. But pride suddenly held him rooted to the spot, watching as it disappeared from view. When sufficiently in control of his temper, he strode back through the copse towards the Lodge. He had no quarrel with Maude Jackson; in fact, he owed her his gratitude for championing him. His intention in returning was to simply leave with her a message that he would, regrettably, be otherwise engaged and unable to take her mistress out for a drive later.

She did not love him. She had been a woman awakened to sensuality, but unfulfilled. He had satisfied a natural craving. That's all it was. She did not love him…she must not. So ran Sarah's thoughts as the dogcart jogged over ruts bearing her into Willowdene. But even with a logical explanation for the overwhelming happiness that filled her being, still she could not control the wild thump of her heart at the prospect of soon seeing Gavin again. Last night he had made love to her with an enchanting mix of tenderness and raw sensuality that made her body tingle anew as she dreamily dwelled on it. Then when they both were sated he had held her while she slept. In the morning he had not left till they had taken tea together and arranged the hour for him to come and call on her to take her for a drive. A wonderfully lingering kiss had been his parting gift to her.

She wanted to carry out her errands swiftly so she might return home and dress prettily for her outing. Although she had said to Maude he would soon return to London, a secret hope was lodged in her heart that he might eventually come to like her, and country living, well enough to settle here. And then, when she was sure that she could trust him, she would tell him what she must and hope he would listen sympathetically to the tale of her father's greed and chicanery and how it had led to their family's ruin. She knew in her heart that Maude was being honest and courageous in warning her of the risks of dissembling. She prayed that soon there would be no more need for any of it.

A sorry sigh escaped Sarah as she saw Joseph Pratt, deep in conversation with Daniel Bloom outside his apothecary. Both gentlemen noticed her and seemed to give her a deliberate sideways stare before turning their attention to a point across the street. Sarah sensed that something significant lay behind their sly gazes. She looked in the direction they had turned and saw a woman preparing to take a promenade with her maid. A small parasol was being opened and closed as though in readiness to be employed. Sarah did not recognise the lady and immediately guessed she had arrived from London; she had the polished confident air that wealth and good connection bestowed. An unpleasant ominous sensation tipped over Sarah's insides. Instinctively she knew what had caused the gentlemen to swing a glance between her and the attractive brunette—the young woman had come to Willowdene because that's where Gavin was.

With a murmur Sarah directed Matthew to stop so she might buy laudanum. Daniel Bloom went back inside his shop and Joseph Pratt sauntered in her direction, making a show of helping her alight, the glee in his eyes unashamedly apparent.

'Good day, Miss Marchant,' he jovially boomed.

Sarah would have preferred to get down unassisted rather than take his aid. She snatched back her fingers whilst returning him a cool greeting.

He positioned himself so as to trap her between his portly figure and the vehicle. 'I fear I might have misled you into thinking that Mr Stone had gone to London. I now know he is residing at the Manor.'

Sarah dipped her head in acknowledgement of the information and tried to pass him.

'Perhaps he may stay a while now he has his friends around him,' Joseph continued, his low-lidded eyes fixed on her tense features. 'A short time ago I was speaking to his charming friend, Mrs Warren. She arrived just last evening from town and has taken a suite of rooms at the Red Lion. She is an extremely lovely young woman, is she not?' Joseph prodded home his victory with a meaningful glance across the street. 'Are we not lucky to have such fashionable people come to join us? You have missed Sir Clayton; he was earlier conversing with Mrs Warren. I expect he left so speedily to inform Mr Stone of the good news of her safe arrival.'

A chuckle erupted from him that was spiteful enough to make Sarah want to slap him. She bit her tongue, adopting an air of apathy, and let him have his say.

'Perhaps Elizabeth Warren and her retinue might move into the Manor with the gentlemen. What fine entertainment they'll have to be sure.'

That *was* enough. With a determined side-step Sarah was past him and endeavouring to ignore the low laughter that followed her into the apothecary shop.

Boldly she met Daniel Bloom's eyes whilst giving her order. Sarah thought she detected a light of pity in his eyes as he handed over her purchase and it wounded her more than had the lawyer's malice. With her chin elevated, she exited the premises, relieved to see that Joseph Pratt had taken himself off.

She must not jump to conclusions, Sarah exhorted herself as she headed off on the cart to see Tim and Aunt Bea. She would see Gavin very soon and take a drive with him. She felt now enough harmony and honesty was established between them for her to ask him about Mrs Warren. She trusted he would tell her the truth. This morning they had parted as friends and lovers; no amount of Joseph Pratt's poisonous words could alter that.

Chapter Sixteen

Sir Clayton Powell had expected his tidings might be badly received. What he had not expected was to find his friend already in the foulest of tempers.

On quitting the Manor earlier that day, Gavin had been in excellent spirits. It had not taken much imagination on Clayton's part to guess why that was, or whither his friend was once more headed. He had been sure Gavin might not tear himself free of Miss Marchant's embrace for a day or two. Thus he had not anticipated finding his friend at home and had been about to pen a note for Gavin to read on his return.

He knew that Gavin had fallen in love for the first time in his life and, if he were to be honest, had at first felt a tad miffed at playing second fiddle to the sweet chit who had stolen Gavin's heart.

Ordinarily, rather than play gooseberry, Clayton would have returned alone to Mayfair where his popularity would be better appreciated. Yet he found he was loitering in the vicinity, as Gavin's houseguest, for the same reason that kept his friend here—a woman had captured his interest.

Ruth Hayden was a beauty; he had noticed that the first time he saw her driving her little pony and trap. He'd learned from Gavin that she was a widow; he'd also been told that Ruth was a good friend of Sarah's and strictly out of bounds of any predatory intentions. With unconvincing indignation he had declared himself innocent. And, indeed, there was more to it than his attraction to her. He had a niggling feeling that some intelligence about her was stubbornly evading his memory. Unfortunately, because she was in full mourning, he was unable to engineer an opportunity to properly talk to her and satisfy his curiosity.

Putting thoughts of Ruth to one side, he brought his concentration back to his friend. He'd come upon Gavin in his study, slouched behind his desk, with a grim expression on his face and a full brandy balloon in his fist. From the dishevelled look of him, and the fiery glint in his eyes, it was obvious Gavin had been imbibing for some while.

The cognac was swiftly dispatched and Gavin refilled the glass. With a brief flourish of the decanter, he wordlessly indicated that Clayton should help himself and continued glaring into space through a fog of cigar smoke.

'Bit early for a serious session, isn't it?'

Gavin shot his friend a dark look and drew deeply on the cheroot clamped between his lips.

'Hell's teeth, Gav! It ain't that much of a calamity.
Pack her off home with a flea in her ear.'

'What in damnation are you on about?' Gavin
barked, having snatched the cheroot from his mouth and
slammed down his glass.

'From the look of you I thought you must already
have found out about her…' Clayton hesitated attempting to gauge whether Gavin was aware that Elizabeth
Warren had followed him to Willowdene.

'What should I have found out?' Gavin slurred with
a nasty smile, whilst watching his fingers grinding out
the cheroot in the ashtray. 'That Miss Sarah Marchant
is a traitorous little bi—' The insult was bitten off early.
Snatching up the glass, he gave the liquid a savage
swirl before downing it in a swallow. 'I already know
about her, so save your breath.'

'Ah…' Clayton said, and rubbed the bridge of his
nose with a long finger. 'You don't know.'

'What the devil is that supposed to mean?' Gavin's
palms slammed on the edge of the desk and he shoved
himself to his feet. 'What do you know about her?' he
demanded harshly.

'Nothing…I swear, nothing,' Clayton assured
soothingly.

Seemingly satisfied with that, Gavin braced a hand on
the wall and soon seemed lost in morose thoughts that
kept his eyes directed through the wide lead-paned
window.

'But I do know something about another lady.'

Clayton sighed before launching into, 'At the risk of considerably worsening your mood, I'll tell you that I have just been talking to Elizabeth. She's turned up in Willowdene, looking for you.'

Gavin half turned and frowned in incomprehension at his friend from beneath a lank fringe of dark hair. 'Elizabeth?' he echoed. 'What in God's name does she want?'

'That's exactly what I asked her,' Clayton supplied carefully. 'Her answer was…she'd tired of waiting for you in Mayfair and had come to the godforsaken sticks to find you.' On the few occasions he had witnessed Gavin enraged, he had learned it was best to be elsewhere until he calmed down. But Gavin surprised him by suddenly tipping back his head and roaring with laughter.

'There's only one thing for it, then,' Gavin drawled, wiping a wry, mirthful tear from his eye. 'I'm heading home.' As though to impress on his friend that he'd made a serious decision, he strode out of the study and went in search of Drayton, the butler, with the intention of ordering him to make the necessary arrangements for their departure.

A few minutes after Gavin arrived at the stables, in order to direct the grooms to make ready the travelling coach and horses, a maid sped towards him with the information that an urgent message had just arrived for him.

The light breeze that stirred the autumn treetops had

also dispersed some of the intoxicated haze clouding Gavin's mind. More alert he strode, thin-lipped and impatient, into the hallway to be confronted by Drayton. With great aplomb the elderly servant extended towards him a silver salver on which reposed a letter. Gavin had been expecting a note. He guessed this to be from Elizabeth, demanding an audience, although he hoped very much it might be from Sarah, demanding an explanation. He was in just the mood to go and give it to her. But he would not…he must not. He must avoid her at all costs. He still wanted Sarah with a hungry yearning that shook him to his core, despite his knowledge she loved another man and wanted to be with him.

He would leave this damnable place without seeing her again, for the violence of his emotions was disturbing him. He felt on the brink of succumbing to some insanity he was sure to regret, once he'd conquered the mawkish sentiment that was destroying his reason.

In pent-up frustration he flung back his head and sent an oath flying at the ceiling, making old Drayton start to attention and peer at him queerly. Gavin dismissed him with a hand flick. Now the staff would think he was mad and he couldn't blame them for it. For the first time since he'd met her…and lust and obsession had possessed him…the savage throb in his loins was a lesser torment than the constriction in his chest.

He wheeled about, stuffing the note into a pocket,

and returned to the stables to hurry the preparations for his travel home. He was going back to London, and women like Elizabeth Warren, and a life he understood.

While the grooms toiled to make everything ready, Gavin ripped open the seal and unfolded the parchment. Impassively his eyes scanned the news that his uncle, Viscount Tremayne, had passed on. The writer went on to implore Mr Stone to visit the offices of Venner and Styles in Cheapside at his earliest convenience to receive news of great import.

'Is that all he said?' Sarah asked in bewilderment.

Maude nodded and wiped her floury hands on her pinafore.

'Did he seem cross about something?'

Maude shook her head. 'Seemed like a fellow keen not to give anything away. Just said he wouldn't be back to take you out.' Maude sent a meaningful glance across the room at her husband. After a doleful shake of the head, Matthew dutifully left them alone and went outside. 'Polite he were, of course,' Maude continued. 'But if I were to take a guess, I'd say Mr Stone had something weighing on his mind.'

'I see.' Sarah stripped off her bonnet and placed it down on a chair.

'I said no good 'ud come of being deceitful.' Maude's voice held a soft sadness.

'Yes, I know,' Sarah said quietly. 'And while I was out I thought about what you'd said. I had decided you were right and that this afternoon, when we were alone, I would confide in him.'

'It would have been for the best,' Maude said kindly.

'No…it would not have been,' Sarah said on a choke. She gave Maude a teary look. 'When in town I saw a beautiful, stylish lady just arrived from London.' She'd drawn closer to the table whilst talking and looked at the pie Maude had made. It was more than enough for two, but she would again be dining alone. 'Mr Pratt made sure I understood who she was,' she steadily resumed. 'Mrs Elizabeth Warren is her name and she is Gavin's mistress. You see…I know why he has made his excuses. He has gone to her, that's why he could not take me out.' As Maude clucked sympathy and enclosed her in sturdy arms, Sarah's tears were unabated. 'How stupid I was to ever imagine there could have been something fine between us,' she choked. 'Edward told me about his womanising rogue of a brother. I cannot plead I did not have fair warning of his character.'

Three weeks later a letter was redirected from the Lodge to the cottage where Sarah was staying with Tim and Aunt Bea. Simply from looking at the firm masculine hand that had written her name and direction, she knew it to be from Gavin. She broke the seal and read, with mounting dismay, the brief message:

I trust this note will eventually reach you, although I imagine you are now moved to live with Tim. I fear he must spare your company for a month or two as I wish you to come and join me. I will assume that the twenty-first of this month will give you adequate time to prepare to travel and will make the necessary arrangements for a carriage to be despatched to collect you from the Red Lion in Willowdene on that date.

Sarah sank down on the side of her bed, her complexion sickly. Her eyes devoured the words again, but her brother's name was there in black and white. He knew of Tim's existence! Her mind vaulted from that fact to another—he surely must be acquainted with all her woeful history too. She must pray he kept what he knew to himself. The shock of that discovery was swiftly supplanted by other, equally disturbing, intelligence. This was no request. He was *commanding* her to do his bidding and was planning to despatch a coach to fetch her.

Sarah's mouth pursed and her hackles rose. How dare he act with such vile arrogance and demand she go to London to sleep with him for a month or two. No doubt after that time he would send her packing and Mrs Warren would again be in favour.

He had left Willowdene without sending her word of his departure. Sarah had discovered that Mrs Warren had quit the Red Lion and returned to London the same day. She was obviously a tenacious mistress and one who put the lie to his claim that he avoided women likely to be possessive. But then she ought to have known she could not believe a word he said. Thank heavens she had discovered in time that his notoriety was deserved. Had she foolishly fallen in love with the heartless beast…how dreadful that would have been. Yet despite being sure she had been sensible and protected her heart a depressing sense of loss…of emptiness…was constantly with her. She felt more bereft and lonely than she had after Edward's death. It was no more than companionship she missed, she told herself, time and again. She would fill the void she had joyously anticipated he might occupy by spending time with someone she most certainly could trust and liked very much. She was determined to pay a visit on Ruth later in the week.

'You look very well.' Such was Ruth's smiling greeting when Sarah stepped over her threshold.

'And I must return the compliment,' Sarah told her friend on giving her a little hug.

'Come through to the garden,' Ruth invited. 'It is such a glorious afternoon. The roses are still in bloom and make quite a picture.'

The two young women walked the hallway and through the dining room, exiting the cottage through the double doors that lead on to a paved patio. A blaze of autumn colours, interspersed with the pastel shades of roses trailing trelliswork, met Sarah's appreciative gaze.

'I shall fetch the tea. The kettle is boiled so I shan't be long,' Ruth said, having led the way to a small wooden bench, and inviting Sarah to sit down.

Sarah smiled her thanks and settled back, allowing her senses to be pleasantly soothed by birdsong and the powdery scent of flowers.

Soon Ruth reappeared, bearing the tea tray. 'Is Tim well? And your Aunt Bea?' she affably enquired as she placed the tray down on a circular stone table.

A rueful smile preceded Sarah's answer. 'They are well, although they are sometimes reluctant to let me know it. At times I very much miss the peace and quiet of Elm Lodge.'

'Will you move back there?' Ruth asked, handing Sarah her tea.

'No…not unless…' Her voice drifted into silence.

'Not unless Gavin Stone returns to Willowdene,' Ruth supplied.

'I doubt he will,' Sarah dismissed quickly. She gave Ruth a quirk of a smile. 'He has written asking…nay, demanding…that I join him in London for a month or so.'

Ruth placed down her cup and her brown eyes looked troubled. 'And will you go?'

'Indeed I will not,' Sarah answered pithily. She gazed into the distance. 'He mentioned Tim in his letter. From that I must assume that he is now aware of my background. I imagine he was disgusted to discover that a shocking scandal has blighted my life. Perhaps that knowledge caused his abrupt departure…together with his mistress's cajoling, of course.'

Ruth clasped one of Sarah's hands and looked into

her friend's peaky features. Only moments before Sarah had looked blooming and she had told her so; now her friend looked fragile, as though she were ailing. 'You have gone quite pale, Sarah. Do not upset yourself over it all.'

'Oh, it is not her…or him,' Sarah said on a gruff little laugh. 'I swear daily I will not let memories of Gavin Stone bother me. It is just that lately I have been feeling rather nauseated. Perhaps something I ate has not agreed with me.'

Ruth sat back and looked keenly at her friend. 'And have your aunt and brother felt ill, too?'

Sarah shook her head. 'I don't think so. It is nothing…just a queasiness, and usually the feeling leaves me towards the afternoon.'

'Are your menses late?' Ruth asked quietly.

Sarah looked startled, but then gave Ruth a most quizzical look. 'Why…yes…how did you know that?'

'I have been with child,' Ruth said softly, 'That's how I know the signs. I think you are increasing, Sarah.'

'But…but it cannot be.' Sarah stared at her friend, her golden eyes widening in shock. 'I lay with Edward many times and feared I might conceive. But I did not, and of course I was greatly thankful of that, given my circumstances. I thought the trauma of my accident had affected me in some way.'

'I have heard that it is not only a woman's fault if she fails to breed. Did Edward have children with his wife in their early married years?'

The awfulness of what Ruth had brought to her attention was slowly penetrating Sarah's mind. She shook her head in response to Ruth's question. Instinctively she knew that what her friend had suggested was the truth. A hand curved with innate care over her belly. She had felt odd for some weeks. But the niggling discomfort in her breasts, and low in her abdomen, she had dismissed as due to anxiety and her fraught emotions. Her eyes sped to Ruth's face. 'Are you sure you know the signs?'

Ruth nodded. 'I gave birth to a daughter,' she murmured.

Sarah looked expectantly at her friend, her own worries in limbo.

'She was stillborn,' Ruth said bravely and forced a wobbly smile. 'It was quite a time ago now.'

'I'm so sorry…'

Ruth gripped both Sarah's hands and gave them a brisk shake. 'What we must now concentrate on is what you are to do about it all.'

The full force of her terrifying predicament suddenly hit home like a physical blow. Sarah folded forwards a little and her arms crossed over her midriff as though to conceal the child within. 'What *am* I to do about it?' she echoed in a tiny panicky voice.

There was no room for delay on a matter such as this, Ruth had told her, and Sarah had known that to be very wise advice indeed. Since their conversation her

morning sickness had occurred with alarming fre-
quency and she had noticed Aunt Bea looking at her
queerly. Soon her aunt would ask what ailed her, and
if Sarah did not tell her, the woman would know soon
enough simply by using her eyes. Her swollen bosom
was already straining her bodice buttons, although her
stomach was quite flat.

Just a short while ago she had been determined she
would defy Gavin's demand that she join him in
London. Now she had no choice but to go and immediately inform him that she was pregnant and needed
his undertaking to provide for their child. She could not
wait weeks, fretting and growing larger, until he sent a
carriage to Willowdene to collect her.

She had not sent him notice of her imminent arrival.
What would she write? She could hardly communicate
in a letter that he had fathered a bastard. Such delicate
yet explosive news was best conveyed face to face, in
private. Neither would she prevaricate and coyly imply
she was arriving earlier than arranged because of her
impatience to see him. Her pride would not allow her
to do so…even though partly it was true. Despite
knowing him for a callous rogue, and a lover who
would cruelly deny her even the briefest farewell, a
fragment of her heart still leaped at the thought of
seeing him again. And very soon she would, for in an
hour or so they would reach the city…

Her introspection was interrupted as the woman next
to her on the cramped seat started to bounce the fretful

child on her knee. Sarah shifted an inch or two further into the corner and leaned her head against the side of the mail coach, longing to doze, yet knowing it a vain hope stuck as she was in such strident squashed conditions. The young man opposite, who looked to be a farmhand by trade, caught her eye and gave her a wink.

Sarah closed her eyes, idly wondering what brought that bluff-looking individual to the metropolis. Her musing was rudely curtailed as an elbow dug in to her ribs. 'Be a kind soul, would you, miss?' the woman by her side implored. 'Take little 'un off me for a bit. Me legs've fair gawn ta sleep. She's a bonny little lass as you can see, but hefty with it.'

'Oh…of course…' Sarah gave the woman a faint smile. Tentatively she lifted the chubby child on to her lap. She settled her down; she was indeed a solid little thing. Immediately the child swivelled and made a grab for her bonnet strings. Seeing that she had a fascination for the ribbon, Sarah untied her hat and let the child investigate its floral decoration with inquisitive fingers, her small features crumpled in concentration.

'Where you off to?' the woman asked as she massaged at her knees beneath her brown serge skirts.

'London.'

'Oh…'course I know that,' the woman scolded with a chuckle. 'You off to see family in town?'

'A friend,' Sarah replied briefly. She nodded at the child. 'What is her name?'

'Deborah. We calls her Debbie. She's me granddaughter. Well, one of 'em. I've got four in all, and two grandsons.'

'You're very lucky.' Sarah swept a finger over the child's soft cheek.

The woman beamed. 'I'm taking this one back to her ma and pa in Hackney. Took her to stay with me for a while as her ma's in the family way again.' She chuckled. 'Betime I get to their place I dare say I'll have a new little 'un to swing in a crib.'

Sarah smiled slightly, unable to make a comment, for thoughts of newborn babies caused a lump to clog her throat.

'Lodging with yer friend, are you?'

'I expect I shall...' Sarah murmured evasively and quickly clucked at the boisterous child in an attempt to soothe her restless mewing.

The woman gave Sarah a long assessing look. 'Well, now...if'n yer friend can't manage to put you up, I know of a real respectable place in the city.' She leaned closer to whisper conspiratorially, 'Mrs Draper, Walton House, Gracechurch Street. She's got a right nice establishment for genteel ladies such as yerself.' With that piece of kindly advice she lifted the child back on to her lap. 'Don't forget...' she said to Sarah in a confidential tone. 'Walton House, and tell Minnie Draper that Vi Spooner sent you. She'll see you right.'

'Thank you...' Sarah said softly and felt the lump again thicken her throat at the woman's unexpected concern. She again closed her eyes, and leaned her head back against the cushions. She hoped that her desperate situation was not somehow obvious to strangers.

Chapter Seventeen

'Old Vi?' The woman gave one of her hips a gleeful thump with an open palm. 'I haven't seen Vi Spooner in a long while. How does she fare?'

'She seemed very well indeed,' Sarah politely told Mrs Draper.

A gap-toothed grin met that information. 'Well, now…if my friend told you to come and see me, she wants you looked after. So looked after you shall be, my dear,' Minnie Draper promised on ushering Sarah over the threshold of Walton House.

Sarah's eyes darted about as she followed the cheerful landlady along a gloomy corridor to a doorway. In contrast to the depressing appearance of the stark reception hall, the back parlour was bright and quite adequately furnished with a plush sofa and two wing armchairs.

At the landlady's invitation Sarah perched on velvet

and accepted a glass of lemonade. Despite being quite exhausted, and longing for a nap, she listened obligingly as the woman recounted a little bit of history surrounding her acquaintance with Mrs Spooner.

'Vi was a good friend to me when me husband passed on. Albert used to help me run this place. That were eight years ago. Vi's a widow, too, but she's got quite a brood of grandchildren to keep her on her toes. We don't see so much of each other nowadays. Would you like some dinner, miss?' was incongruously tacked on the end of her reminiscence.

'Oh, yes…thank you.'

'I've got a nice clean room you can have at the front.' Sarah got another uneven smile. 'Special rate too for friends of friends.' She tapped at her nose and winked. 'And the dinner is just a shillin' and you won't get no better victuals from fancy chefs up west.'

'I'm sure I won't,' Sarah said appreciatively. She shifted further forward on the sofa, about to stand up. 'Might I be shown my room, Mrs Draper? I should like to rest after my journey.'

Minnie clucked solicitously at her. 'I'll get one of the girls to fetch you up some hot water. I expect you'd like to freshen up. Then I'll have your dinner sent up at about five of the clock.'

An hour or so later, having catnapped on a surprisingly comfy bed and eaten her fill of a tasty piece of beef-and-oyster pie with roasted vegetables, Sarah felt refreshed. In fact, so recovered was she that she was pacing restlessly about the chamber. She peered through the window at the busy street below. The area around Cheapside was renowned for being a hub of commercial activity. Even at this late hour in the afternoon the pavements were thronging with people hurrying about their business. Such industry reminded Sarah that she also had a task in front of her. A daunting ordeal it was, too, and pondering miserably on it rather than taking action had never been her way.

She knew Gavin lived in Lansdowne Crescent. And she knew exactly where that was, for once she had lived within walking distance of the fashionable quarter. In a decisive snap Sarah began stripping off her travelling clothes. She swirled a finger in the water in the copper pitcher, pleased to note that it had cooled to a good temperature. She tipped up the jug and, plunging the washing cloth into the bowl, began briskly making ready to go out.

'The hall is a magnificent edifice in the Palladian style. The gardens are vast, and a joy to behold. I am able to comment with such conviction, my lord, as I had the rare privilege to gaze upon it all with my own eyes. Your late uncle bade me accompany him there. Urgent business, you understand, about a year ago now…' Apparently unperturbed by his new client's lack of participation in this conversation, the lawyer pushed his spectacles further up his nose and continued listing the extraordinarily fine attributes of the Tremayne estate. 'Beyond the east wing lie stables renowned to house the finest horseflesh in the country. It was the late Viscount's passion…his downfall too, of course,' Mr Styles added in a respectful under-breath that conveyed his regret at the accident. 'The steward and most of the senior staff were taken on personally by the late Viscount. He wanted about him people of the highest order.' The lawyer peered studiously over his spectacles. 'I am aware that a family rift caused you and your uncle to remain strangers, nevertheless I think you would approve of it all. No doubt you are planning to soon travel there to see for yourself.'

Gavin roused himself to nod meditatively at the lawyer over his steepled fingers. He hoped he was giving the impression of a man who was conscious of his astonishingly good fortune…otherwise the fellow might wonder whether he was lacking in the attic. He had not known his father's brother; he had hardly known his father, for that matter.

Over the past week or so he had learned that, not only had he become a peer of the realm, he had also acquired an estate that covered ten thousand acres in Surrey. With it came one hundred and fifty staff, three hundred cottages housing five hundred tenants, and a few million pounds to add to the smaller fortune that his brother Edward had left to him. Yet no amount of land, property and riches could oust from his concentration the woman he'd inherited…who wanted another man. He was tormented by the idea that the brute might hurt Sarah because he feared his meal ticket was slipping away. Then, when rational, he reasoned that she had made her bed so she must lie on it…with him…for she had said she would always love Tim…

His startling succession to the viscountcy had been gazetted a week or so ago. Since then he had been exceedingly popular with ambitious parents who had débutante daughters. A deluge of invitations to balls and soirées arrived at Lansdowne Crescent daily. The *grandes dames* of polite society cajoled him mercilessly to attend their insipid dances at Almack's. Why they imagined he might do so when he had studiously avoided entering the place for over a decade escaped his comprehension. He had no desire for a wife.

But if Sarah was not a schemer…if she did not love another man…if she had not played him for a fool… if…if… Mentally he shook himself to remove from his mind the haunting image of a fair goddess with an enchanting shy smile and a bewitching figure.

Since he had quit Willowdene he had fought a hopeless battle to erase her from his mind. No amount of carousing could banish the memory of her soft sweet body merging with his. So he had succumbed to the need to contact her. She would ignore his summons to join him in town, he knew that, so eventually he'd return to Willowdene and claim her company, as was his right.

Gavin had been gazing sightlessly out of the window

whilst brooding. A sudden boom of thunder focused his eyes on the street scene. The storm was unexpected; barely a few minutes ago a hazy sun had been warming his profile.

'My goodness!' Mr Styles proclaimed, frowning as jagged lightning momentarily scarred the sky. 'Look how dark it has got.' He pulled his spectacles off his nose to peer at the startling tempest beyond the window.

Gavin got up, glad of an excuse to stretch his legs. He had been ensconced within the armchair for almost an hour. He strolled to the window and watched relentless rain slant down to bounce off the pavements. The people who had been thronging the street were darting hither and thither to find shelter in doorways or under shop awnings. About to turn away, he became quite still and his eyes whipped back to a lone figure huddled in the tiny aperture that led into the barber's shop.

The woman's head was down and she was huddling into her cloak, pulling the hood about her face. But wisps of blonde hair were visible and there was something so achingly familiar about the way she tried to tuck them back behind an ear. And then she looked up. Before she ducked down again, her beautiful face was momentarily visible as she frowned at the elements. An exhalation of pent-up breath whistled though Gavin's set teeth.

'My goodness,' Mr Styles exclaimed from Gavin's shoulder, for he had joined him at the window to better observe the spectacular storm. 'That looks just like…but it couldn't be…quite a beauty, too…just like that poor mite…'

Gavin was not listening to the lawyer's disjointed mutterings. With a curt excuse flying in his wake, he was already striding swiftly from the room. He dashed along the corridor of the offices of Venner and Styles. In a trice he had yanked open the front door and sprinted down the stone steps to stare in frustrated disbelief at the empty doorway opposite. His head swung savagely from side to side as he scoured the street for a sight of her. But everyone was again on the move. The torrential rain had stopped as abruptly as it had started. Just a misty drizzle remained and a tepid sun, low on the horizon, was slanting glittering gold on to the pavements.

With a flick of his hand he summoned his carriage. Having barked instruction to the driver to slowly patrol the street, he was soon inside and studying every cloaked female pedestrian he saw with fanatical interest. Once or twice he jumped out whilst the carriage was still moving, making Todd, his driver, pull up in alarm and set the thoroughbreds skittering. Not every lady he accosted was annoyed by his attention. Quite a few female heads turned to disappointedly watch the handsome gentleman as he stepped away with a muttered apology.

Sarah settled back into the squabs in the hackney, thanking her lucky stars that she had been first to hail it. Had she not bolted from her shelter whilst it was still raining hard, she might have lost her ride to someone else. She imagined that now the storm had passed, every hackney in town would be busily taking home people who had been drenched through by the sudden downpour. With a sigh she pushed back the sodden hood of her cloak and patted at her damp hair. When she had quit Mrs Draper's lodging house she had been pleased with her neat appearance. She had donned her smartest day dress and her new cloak. Now she must look a bedraggled wretch. But she would not go back to change. It was too late to again set out today, and tomorrow she might not find the courage to travel to Lansdowne Crescent and demand an audience with the father of her unborn child. Tomorrow she wanted to be travelling home to her brother and aunt with her mind somewhat eased that Gavin would do his duty by her and her baby.

Briskly she opened her reticule, withdrew a handkerchief and began mopping the moisture from her person. Satisfied that she had done all she could to improve her appearance, she looked out on to glistening pavements as the cab bore her ever closer to Mayfair.

Another lady was surveying the wet conditions from the sanctuary of a carriage. Christine Beauvoir peered up at the clouds with an indelicate curse beneath her breath. She slanted a glance at her maid. The girl looked back at her with an expression of mute inso-lence. Fanny thought she was quite mad. She could not really blame her. But now it was getting a little brighter she would again get out of the carriage and take a promenade. Sooner or later he must return home and in a way the storm might have proved to be a help rather than a hindrance—the best place to be in such atrocious weather was indoors.

With a snapped instruction to Fanny to carry the umbrella, Christine allowed the footman to help her alight. Having taken care to straighten her attire, she was soon beginning another slow promenade along Lansdowne Crescent with Fanny's damp little figure sullenly trailing in her wake.

Christine was only a few yards away from her carriage when her spirits soared and a satisfied smile twitched her lips. The gentleman she had spied was not the one she had hoped to see, but was certainly a pleasing alternative. The tall blond figure of Sir Clayton Powell was instantly recognisable and he was striding straight towards her.

'Why, sir, what a surprise to see you here,' she breathily greeted him and stepped in to his path so he must stop.

'Mrs Beauvoir,' Clayton exclaimed. He halted at once to avoid bumping into her and politely accepted her limp hand. 'I had no idea you were in town. Are you visiting friends?'

'Oh…my sister lives quite close by in Fontaine Street.' It was the truth. Christine simply omitted to add she had not seen or spoken to Denise since she had been caught *in flagrante delicto* with Denise's husband. Christine had thought her sister had overreacted to something quite trivial, she'd had no serious designs on her dull brother-in-law but, having been newly widowed and missing a man's company, a little dalliance had been too tempting to resist.

'Do you reside hereabouts?' Christine looked at him coyly.

'Quite close by,' Clayton supplied. 'My friend lives in this Crescent.'

'Mr Stone, you mean?' Christine asked, all wide-eyed innocence. She clucked her tongue in self-scolding. 'Of course, I should say Viscount Tremayne, for I know that he has had mixed fortunes since he left Willowdene. How sad he lost his uncle…and the late Viscount was about to be wed, I believe.'

'Indeed…how sad…' Clayton mimicked whilst attempting to keep a cynical curve from his top lip. 'I am just on my way to pay Gavin a visit and hope I find him at home. If you will excuse me, ma'am, I must bid you good day.'

Christine sought to delay him, but suddenly a glimpse of someone in the distance made her halt mid-sentence and stare in slack-jawed amazement. Soon her demeanour had hardened into repressed fury. Hoping to conceal from Sir Clayton her violent emotion, Christine quickly took her leave of him. She swept on purposefully, with Fanny skipping to keep up with her.

If the little hussy had come to town with the ambition of snaring Gavin, she would do all in her power to thwart her impudence. Christine had ambitions of her own and she was not about to be bested by a sly minx with nothing but a pretty face and light skirts to recommend her.

She had heard on the grapevine that Elizabeth Warren had been pensioned off by Gavin and was looking for a new protector. Christine wanted to fill the place Elizabeth had left in Gavin's bed. And she was not about to share Viscount Tremayne with a little provincial miss who had been fortunate enough to entertain him whilst he was out in the sticks.

She knew how the little harlot had earned the right to stay at Elm Lodge. It had been no hardship for Christine to do without Edward's tedious company on occasion and let the Marchant girl have him. But Edward's handsome younger brother was another matter entirely. He was a viscount and rich as Croesus. Even without those wonderfully tempting lures she would have wanted him. He was the most dangerously charismatic man she had ever met.

'What brings you to town, Miss Marchant?'

Sarah spun about on hearing her name spoken, and with such sneering emphasis. Her golden eyes became round with surprise, as did her full pink mouth. She was as astounded to see Christine Beauvoir so far from Willowdene as she was to receive her direct attention. The woman had never before deigned to acknowledge that she existed. Quickly she collected her thoughts and slipped some coins in the palm of the hackney driver who was patiently waiting for his fare. A solid weight of disappointment was crushing her courage. She had no wish for Mrs Beauvoir to know any of her business. Instinctively she knew they each understood the other's motives for travelling to precisely the same spot in London. They were both in Lansdowne Crescent hoping to see Gavin.

'I might ask you the same question, Mrs Beauvoir,' Sarah replied with admirable aplomb. 'Why are you so far from home?'

'I have family in the area,' Christine snapped, narrowing her dark eyes on Sarah. She resented the girl's unexpected self-possession. '*I* can class this as home. And you?'

Sarah's hesitation in answering prompted a sly smirk to twitch Christine's mouth. 'If I were to hazard a guess,' she said with silky satisfaction, 'I would say you are here hoping to accost Viscount Tremayne and remind him of the services you recently provided for him.'

'I have no idea what or who you are talking about,' Sarah returned icily and tried to pass Christine.

'Don't try to fool me, you little trollop,' Christine hissed beneath her breath, bumping a buxom hip against

Sarah to foil her escape. 'You have brazenly followed Mr Stone, hoping to hook him now he's a viscount with a fortune. And if you think he won't realise straight away what a vulgar harlot you are to pester him so outrageously…'

Sarah halted then in her attempt to dodge past Christine. Her vivid tawny eyes scoured features veiled by artful maquillage. But instinctively she knew she was telling the truth. The shock of knowing Gavin's prospects had leaped dramatically numbed Sarah's mind and her sole reaction was to frown at the elegant crescent of townhouses. 'Does he still reside here?' A practical worry had tripped awkwardly off her tongue. If he had moved away, she had squandered the cost of this journey.

On hearing the quiver of desperation in Sarah's voice Christine gave a gratified chuckle. She tilted her chin so she might better peer down her nose at her rival. 'I have no idea,' she glibly lied. She knew Gavin was in residence as his friend was even now paying him a visit. 'What I *do* know is that he now has a magnificent estate in Surrey and a vast amount of female attention.' She glanced at Sarah from beneath her sooty lashes. 'I shall give you a piece of advice, Miss Marchant, and you would do well to heed it. Mr Stone is most sought after by well-bred young ladies. It is rumoured he is soon to make a most advantageous match…' Christine guessed rather than knew this to be true.

'In that case, perhaps you would do well to heed your own advice, Mrs Beauvoir.' With a little push to move the woman aside, Sarah briskly walked on. She swiftly gained the end of the Crescent and, with her mind in turmoil, turned the corner and kept going with little thought as to where she was heading.

Sir Clayton pulled out his pocket watch, gave it a cursory glance, then cursed. He had been shown to Gavin's study to await his homecoming. Having twice paced the length of the oak-panelled room, he was growing impatient and on the brink of leaving to seek Gavin elsewhere.

Whilst in his club this afternoon, Clayton had heard news of which he was certain Gavin would want to be apprised. A woman was intent on receiving an immediate marriage proposal from Viscount Tremayne. In fact, so serious was the lady that, rumour had it, she and her brother were due to pay an impromptu visit on Gavin to thrash out the matter this very afternoon.

Clayton's thoughts returned to the silly spectacle Christine Beauvoir had made wandering about the Crescent whilst awaiting an opportunity to waylay Gavin. He knew she had no such lofty ambition as marriage on her mind. She would happily settle for a stint as Gavin's mistress. He also knew that she was wasting her time pursuing his friend. Elizabeth Warren had learned, to her cost, that Gavin was irritated rather than flattered by being stalked and spied on. But there was another woman who was deluded enough to believe she had every right to become Gavin's wife.

Jack Stone, the late viscount, had announced his engagement to Stella West just a month before his untimely death. His betrothed had been his mistress too and was, Clayton supposed, entitled to feel miffed at the cruel hand fate had dealt her. After pleasuring a man old enough to be her father and being clever enough to secure an official proposal, she had been but months away from having Jack make an honest woman of her...and a viscountess to boot. According to the tattle in White's, Stella and her brother were of the opinion that it was Gavin's duty to step in to his dead uncle's shoes and honour the marriage contract so the wedding could go ahead as planned.

Ordinarily Clayton would not have felt so disturbed by it all; Gavin had always been perfectly able to take care of his own affairs, and with ruthless efficiency when necessary. But since their return from the country Gavin had been different. He seemed unimpressed by his excellent good fortune and, because he was constantly preoccupied, neglected to deal with simple things. Although they still socialised much as they always had, Gavin's heart was no longer in having a rollicking good time. It was in Elm Lodge, and Clayton knew that sooner or later Gavin would conquer whatever pride and problems kept him from Sarah Marchant and return to Willowdene to propose to her. And that brought Clayton again to musing that it would be as well if Gavin were informed that gossip was circulating about him soon plighting his troth elsewhere.

Before the carriage was completely still, Gavin jumped to the pavement. His dark expression was not lightened on seeing Christine Beauvoir speeding along the pavement towards him. It wasn't the first time he had glimpsed her loitering in the vicinity of his house. With a curt greeting Gavin strode past her without slowing his pace, or touching her coyly extended fingers.

Open-mouthed, Christine watched his broad back as he took the steps to his mansion two at a time. A muffled giggle from behind prompted her to swing about and glare at Fanny. 'To the carriage,' Christine snapped. 'It is coming on to rain again.' She pivoted about and marched towards the coach, her face blazing with humiliation.

Christine settled back into the cushions, still smarting from the snub. In fact, he had not so much given her a set-down as ignored her, and that was worse. She cast a look at Fanny huddled in to the corner. She might look sorry now, but she was determined to make the snivelling wretch pay for her insubordination.

About to tell the driver to take her to her rented apartment in Marylebone, she bit back the instruction. She peered through the window as a fancy landau passed smoothly by, braving the weather with its hood down. Obviously the elegant couple within were more interested in being seen than keeping dry. Christine watched avidly as it drew up outside Gavin's residence. Within a short time a beautiful young woman and her gentleman companion had, with some parade, climbed the steps and gained entrance to Gavin's townhouse.

A malicious smile hovered over Christine's lips. She had heard a rumour that the old viscount's be-trothed was not giving up without a fight and had enlisted the aid of her brother in trying to cling to her engagement. She imagined it was not that difficult to guess the identity of the unsmiling people who had passed over Viscount Tremayne's threshold. She settled back with a vindictive smile, feeling better, then ordered the driver to take her home.

Chapter Eighteen

By the time his would-be wife and her brother were announced, Gavin had been sufficiently briefed by Clayton to know the nature of the impertinence that had brought them to his door.

He had been informed, weeks ago, by Mr Styles that his uncle had been about to marry for the first time in his life. He had learned from the same source that unfortunately the late viscount had made no provision for his prospective bride in the event of his untimely death. He was also aware that the deprived young lady was hopping mad at the turn of events. That she would expect her lover's successor to take her on, in the same capacity, he had not known, nor in his wildest dream anticipated. The sooner Miss West was made aware that she could count on nothing from him other than his condolences, and an *ex gratia* payment to hasten her on her way, the sooner he could again concentrate on finding Sarah. But for now he supposed this infernal matter must take precedence over all others.

Despite that sensible conclusion, Gavin's mind again deduced that his search of the environs of Cheapside had been thorough, thus Sarah must have been spirited away in a carriage. In turn, that led him to consider that she might have had a companion. Perhaps her lover, Tim, had been with her. Had they come to London to hound him for more money? Then he reasoned that the woman he had spotted in the barber's doorway had seemed to be very much alone. Had it been a case of mistaken identity? What actually had he viewed through a window blurred with rain? It had been just a momentary glimpse of a slender female with blonde hair huddling into her cloak. But instinctively he had known her. It had been real enough to make him hare dementedly into the street to try to catch her.

As the brother and sister were announced by his butler and shown into his study, Gavin strode to stand by the window, his mind still defiantly cluttered with thoughts of Sarah. It *had* been her. He was certain of it. It was not simply how she looked; little mannerisms and a familiar graceful bearing had contributed to convince him.

He forced himself to face the couple. They were dressed in stylish finery…courtesy of the late Jack Stone, Gavin shrewdly supposed. The brother looked to be about twenty-three and younger than his sister by a few years. The woman was a redhead and good-looking. Momentarily their eyes held and Gavin knew she was a practised flirt. She was pleased she had got his attention and wanted to reward him for it. The flimsy shawl that covered her arms was allowed to slip revealing a decolletage that was smooth and white and framed by a gown of green to match her slanting eyes. Not so long ago he would have taken up her invitation. He knew well enough that she would settle for a less formal arrangement than marriage. Her brother was simply starting the bidding high. His indifferent eyes slipped over her exposed flawless flesh and again Gavin ached for a less perfect body. He fought to keep his yearning for Sarah from distracting him from the business in hand.

'We must beg leave to apologise for this unsolicited visit, my lord, and hope it will not too much inconvenience you,' the fellow began. He hesitated, perhaps hoping for some demurral.

Gavin raised dark brows at him, his expression a study of impatience.

David West flushed at the blunt inference that my lord was feeling very inconvenienced indeed. 'We beg leave to speak to you privately.' He indicated Sir Clayton with a flash of dark eyes.

'There is nothing you can possibly have to say to me that is too private for my friend to also hear.' With a gesture of exasperation Gavin decided he could not be bothered to beat about the bush. He was wasting valuable time that could be better spent elsewhere, discovering Sarah's whereabouts and what brought her to town. He doubted it was to see him! He had told her where he lived. If she wanted him, she would have by now arrived or sent him a message.

Abruptly he launched into, 'I believe this unexpected visit is prompted by a sense of grievance you have regarding the prospective marriage contract between my late uncle and Miss West.' Gavin gave the young woman a glance and she tilted up her chin, elongating an alluring column of throat. He rewarded her with an impassive stare. 'My condolences, ma'am, that it came to nought.'

Stella West's almond-shaped eyes widened and in alarm she darted a feline glance at her brother for guidance.

'We believe, my lord, that it should not come to nought,' David West firmly began his appeal.

Gavin raised a silencing hand; with a bored expression he strolled closer to the couple. 'In recognition of your attachment to my late uncle, and your eagerness to still attain the marital state, I am prepared to put by some funds...' He broke off to grunt a laugh as he noticed an excited look pass between them. They really were quite engagingly blatant in their greed. He coughed, languidly moving a hand to excuse his lapse. 'The fund will be paid as a dowry on the marriage of Miss West.'

Again the siblings exchanged a meaningful look.

Giving up any pretence at moral injury, the fellow demanded baldly, 'How much?'

'Enough to make your sister an attractive prospect to a peer with pockets to let,' Gavin drawled. 'The sooner you set to and find her a title going begging, the sooner my lawyers will be able to deal with the matter.' Gavin executed a very slight bow, indicating that he had nothing more to add and their time was up.

Sir Clayton, who was quite cheered to find his friend was still perfectly in possession of his faculties, despite being madly in love, made it his business to curb his amusement and usher the couple to the door.

'Oh…and know also,' Gavin said just as they were about to exit the room, 'a legal document will accompany the transfer of the fund. Should you at any time approach me again on this matter, it will furnish me with the right not only to reclaim every penny, but to sue punitively.'

Stella West glared at him and flounced from the room; her brother hesitated and said in defeat, 'The old viscount was your kin. It's you should marry the poor mite.'

Gavin's lips curved sardonically, but the smile rapidly faded. He recalled having heard a similar phrase quite recently and, because it seemed to have great significance, he knew it must have a connection to Sarah.

Having spent the past hour or so reasoning that it would be the height of foolishness…as well as extremely craven…to return to Willowdene without speaking to Gavin, Sarah was now desperately attempting to pluck up the courage to do what she had set out to do. As she made her way back along Lansdowne Crescent, there was not a rain cloud in the sky. But the shadows were lengthening and she knew she must act swiftly if she were to get back to her lodgings before dusk. She spied a young maid, clutching a package, hurrying towards the servants' entrance of a house she was passing. Having beckoned her, and asked a question, the girl obligingly pointed and told her that Mr Stone lived behind the green railings. Sarah gave her a small smile and bravely set off again, her mind churning with the possible consequences of her audacity and how she might cope with them. At worst, she supposed, she might be summarily ejected from the house and told never again to darken his doorstep.

Even as she slowed her pace to stare at the huge door, it opened and a lady and gentleman came out. Sarah shrank back against some shrubbery as a stunningly attractive woman with vivid sherry-coloured hair descended the steps with her companion. Sarah watched, mesmerised by the sight of her nude white shoulders. The emerald-coloured gown the woman was wearing was a magnificent foil for her pure pale skin. As though suddenly chilled, the young woman covered her bare arms with her shawl. Within a moment the couple were in the landau and it was moving away… and so was Sarah.

Having hastily turned the corner, she this time halted to scour the street for a cab to take her back to her lodgings. Thoughts of babies and family duty and security—all those sensible reasons that had prompted her to swallow her pride and come to London were now pushed aside. Gavin had moments ago been in the company of a lady who was proud to display to the world her unblemished beauty in a low-cut gown. Inwardly Sarah railed at herself for allowing a silly insecurity about her disfigurement to rob her of the temerity to see through her plan. Of course he socialised with such attractive women. She had always known he enjoyed a host of female companions. What on earth was the matter with her? He was at home, and his visitors had left. It was an excellent opportunity to rush back and do and say what she must. Yet stupid vanity held her rooted to the spot, unable to conquer a mocking image of perfect luminous skin that had burned indelibly into her mind. As a cab approached the jarvey looked at her expectantly. Choking back tears of angry frustration, she nodded at him.

Mr Styles was in the process of locking his office door when his esteemed client strode in from the street.

Having waited, twiddling his thumbs for over an hour and a half, for Viscount Tremayne to return so they might continue with their meeting, Peter Styles had eventually concluded that his commerce was finished for the day. He had thus tidied away his papers and decided he was very much ready for his dinner. Beneath his breath he sighed as the saturnine fellow came purposefully closer.

'Ah…I wondered if you would return, my lord…'

'You said something earlier and I would like you to explain what you meant by it,' Gavin stated without preamble.

Mr Styles unlocked his door and again went within. He had no desire to repeat the intricacies of various stockholdings and bonds whilst his stomach grumbled and the viscount gazed moodily off into space. He took a peer over his spectacles. The fellow was an odd cove indeed! Earlier he had sat looking little interested in knowing he'd inherited a catalogue of possessions that would have made a prince's eyes pop.

Peter Styles took up position behind his desk and adopted an official air. When the viscount strode straight to the window, Peter half-rose from his chair. With his posterior hovering over the seat, he enquired wearily, 'How can I help, my lord?'

'Earlier today there was a woman in the doorway opposite, sheltering from the storm. I thought I recognised her. I have recalled you saying something that has made me believe you might know her too.' Gavin turned from the glass to send an enquiring look at the lawyer.

Having conquered his shock at such an unexpected enquiry, Peter swivelled his eyes about in concentration for a moment, trying to bring to mind the incident.

Eventually he brought together his jaw, raised a finger and wagged it. 'Ah…yes. That's it.' He straightened up and flexed his knees. 'But I don't think it was her; the light was bad…and of course she would by now be a woman, not the child I remember.'

'Who was it?' Gavin hoarsely demanded to know.

'I thought it to be Miss Poole.'

Gavin's features hardened in disappointment.

'Not Miss Sarah Marchant…'

'Why…no… But oddly, Marchant was the mother's maiden name and I believed the child to be called Susan…or it might have been Sarah, now I think on it.' He frowned, looking intrigued. 'Valerie Marchant was married to Eric Poole.' He heard the Viscount's sharp intake of breath and guessed he recalled the family, and the awful scandal that had destroyed it. 'I expect Valerie rued her choice of husband to her dying breath. Her family most certainly did. They soon had cast her off for marrying such an obnoxious fellow. But by all accounts Valerie stayed loyal to Eric despite the despicable way he heaped humiliation on her head.'

'I remember he was an indiscreet adulterer, amongst other things.' The harsh statement tore from Gavin's throat as his mind sped back through the years and he saw again the debauched visage of the wretched felon who had sired Sarah. And he knew instinctively that she was a product of that sorry union.

I have my codes, she had said to him when fretting he might have a wife or a mistress who loved him and who might be hurt by his attachment to her. Sarah had been reared watching her mother's distress and humiliation as her father flaunted his squalid affairs. And he had cynically doubted she was a courtesan with a conscience.

Peter nodded grimly. 'An indiscreet adulterer, indeed!' he echoed. 'It was rumoured Eric propelled his wife into a decline, and an early death, with his constant whoremongering. A sweet-natured woman she was, and a great beauty. Sarah was her likeness. And then, of course, there was that *dreadful* business. In a way it was fortunate Valerie had died before she could witness his shameful thievery.' Peter shook his head and lowered his eyes. 'No doubt you recall it,' he whispered. 'The worst fraud. The very worst I have known.'

An agonized expression tautened Gavin's features to a white mask. Snippets of the outrageous scandal to which Mr Styles was referring were slowly being retrieved from his memory. He spoke them aloud as they came to him. 'He embezzled money, then committed suicide. A host of people were out for his blood. My brother was one of them.'

Peter nodded vigorously. 'The devil was a coward to the end. Eric took the easy way out after stealing a fortune from a commercial syndicate. He could never have hoped to repay the other investors, the amount was so great. Many families never recovered from the swindle. Nothing was clawed back. He had squandered the lot. Charles Beddowes took his family to the

Americas to start a new life. The Forsythes went the same way. There were similar stories of terrible hardship.' Peter glanced at Gavin, noticing his absolute stillness and the ravaged look on his face. Bluish grooves bracketed his mouth and his eyes were un-blinking, betraying him to be lost in savage introspection.

Sensing something of great import was at hand, Peter continued recounting what he knew. 'I used to deal with your brother Edward's affairs when he lived in town as well as your uncle's. Edward's losses were not devastating, yet I recall he was quite bitter and vengeful. But how do you exact retribution from a dead man?'

'You don't,' Gavin said in a raw mutter. 'You make his daughter pay instead.' He pushed a shaking hand roughly over his face as the awful truth of his own brother's wickedness penetrated his mind.

'Oh, no, the poor little mite could not have made amends even if she'd wanted to. There were no assets to have. Their home was mortgaged to the hilt. Besides, the day her father killed himself, Maybury House was rendered to ashes.' Mr Styles was startled in to silence as the viscount suddenly threw back his head to howl an oath at the ceiling. It was indeed a tragic story, but its ghastliness had been diminished by the passing of time, so most people thought.

The disaster obviously held for the new viscount a dramatic significance of which he was ignorant. The fellow looked to be in the throes of a very great torment.

Gavin's eyes slowly closed. 'Did he set the fire deliberately?'

Peter muttered a vehement denial. 'He shot himself while his children were abed. Nobody truly believed him evil enough to start the blaze, but the candle on his desk went down as he did…'

Swiftly Peter concluded what he knew of the catastrophe. 'Had Eric Poole's widowed sister, Beatrice, not been in residence at Maybury House, the children would have perished for sure. She roused them from their beds and helped them escape. But both were injured in the fire and Beatrice's hands were badly burned too.'

Gavin slowly raised his face and looked at the lawyer with eyes that were ablaze with anguish. 'The boy survived?'

'I believe he did. And when they were recovered well enough to travel, they fled from town and the creditors baying for blood. Whether the boy still lives, I do not know. Timothy was far more badly injured than was his sister.'

With his story at an end, and the viscount now apparently lost for words, the lawyer set about locking and bolting the office. Having executed a low bow and a polite farewell, he set off home. Only once did Mr Styles turn his head to peer over his shoulder. He observed his eminent client still to be in the exact spot where he had taken his leave of him, hunched against the wall with his head down and his hands plunged into his pockets. He looked like a fellow who had the cares of the world upon his shoulders rather than an astonishing fortune under his belt. Peter shook his head sadly, then went determinedly in search of his dinner.

Gavin jerked up his face, revealing tortured features. The back of his head hit brick once, twice, three times as though he mercilessly punished himself. In his mind whirled the same anguished phrase. What *had* he done?

How could he have cruelly abandoned the woman he loved, a woman who he had just learned had suffered unspeakable pain in her short life, because he was jealous of her brother? Heat filled his eyes and immediately a finger and thumb pressed between them to stem the prickling salt. He'd readily assumed the love Sarah had declared for Tim would be carnal rather than platonic. But then what else would spring to the mind of a cynical rake? The wounding sense of shame that pervaded his being shook him to the core.

He'd known before the lawyer recounted to him any of her harrowing history that he loved and desired Sarah in equal measure. Now the instinct to protect her dominated his emotions. Never again must she be left to the mercy of cruel fate or devious men. He must find her urgently and beg her to marry him.

At one time he had been sure she was softening towards him. They had shared tender as well as passionate times together. If she hated him now and rejected his love—and he could not blame her for it—he must convince her of the sense in sheltering beneath his name.

The thought of being her husband, but not her lover, was a bitter pill to swallow, but he knew he deserved to suffer.

A raw mirthless laugh clogged his throat. Suffer! What did he know of suffering? He had thought his own childhood bleak, yet it was nothing in comparison to the wretched existence Sarah had endured in her tender years. He'd taken beatings and abuse from his father and, by the time he reached sixteen, had been strong enough to return them. At sixteen his life had started to improve. When Sarah reached sixteen, she met Edward and her life altered. In her innocence she believed her lot in life had been improved by becoming Edward's mistress. Gavin knew it had not. Nor had Edward intended it should.

But he would not dwell on Edward now. There were far more important things to do than brood on his brother's iniquitous malice.

Gavin massaged the stubble on his face whilst drawing a calming breath deep into his lungs. He had learned some dreadful debilitating news this afternoon. Pondering on it further would serve no purpose. Action was needed. In his mind he regimented his thoughts. He had no proper proof that Sarah was in London. Prowling around the darkening streets of Cheapside in the hope of finding her lodging somewhere was likely to result in nothing but a waste of valuable time. He would be better served travelling immediately to Willowdene and seeking her there. If he discovered from the Jacksons that she *had* journeyed to London, they might also supply her direction in the City. It was frustrating knowing he might journey through the night simply to turn about and return to town. But one thing he was sure of: he would not rest until he'd done his utmost to put things right for Sarah.

Chapter Nineteen

'Nag's pulled up lame, miss. Gotta turn about and get to the farrier sharpish or it'll be the knacker's yard fer 'im.'

Sarah started from her solemn reverie to comprehend that she was being ejected from the cab. The jarvey opened the door and gave her an apologetic look.

'Yer in Cheapside and yer lodging be just a short walk along there.' He pointed off up the road. 'Won't take yer no more'n a few minutes if'n yer get going brisk like.'

It seemed the whole day was to be a disappointment in one way or another. Sarah slipped, with a sigh, from the vehicle and held out some coins.

'Nah.' He declined payment and gave her a grin. 'G'wan. Off yer go 'fore it gets proper dark. Soon be home if'n yer scoot.'

With a slight smile of appreciation, Sarah slipped the

coins back in her reticule and took his advice. Pulling her cloak tight about her, she set off at a brisk pace towards Gracechurch Street.

Melancholy thoughts kept her eyes downcast, but Sarah was alert to her surroundings and the few people she passed. She might have troubles that kept her pre-occupied, but she was conscious of the need to be vigilant when abroad in the evening. She was certainly not in the best part of town. She raised her head to take a circumspect look about at the same moment that he glanced her way.

It was a moment before Sarah's brisk pace faltered and her face twisted fully towards him, just as a second had elapsed before Gavin realised his yearning was not mocking him with an apparition.

Sarah felt her heart vault to her throat as vague instinct turned to full recognition. It *was* him. And he had seen her. She skittered back against brick, startled by the speed with which he suddenly launched himself across the road towards her.

Sarah gazed up into his face, wondering at once what was wrong, for his dear handsome face was gaunt and lined as though he endured some agonising pain. She allowed him to trap her back against the wall and closed her eyes in mute bliss as his gritty palms rose to tremble against her cheeks. Then she was in his arms, held so tightly that she felt she might gladly suffocate. The memory of his callous abandonment, and of the daunting revelation she'd yet to make, was subdued by her joy at being with him. She clung to him, revelling in his solid strength and the scent of sandalwood and cigars that clung to his clothes.

'What are you doing here?' The words were breathed hoarsely against her hair.

'I might ask you the same thing.' Sarah's voice was light, muffled by his coat. 'This is not Mayfair.'

'I've been with my lawyer.' Gavin flicked his dark head to indicate the office he had recently vacated. 'Styles had vital news for me...'

Sarah moved back a little and tipped up her face to look into his blazing dark eyes. His long child's lashes looked clumped together as though he had got wet or been crying. 'I'm sorry you have suffered another bereavement,' she said solemnly, seeking to comfort him. 'I had heard your uncle had died and you had succeeded him.'

'I learned that news some time ago from Styles,' he said with a hollow bark of a laugh. 'Did you come to London to find me?'

'Yes...' Sarah honestly admitted, then blushed in awkwardness. 'Oh...I did not know of your better prospects when I left Willowdene. I'm not here to ask for more from you now you are a viscount... Well...that is not strictly true,' she added miserably, aware she was making a mess of it all.

This was not how it was meant to be. She had been sure she would tell him of their child in a calm and dignified manner. But she had not anticipated such an un-

expected meeting between them. All her reasonable, re-
hearsed conversation had fled her mind. She cleared her
throat. 'I'm sorry, but there is no easy way to tell you
what I must. I too have some vital news for you,' she
began shakily.

A natural consequence of their passion had not
occurred to Gavin before, and yet it should have.
Usually he was adept at not leaving his seed where it
might grow. But with Sarah it had been different…ev-
erything with Sarah was different. Slow fingers cradled
her face, smoothing tenderly against her flushed skin
whilst turning her to shyly look at him. How would he
ever beg forgiveness for abandoning her so cruelly?
He'd made it necessary for her to courageously leave
everything she held dear to follow him. She had conquered her pride, and her fear and hatred of a place that
held such harrowing memories. She'd had to come to
London to find him to ask him to support their child
because stupid groundless jealousy had prompted him
to turn his back on the woman he loved.

He watched her golden eyes flit to his face, then dart
away as she sought some delicate yet assertive way to
demand he help her. And he couldn't bear to be the
cause of any more hurt to this beautiful brave woman.
His heart…his whole being…felt swollen with admiration and love for her and he silently vowed he would
kill any man who again wronged her with so much as
a look.

'A baby?' he pre-empted gently. 'Are you pleased?'

Gratitude and relief rippled through Sarah as he saved her the embarrassment of telling him she was increasing. Instinctively a hand slipped to curve on her belly. Her eyes whipped to merge with his. 'No…of course not,' she murmured.

Gavin moved a hand to cover the slender fingers that had immediately sprung to protect their child. When he simply kept staring at her with soulful penetrating eyes she dropped down her head and nodded. 'I thought I would not be,' she whispered. 'I *should* not be…' Defiantly she looked up at him with tear-glossed eyes as she recalled what she had come here to do for the tiny life flourishing within. 'You must ensure that, if a boy, he is well educated and able to make his way in the world. And if a girl…'

Gavin swiftly pressed his mouth to hers to silence her. 'And if a girl…' he said softly against her lips '…she will look like you…act like you, too, I expect and twist me about her finger till her papa gives her all her adorable heart desires.'

With a gasp Sarah grabbed at his lapels whilst gazing deep into his eyes. 'You are not angry? You want our baby?'

'I want our baby, and God knows I want you…'

Spontaneously Sarah flung her arms tight about his neck. 'I want you, too,' she burst out. 'I've missed you so much and still want to be your mistress. Truly I do. I know you think I have been cold towards you at times. But I deliberately held my feelings in check. I couldn't bear to grow fond of you, then pine for you when you went away, perhaps never to return.'

'Hush…' Gavin soothed. 'I swear I'll never leave you. And I hope so very much you might grow fond of me, yet I fear you have every right to despise me.'

Sarah fiercely shook her head. 'I do not…I never have. Even when we first met I held you in respect, despite what Edward had said about your character. Since then I have known him to be wrong to make you out an irredeemable rogue, for you have proved to be fair and generous and kind.'

'Hush…' Gavin said again and looked away, a diffident expression lending his rugged features a boyish air. 'I might not be an irredeemable rogue, but neither am I a perfect gentleman. Can you ever forgive me for leaving you the way I did?'

'No,' she answered immediately with a catch to her voice. 'But I understand why you did and so it is best forgotten.'

Gavin grimaced his disappointment as he gently moved a stray tress that was caught on her curly downcast lashes. 'Tell me why you believe I left you.'

A stab of jealousy tightened her insides and Sarah fought to control it. She did not want to spoil this blissful reunion and, besides, Elizabeth Warren had more claim on this man than did she. Gavin might have been Elizabeth's lover for years, not months. 'I know your mistress came to Willowdene looking for you.' Small teeth nipped at her lower lip as she dwelled on how Mrs

Warren must have craved his return. That brought to mind those sad times when, believing herself to be unobserved and her children safely tucked up in bed, her mother would silently weep whilst her father was out fornicating. 'She must have missed you dreadfully to have made the journey to fetch you,' she quietly concluded.

'She did not,' he tenderly reassured. 'Leastways, not in the way you mean, Sarah. No proper love or commitment existed between us. Elizabeth is not at all humiliated by my ending our relationship, just a trifle petulant. She is financially secure and content to find a new gentleman friend. There is nothing for you to worry about. I swear you have done nothing to hurt her.'

Sarah's eyes searched his face and she frowned. 'If not to please your mistress, then why *did* you leave me?' she gasped. 'Why did you go away without even a word of farewell? ' she keened in anguish.

'Because I was jealous.'

Sarah's eyes whipped to his and her mouth parted in readiness for her to speak, but he had not yet finished.

Long fingers pressed to her soft lips, stopping her words. Humbly he continued to say what he must to prove his deep sorrow and regret. 'I went away because I overheard a conversation between you and Maude. I heard you say you loved Tim and, because I'm a stupid cynical fool, I thought he must be your lover. I let my pride overrule all else and never will I forgive myself for it.'

'In the letter you sent me you mentioned Tim,' she whispered. 'How long have you known about my family?'

'About…thirty minutes or so,' Gavin admitted wryly. 'That's not strictly true,' he added, newly grave. 'I've known for years about the scandal surrounding Eric Poole's death, but I did not know you were his daughter.' He gazed at her with eyes brimming with adoration. 'How could you have endured it all and still be so sweet…so beautiful? Why are you not embittered?'

Sarah averted her face and a solemn frown crumpled her brow. 'I have days when I feel that way…many days…but, then I think of how much worse it might have been and I feel blessed. I still have some family left to me. We have our lives and each other.'

'And you have me.' Gavin told her in a voice that resonated with the depth of his sincerity.

She snuggled into his arms, displaying rather than voicing her gratitude. 'I know you like your life in London, but will you stay in Willowdene with me?' Sarah asked huskily. 'At least for some of the time?'

'I'd go to the ends of the earth with you, Sarah.'

Sarah raised twinkling eyes to his. 'In that case I must demand you stay at Elm Lodge with me *all* the time.'

He chuckled and drew her close against him. 'Come…it is getting cold and late and there is still much for us to talk about.' With a brusque flick of long fingers Gavin summoned his driver. Immediately Todd set the elegant coach, stationed across the road, in motion.

'Where are we going?'

'I don't know,' Gavin answered truthfully. 'You choose…'

He helped her aboard and when they settled back into the squabs, opposite one another, his sigh was weary yet content. 'Where have you been staying? You shouldn't be out alone so late. Will you come home with me?' His questions streamed out urgently.

'You know I cannot!' Sarah answered the last with a scandalised smile.

He leaned forwards and took her hands between his, slowly bringing the small slender fingers to his mouth to salute them and drop his forehead to them as though in obeisance. 'Why are you not angry with me?' he asked hoarsely. 'I should not have snooped on your conversation. It is said only ill comes of doing so.'

'It is not all your fault it went so horribly wrong,' Sarah answered graciously, laying a hand on his glossy bent head. 'I recall that day and that conversation. Maude was upbraiding me for not being completely honest with you. She said no good would come of being deceitful. If I had told you sooner about my brother and my past, you would not have been jealous of Tim.' A regretful sigh escaped her. 'You may not be a perfect gentleman, but neither am I a perfect lady, despite your kind praise.' She lowered her eyes to admit, 'I was prideful too. I didn't want you to know of my scars or the shameful scandal in my past. I couldn't bear to see you look at me with disgust.'

With a groan Gavin hauled her across the coach and into the comfort of his arms. 'Never,' he uttered in a harshly vehement voice. 'Me? Disgusted by you? I'm not fit to touch the hem of your skirt and neither was that fiend of a brother of mine. I wish he were alive so I could kill the bastard.'

'Why?' Sarah asked, shocked by his savage outburst. She angled her face to look into his. As he tried to avoid her eyes, she whispered, 'Have you discovered something awful about him?'

Gavin repositioned himself on the seat, easing Sarah down to sit cosily against the squabs.

'I know you did not like him, and think he wronged me,' she began cautiously, 'but in his way he was good to me…'

Gavin barked a bitter laugh. 'Don't say that! You don't know…' He passed a shaking hand over features that were now tight and livid. 'Just promise me you won't say it again, Sarah,' he pleaded.

'You know something,' Sarah murmured with suspicion narrowing her eyes.

He swung his head away from her searching gaze. Destroying his blissful contentment was knowledge of the vengeful lechery perpetrated by his own brother. He recalled the time when Sarah had accused him of using her as though she were an opportunity he were entitled to take, whereas Edward had treated her better. It was his wretched hypocrite of a brother who had cruelly used her over several years because he thought he was entitled to do so. The spiteful miser had borne a grudge over his financial losses and made a sixteen-year old girl atone for her father's sins.

While Gavin had been loitering outside the lawyer's office, brooding on the shocking information Styles had imparted, it had suddenly become damningly clear why Edward would bequeath his innocent courtesan to a man he believed to be a ruthless libertine. Edward had attached strings to his inheritance in the full knowledge that being manipulated in such a way was likely to infuriate him. But Edward had not wanted him to like or respect Sarah. He had intended him to resent her and degrade her until her spirit was broken and she became a coarse jade because he was unwilling to show his true colours and do it himself.

Whilst alive, Edward had striven to maintain his reputation as a good, upstanding fellow. He would not have wanted any tales of vice to tarnish his image. But Sarah was no victim despite the injurious events in her early life. Edward would have known she would have reported his abuse because she was strong and principled and wonderful…so the fiend had deliberately devised a way to continue to persecute Sarah from the grave.

Gavin closed his eyes and subdued the awful truths he longed to air. Sarah had given Edward her virginity and her affection and her loyalty, and knowing he had betrayed her trust so completely would scar her mind. He could never hurt her, no matter how greatly he wanted to expose Edward's devilry.

He turned to look at her and tilted her a lop-sided smile. 'It's nothing,' he finally replied. 'I'm jealous of him, that's all.'

'I know you must be angry that you agreed to his terms when it was all in vain,' Sarah said.

'In vain?' he echoed.

'You need not have got entangled in Edward's scheme at all. Had you only known what fate had in store, you could have rejected his rules and his fortune. I know you now have a greater inheritance. I bumped into Mrs Beauvoir and she told me that you have a magnificent estate in Surrey and much female attention. She expects you to soon make a good match, and of course we must talk about that,' Sarah added very quietly.

'The woman's a mischief-maker.'

'But it is true?' Sarah's eyes clung soulfully to his. If he were to marry, she would be racked with guilt over causing hurt to his wife. Or perhaps she would be the one bearing the greatest pain.

'Yes, I'm wealthy and titled and popular. I need none of it. For Edward, unbeknown to him, gave me something far above riches. I pray he is grinding his teeth in his grave to know it,' he finished on a triumphant chuckle.

A gentle touch of his lips on hers distracted her from pursuing the matter, as did his next question. 'Why did you not marry to support your family? With your beauty there would have been plenty of gentlemen keen to pay court.'

Sarah blushed prettily at his compliment whilst choking a wry, mirthless chuckle. 'I was not launched into society to meet anyone suitable, and looks can be deceiving…as you know.' She cast him a quick glance from beneath low lashes. 'When I was sixteen, and I first met Edward, he knew of my past—I did not tell him. He had recognised Aunt Bea as my father's sister. He said he wanted to be our friend, and we had nobody else to turn to. We had fled to Willowdene because my aunt's sister-in-law lived there. She was older than Bea and unfortunately passed on within six months. But there was a small silver lining for we were able to take on her cottage. My aunt and Tim still live there.' She paused, raised her eyes to his. 'When Edward came into our lives it seemed like a godsend, for we were close to being forced on the parish. He and my aunt discussed trying to find me a husband as a way to make ends meet. But it was concluded that no suitable match was likely. Edward pointed out…quite sensibly, I suppose…that his protection was preferable to a union with a mean fellow who might refuse to support my kin. I have an ugly disfigurement and such dreadful family connections. What gentleman would want such a wife?'

'This one,' Gavin said hoarsely. 'I would.'

Chapter Twenty

'Please don't joke…' Sarah's open expression crumpled and she abruptly averted her face.

'It's no joke,' Gavin said in a voice that vibrated with emotion. 'I love you, Sarah. God knows I love you so much. I would have told you so a long while ago… probably on that day in Willowdene when I came to Elm Lodge to take you out. But my stupid pride and jealousy ruined everything. Since I've been back in town I've done little else but pine for you.' He gave a forlorn chuckle. 'You may ask Clayton what a disappointing carouser I've become. He says I'm no fun any more.'

Honesty flared in Gavin's steady gaze, was apparent in the rigid set of his features; still Sarah's astonishment at what she'd heard made her hesitate in answering him. Moments ago she had been overjoyed to think he still wanted her as his mistress. She had expected no more than his care and affection for her and their child. A gentleman of modest means would baulk at the idea of wedding a woman whose reputation and family connections were as bad as hers were. An exceedingly eligible peer of the realm certainly should shy away from any such absurd idea.

'Your name would be tainted by an association with mine,' Sarah warned him huskily. 'It is not just that I am unchaste and have lived a shocking life as a courtesan. Many people are sure to still bear grudges against the Pooles because of my father's fraud.'

'Do you think I care about gossip? I have already thought of all of that and dismissed it as irrelevant.' A slow hand reverently touched her face. 'Let them tattle. I know the truth about you and nothing would give me greater honour…greater happiness…than to have you as my wife. I'm asking you to marry me, Sarah, because I love you and want you and you're to be the mother of my firstborn. I know I've no right to expect you to care for me after what I've done…but say you'll marry me, for our baby's sake if no other.'

Sarah slowly raised her eyes to his face, her heart commencing an irregular tattoo as ripples of joy weaved through her veins. Still she hesitated, fearing the miracle might be snatched away. 'You would risk so much for me?'

'I would if it were necessary. But there is no great disaster afoot, sweetheart, I promise. Polite society is founded on hypocrisy. It worships at the altar of money and status and now I have both we will be welcomed everywhere. In a few months' time you'll be invited by society hostesses to attend their little salons. You could be a society hostess too…if that's what you want.'

Gavin saw her uncertainty, but something else too. Hope was glimmering at the back of her tawny eyes. She wanted to believe him, and she cared for him. 'Shall I prove it to you? Shall I prove how much I want you…how much I love you?' He dipped his head, smiling against her full pink lips, and when they readily parted he kissed her gently, teasingly.

With a sigh of surrender Sarah tilted up her face and snaked her arms about his neck, holding him as though she would never let him go.

Gavin felt little sobs jerk her and her tears were hot and damp against his neck.

'If you leave me again…'

He captured her lips with his, proving in his own way just how ardently he'd meant every word he'd said.

On catching her breath, and gazing into eyes warmed equally by love and desire, Sarah realised she had yet to declare her own adoration for this noble rogue who had, despite her worst fears and expectations, turned her life to rights, not upside down.

'I love you, Gavin. I do truly care for you,' she told him fiercely.

'I've waited a long while to hear you say my name.' It was a gruff complaint.

'I know you have, Gavin,' she said and laughed. It

started as a giggle, but soon became more hearty, and so infectious was her amusement that he joined in the cathartic laughter.

Finally, clinging together in the coach, face to face on the comfy seat, Gavin wiped a tear from his eye and then performed the same office for her, gently removing healing salt from her cheeks with his fingertips. Solemnly they gazed at one another.

'Where shall we go?'

Sarah shrugged languidly. 'I don't mind,' she said in total trust and honesty.

'Are you hungry?'

She nodded. 'I must pay my landlady. She has been good to me.'

'Good enough to allow you to bring home a friend?'

Sarah blushed and gave one of his biceps a thump. 'Would you ruin my newly polished reputation, sir?' she lightly scolded.

'Come home with me.'

'No. Would you have your viscountess scandalise the staff before we are even wed?'

Gavin sighed. 'The local hostelry it is, then.'

'Where is that?'

'Just outside Chelsea,' he said rather too quickly and knowledgeably.

Their eyes held and then Sarah said softly, 'I don't mind about your past, because it is your past. I trust you as much as I love you. I know you won't betray me or our children.'

Gavin raised a finger to tenderly caress her cheek. 'No…I won't betray you or our children or your family. And your aunt and Timothy and your servants I humbly welcome into our family.'

'Tim is blind, you know, and very bitter,' Sarah said, a sheen springing to her eyes.

'Well, we must try to improve his lot.'

'He started taking a little laudanum when quite young to ease the pain of his burns. Now he takes great draughts of it nightly and hopes not to wake.'

For a moment Gavin was silent and meditative. 'Does he smoke or drink?'

Sarah shook her head.

'Perhaps he might like to.'

She gave him a look of mock reproof. 'Would you have him add your bad habits to his own, sir?'

'Not all of them…well…not unless he wants to. How old is he?'

'Just seventeen.'

'In that case I imagine he would want to. I'll have a word with him.'

As Sarah's mouth slackened in surprise, he eased her towards him with serious intent and a wolfish gleam blackening his eyes. 'He's a man as well as your brother,' he murmured against her warm lips. 'And I'm a man as well as your betrothed.' His mouth slid to mould urgently on hers, his hands expertly breaching her cloak to stroke against her midriff before slipping to enclose her thrusting breasts.

'We can't allow Todd to freeze on his perch,' he muttered against her lips. 'Please come to a tavern with me…I'll take you back to Willowdene and the Red Lion…we could stay at the Lodge…' he urgently listed out options.

'I imagine poor Todd might like to get home to his dinner,' Sarah stated, but kissed him full on the lips to quieten his protest. 'Will you move from Lansdowne Crescent to your new estate?'

'If you want…' he said, guessing she might be mulling over something of benefit.

'So, if we scandalise the staff, then go away to Surrey, the gossip might not be so very great?'

'My staff are the soul of discretion, my love. They would not dare act otherwise.' Whilst talking, he moved her onto his lap then positioned her so they were face to face with her thighs straddling his hips. His efficient fingers parted her cloak and unfastened the buttons on her bodice, flapping back the sides to expose a swell of creamy bosom.

Sarah felt fire race through her veins as she anticipated the first touch of his hot mouth on her cooling flesh. She sighed as leisurely he tantalised the firm milky globes with lips and tongue. Moist heat was already flushing her pelvis as he dipped his face to the tiny nub blossoming beneath cotton. Immediately her hands sprang to link behind his head and hold him close.

'Oh…we can't go back there…it was a joke,' she

panted. 'The neighbours might see and…oh, we can't…I don't care to be a society hostess, but I should very much like to be respectable one day.'

'Chelsea it is, then,' Gavin growled against her heaving breasts.

'Will you buy Todd his dinner and somewhere to sleep?'

'Right now I'll buy him his own tavern if you say you'll come with me.'

Sarah lifted his head, gazed at him with hot golden eyes. Her soft palms ran agitatedly against his abrasive dusky jaw. 'Take me there, Gavin,' she pleaded with a sweetly sensual smile.

And he did.

* * * * *

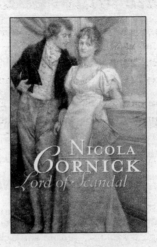

Celebrate 100 years of pure reading pleasure with Mills & Boon®

To mark our centenary, each month we're publishing a special 100th Birthday Edition. These celebratory editions are packed with extra features and include a FREE bonus story.

Plus, you have the chance to enter a fabulous monthly prize draw. See 100th Birthday Edition books for details.

Now that's worth celebrating!

July 2008

**The Man Who Had Everything
by Christine Rimmer**
Includes FREE bonus story *Marrying Molly*

August 2008

Their Miracle Baby by Caroline Anderson
Includes FREE bonus story *Making Memories*

September 2008

Crazy About Her Spanish Boss by Rebecca Winters
Includes FREE bonus story
Rafael's Convenient Proposal

Look for Mills & Boon® 100th Birthday Editions at your favourite bookseller or visit
www.millsandboon.co.uk

2 FREE

BOOKS AND A SURPRISE GIFT!

We would like to take this opportunity to thank you for reading this Mills & Boon® book by offering you the chance to take TWO more specially selected titles from the Historical series absolutely FREE! We're also making this offer to introduce you to the benefits of the Mills & Boon® Reader Service™—

- ★ FREE home delivery
- ★ FREE gifts and competitions
- ★ FREE monthly Newsletter
- ★ Exclusive Reader Service offers
- ★ Books available before they're in the shops

Accepting these FREE books and gift places you under no obligation to buy, you may cancel at any time, even after receiving your free shipment. Simply complete your details below and return the entire page to the address below. You don't even need a stamp!

YES! Please send me 2 free Historical books and a surprise gift. I understand that unless you hear from me, I will receive 4 superb new titles every month for just £3.69 each, postage and packing free. I am under no obligation to purchase any books and may cancel my subscription at any time. The free books and gift will be mine to keep in any case.

H8ZED

Ms/Mrs/Miss/Mr ....Initials ....

BLOCK CAPITALS PLEASE

Surname ....

Address ....

....

....Postcode..

Send this whole page to:
UK: FREEPOST CN81, Croydon, CR9 3WZ